Hubert
Haddad

Rochester
Knockings

A Novel of
the Fox Sisters

Translated from the
French by Jennifer Grotz

OPEN LETTER
LITERARY TRANSLATIONS FROM THE UNIVERSITY OF ROCHESTER

Library of Congress Cataloging-in-Publication Data:

Haddad, Hubert.
    [Théorie de la vilaine petite fille. English]
    Rochester knockings : a novel of the Fox sisters / Hubert Haddad ; translated from
the French by Jennifer Grotz. — First edition.
        pages cm
    ISBN 978-1-940953-20-5 (paperback) — ISBN 1-940953-20-0 (paperback)
    1. Jencken, Catherine Fox, 1836-1892—Fiction. 2. Fox, Margaret, 1833-1893—
Fiction. 3. Spiritualists—United States—Fiction. 4. Spiritualism—United States—
Fiction. I. Grotz, Jennifer, translator. II. Title.
    PQ2668.A314T47513 2015
    843'.914—dc23
                                        2015013460

*This project is supported in part by an award from
the National Endowment for the Arts.*

ART WORKS.
arts.gov

Printed on acid-free paper in the United States of America.

Text set in Caslon, a family of serif typefaces based on the designs
of William Caslon (1692–1766).

Design by N. J. Furl

Open Letter is the University of Rochester's nonprofit, literary translation press:
Lattimore Hall 411, Box 270082, Rochester, NY 14627

www.openletterbooks.org

In living memory of
Élie Delamare-Deboutteville

*Real or invented, all the facts and characters evoked
in this novel belong to the domain of the imagination.*

Rochester Knockings

Part One

Hydesville

Some things are inescapable;
when they arrive, one must receive them.
—Jan Van Ruysbroeck

I.
The Song of the Iroquois

The sun at dusk lit the staircase through the upstairs window. Seated on a step of unfinished wood, Kate studied the dust motes. They floated inside a shaft of light, one of the many suspended throughout the house. Fascinated, she held her breath. Each particle seemed to follow its own trajectory in the dancing company of its tiny neighbors, of which there were thousands, millions, more than the stars fixed or spinning through the moonless nights. Motionless, so as not to stir the air, Kate tried hard to distinguish a single mote among them with the idea of not losing sight of its capricious flight; the instant after it was no longer the same one, she had lost it forever and the archangelic spear of sunlight crossed painfully over her face, as if to ignite the pollen lining the bottom of her eyelids. She had gathered so many wildflowers that autumn morning to decorate the grave of her dog, Irondequoit, that nausea had clenched her throat and her whole body was still burning from it. And yet Mother had warned her.

There's a creak of the staircase behind her and suddenly it's dark: two freezing hands cover her eyes.

"Leave me alone," said Kate. "I saw you . . ."

"So now you've got eyes in the back of your head?" Margaret sat on a step just above her younger sister. Her torso blocked the ray of sun and its galactic swirls.

"You're bothering me," said Kate. "I was thinking of Irondequoit . . ."

"Oh, Irondequoit, poor old thing! Don't you worry, she's gamboling through Dog Heaven. There's no hell for animals, you know."

"Hell? Do you really believe in that? Why would God exhaust himself by making the dead roast for all eternity? It would be enough to bury and forget them in the ground just the once."

"Don't you see, Katie, that's completely impossible, even for God. Souls are immortal!"

The evening dwelled at length over Hydesville. First tinted blue like the pond's surface in broad daylight, then almost black and wine-dark, shadows spread down to the bottom of the staircase and across the silhouette of the adolescent it slowly obscured. Already Kate couldn't make out her sister's face. Mica-like glimmers flickered between her teeth and on her pupils, giving her the look of a bear cub bewigged with thick black tresses. Straining to fix her attention on where her sister was sitting, Kate thought she was seeing a cruel mask lit from within and in an abrupt jump let out a small cry.

"What's there?" sounded a frightened Margaret, half-turning back toward upstairs.

"Nothing, nothing, it's just the darkness . . ."

"You just made me weirdly afraid, as if you'd seen the devil in the exact spot where I'm sitting."

Margaret considered her younger sister with perplexed irritation. She liked her well enough, her little Katie, she was so pretty and sometimes quite comical, but a compartment or two was missing somewhere in her brain. Kate certainly had brains to spare; even Leah, their older sister who had gone to live in Rochester, agreed; whatever her sustained distractions and funny airs might be, when she focused her cat's eye into space, it betrayed something more than absent-mindedness, something entirely different, as if a part of her was dreaming while wide awake. At eleven years of age, not yet a woman, Katie had the look of an angel, one of "those gracious birds with a human face who populated in myriad the resplendent spheres," as the reverend Henry Gascoigne described them one day in a Sunday sermon.

But suddenly everything was so peaceful. One could hear the faint and metallic sounds from the kitchen where their mother, barely recovered from an awful cold, bustled to prepare dinner. Outside, the cows were mooing in the meadows; the tethered horses fidgeted at the sound of an iron-wheeled stagecoach that passed by without even slowing on Long Road leading to Rochester. When the calm soon returned, the frequent bleating of the sheep and goats announced the return of Pequot, the nickname given to the idiot shepherd with his bright red face who terrified the girls of Hydesville with his postures and antics. Their father, also on his way back from the fields and pastures, was putting his tools back in the stable where he had just unsaddled Old Billy, as he did every night.

Knees tucked under her arms, for no apparent reason Kate burst into tears.

"What's gotten into you?" her sister asked, astonished after their fearful laughter in the dark.

"It's our little brother! I miss him so much."

"He's also in Heaven."

"With Irondequoit, do you think?"

"Not far from her in any case—children would get bored surrounded by old people."

"But we buried him right on top of grandfather in the cemetery."

"Ssh! Skeletons have nothing to do with eternal life!"

Margaret grew quiet, thinking of their former life in another village in Monroe County. Even at fifteen years of age, when one is still dependent on them, adults nevertheless seem about as important as furniture. Maggie had had two precious friends there, soul mates, and even a pretend fiancé, the handsome Lee who frightened all the girls his own age—and then overnight, without warning, they'd decided to empty the house from basement to attic with the help of neighboring farmers, pile an entirety of memories into a big wagon, and that was the end of beautiful friendships and loves, despite promises to see each other again on the occasion of a parish festival or a rodeo. "Three moves equals a fire," was a line from Benjamin Franklin that she had read in an old issue of *Poor Richard's Almanac* dating back to her grandmother. There was a stack of them underneath the armoire in her parents' bedroom. One move, at the age of fifteen, is as bad as all the griefs of love. Katie, on the other hand, seemed to have only a single regret, as violent as remorse: that they had abandoned their little brother there in his grave. Otherwise she appeared perfectly blasé, or else was hiding something in a virtuosic game of concealment.

But now there she was, turning and lifting a night owl's vigilant stare up at her.

"Do you think of him sometimes, the landlord's son?"

"Who are you talking about? Lee?" Margaret cried, shivering from head to toe, her gaze plunged into her younger sister's eyes.

The glow from an oil lamp was flickering downstairs. Mother was arranging chairs around the table. They could hear the creaking of their father's boots who, slightly drunk by this hour, was busy at the woodstove. The smell of lard soup floated up the staircase. Outside, the wolf and the owl were crying into the strong night wind that stirs the air and chases maladies away. It was the Song of the Iroquois that nighttime spirits have taken up from the depths of time. Kate could hear it distinctly through the walls of the wooden farmhouse.

We return thanks to the stars and the moon
That offer us their brightness after the sun's departure
We return thanks to our ancestor He-no
For protecting our children from witches and snakes
And for having given us rain

II.
Maggie's Diary

My diary isn't that long yet. I've promised myself to put down my impressions each night during our period of getting settled in Hydesville. (I felt so pitiful in the carriage filled with trunks and furniture, suddenly reduced to nothing under the laughing eyes of the cowherds! How is it possible that a move could inflict such shame?) The people of Hydesville showed us real courtesy. I suspect that the Reverend Gascoigne sermonized to them about us before our arrival. And then we are a Methodist family, like most people here. Breaking with our old routines hasn't really bothered me. But the absence of Lee and my dear friends pains me to no end. And this sadness—nothing new or exciting comes to make it dissipate. On the contrary I would say it seems to make itself at home in Hydesville. The truth is, I don't like our new house. It's a poor clapboard and slate farmhouse of the most common sort, without even an awning, with a basement of bare earth and an attic carpeted with dust fallen from the sky. Isolated from the village, on the edge of Long Road, you'd think it's abandoned, despite its vegetable garden and fence. The stable, the cowshed, and the hayloft in back under the green oaks and the big cedar, are all housed next to the pond in the same shed that leans slightly due to a landslide. This afternoon, after class with Miss Pearl, the reverend's daughter, Katie and I explored the overgrown shores all the way to the forest where the water disappears, more and more dark. It's surprising, a pond that doesn't reflect the clouds; it was as if every schoolgirl who'd ever died of consumption, smallpox, or meningitis had dumped her inkwell into it. Katie started singing in her high-pitched voice. Based on all the swirls and bubbles, I think the carp and pike were following her all along the bank.

That first night when we went to bed in our new bedroom upstairs, the wind and rain whipped against our uncurtained window. We could hear the old roof groaning. A far-off cloud rumbled in the hills. Autumn was charged with electricity after a torrid end to summer. Lightning pulsed soundlessly in the distance. When the window lit up with a bluish glow, preposterous shadows roamed the ceiling and walls. With the covers tucked under my chin, I was paralyzed like a rabbit beneath a barn owl's wings. Next to me I saw the shine of Kate's open eye, her pupil black as a beetle. She wasn't afraid. Katie was only afraid of herself.

Her slightly strangled voice scolded, "Don't you ever sleep?" She started to laugh softly and then a sigh passed through her. "Do you know what they say in the village?" Without waiting, with her little girl's eagerness, she invented for me the story of our haunted house. The former tenant of the farm, a certain Mr. Weekman, wouldn't have anything to do with their father, Mr. Fox . . . At the first clap of thunder, I started to tremble like tree branches in a tornado. My sister, on the lookout, was silent. The beetles of her pupils ran back and forth across her face, which seemed to me at that moment pale as death. The son of the widow in High Point, a tall youth who'd come to watch us moving in, sitting on the roadside under the pretext of having brought us the keys of Mr. Weekman who had parted in a hurry with his horses and cows, found a way to take my sister's side. He wanted to spare this darling the habit of big chores because of her fragile lungs. With his sealskin face, Samuel Redfield, the widow's son, took the opportunity to tell her that the house was cursed, that it moved all by itself at night, with moaning and scratching on the walls and floor and some sort of floating lights or apparitions; the ex-occupant had to have been scared yellow several times before deciding to leave the place. And I, hardly more educated than our mother or even Old Billy the horse, laughed to the brink of tears. Those are the superstitions of the Iroquois, or the Scots, nothing more. That's what I told myself at the beginning. A new house always makes you worry a little; you think about the people who lived and died there. The dead always outnumber the living, and if you could see them all, it would be dreadful, like the huddled crowds at the rodeo. A new house must be broken in like riding a bull or a wild horse so as not to be thrown off in eight seconds.

Our father didn't really seem to like it here. He came home later and later from the pastures or the bar, where he drank much more than he had before, and one could often hear him grumbling about who knows what. It was actually because of his reputation as a drinker that we'd had to leave Rapstown. Every drunk in the area was his friend. He couldn't go anywhere without a cowboy grabbing him by the arm and leading him off for a drink. Here in Hydesville, based on what I could observe, it seemed like men were watched much more closely by their spouses or mothers, all those sanctimonious devotees of Reverend Gascoigne. The

Methodist church preached moderation in all things, that's what I learned last Sunday. One shouldn't be beholden to anyone, above all the seller of rum and whiskey, and we should love one another, that was the doctrine the pastor gave us to digest, always pointing his finger in the air, himself a widower with large coal-colored eyes. Sturdy in his boots, he wore starched collars and a black hat. When he speaks, you'd swear it was thundering. His eyes blaze and then flash with lightning. A magistrate who was ordering us all to hang wouldn't sound any fiercer.

Miss Pearl, his daughter, in no way resembles her father, as blonde as he is dark-haired, all rose petals. Her hair, her lips, even her eyes gleamed like honey. But at eighteen, she doesn't lack authority in the classroom: that's because of the minister. It is said that her mother suffered from melancholy. Such a pretty word seems so innocuous. Could that be when, under the weight of being sad, one takes a kind of pleasure in one's sadness? Just like how a drinker starts to acquire a taste for his misfortune. Yet Violet, the minister's wife who was by turns elated and depressed, was found one winter morning in the pond. One night she threw herself in wearing just her nightgown, that's what they say. Alerted by Samuel Redfield, the High Point widow's son, stuttering with emotion, some hunters who headed for the woods didn't take long to identify a human form. Mrs. Gascoigne lay suspended in the water under a pane of ice. Her gown had risen up to her face, leaving her naked like one of those large freshwater fish without scales. Lily Brown, the eldest of Miss Pearl's pupils, told me that the minister was publicly accused of having lacked charity for the unfortunate woman. He had performed the act of repentance while preaching the Sunday after her burial. Then, having become easily offended over time, he turned against the faithful parishioners and began to threaten them with hell on Earth, the affliction of those without ideals, since eternal life begins at our birth. Every Sunday for months, Lily Brown claims, he threatened the entire village with damnation. That was his way of grieving. Finally one Sunday, terribly emaciated, his black hair standing up on his head and cheeks, he proclaimed the remission of sins, swearing that all men were resurrected in Christ.

We arrived in the village without knowing any of its dramas. But children are quick to reveal everything to you. Lily told me of the unfortunate Joe Charlie-Joe, the son of a former slave of a Mansfield ranch, who was hung from a great oak in Grand Meadow for taking a walk in the valley with the beautiful Emily. Before committing their crime, the lynchers would have obtained her vow that he had kissed her. If every stolen kiss of the young warranted the rope, there'd be none of us left to marry. It's true, not everyone is black. The beautiful Emily Mansfield was full of remorse. Because of her, a black man hardly twenty years old went to heaven with a kiss for his last rite of Viaticum.

If my dear Lee had been a Negro, the people of Rapstown would've had more than one occasion to put a rope around his neck. Tears come now just from thinking of him. Lee and I had promised to write each other every day. My letters were scented with lavender and decorated with petals. I grew tired after a week: there was nothing in return, not a single word. I dream of Lee almost every night. How can I describe him? He's blond and tan from the sun, with brown eyes, a spice-colored mixture. In my dream, we're riding bareback on a blazing thoroughbred and, impossibly, both of us are holding on by its long mane as if seated side by side. The stallion gallops so fast that it catches up with the setting sun and, suddenly, as if our mount were disappearing into a precipice, it's Lee metamorphosed in flight that I'm astride. I feel that soon, in a convulsion, we are going to melt into each other, rider and mount, and that we will reach the sun while crying out our joy. At that final moment, I wake up in a sweat with a feeling of happiness mixed with dissatisfaction. What could a dream like that mean?

Tonight the old bones of this house are creaking. Undoubtedly because of the north wind. The north wind seeps in between the boards in the walls and in the cracks in doors and windows, it rushes down the chimney flue. It also causes sudden death, they say. Especially in autumn. It's the great sweeper away of leaves and souls. Disturbed by its howling, Katie talked in her sleep. She was saying something about a devil with a cloven foot. And then she started to sing in a soft funny voice:

Oh! it's a boy!
Super! it's a boy
It's a leprechaun, it's a demon!

III.

From a Drinker's Point of View in the Saloon Across the Street

In the sole company of a whiskey bottle, Robert McLeann, the Hydesville marshal, was celebrating the departure toward the Great Lakes of a band of bounty hunters, headed up the trail of the famous "Underground Railroad," as they call the rescue and support network of fugitive slaves from the southern states to the Canadian border. These thugs didn't hesitate to recuperate their losses with the free Negroes of the Union entirely capable of proving their emancipation before underhanded judges who were paid ten dollars a head. There was a barn that served as a "station" on the side of the reservoirs. But the family of eight kids and three wives hidden there by Mormon pioneers, themselves escaped from the Missouri killings, had managed to take the marked trails to other shelters, while the Mormons in their turn went to the port of New York like their predecessors from the *Brooklyn*, in the vain hope of reaching, via Cape Horn, the other side of the Rocky Mountains. To the marshal, hostile to this absurd law of compromise passed by Congress, there was no question of giving the least service to the slave hunters on his piece of land. He already had enough to handle with passing adventurers, the continual stream of starving immigrants in search of Eden, ruined families returning from the West or Indian killers converted into arms traffickers.

At the hour when the hills of the Iroquois disappear beneath the fog, the October sun finished reddening alongside the brick and wooden façades and in the dust stirred up by carts returning from the fields. From his office window, head foggy from alcohol, McLeann saw Mr. Fox get off his horse, fasten it to the ramp above the drinking trough, and proceed to limp into the saloon. Both man and horse were thirsty. He could see the rider's beleaguered air and remembered the previous renter of the farm by the pond, old Weekman, who walked every night to the bar in an uneven step. That ex-buffalo hunter turned farmer who, after settling down beside Long Road, after the death of his wife, and then after several years with no other worries, had developed jaundice two or three times, as well as tachycardia, acute attacks of goose bumps, and the accelerated whitening of his hair. At the bar, in no hurry to get back home, he told of his troubles as a lonely widower: something inconceivable had happened, the house itself was calling for his attention with little noises and intimate movements, creaking from top to bottom at night and flickering faint lights in the thick dark. Weekman ended up sleeping in the barn with his animals; he didn't go back into the house until morning in order to wash and eat. Fright had transformed him; he weirdly began to resemble his horses, with a long face, rolling eyes, terrorized by the least thing. Finally he decided to leave Hydesville with his belongings and the exhumed coffin of his wife.

The marshal struck a match to relight the end of his cigar. In his line of work, instilling fear in people would be rather advantageous, it would keep them a little quieter. Civil peace consists essentially of not meddling in others' affairs; a nice collective dose of being scared stiff would help his sleep as well as that of his fellow citizens. However there was nothing worse—the most dangerous thing for maintaining public order—than an excess of fear, above all fear of the unknown, which worked secretly on men and women who huddled around the same steeple, despite their mutual malice, all ready to turn the panic they feel toward each other onto the first being to come along, provided that it's not from their own flock. McLeann had not failed, on occasion, to learn from some bitter experiments. For example that cursed day when he was unable to prevent the collective murder of a young Mohawk girl, a runaway for some unclear reason from the reservation on the side of the Lake of Two Mountains. This heavenly girl had a devilish beauty working against her in addition to the circumstances: a typhus epidemic was hitting the recently landed Irish immigrant families. Tied to two sticks in the form of a cross, the Indian girl was burned alive at the bottom of a gravel pit and then buried under three meters of sand. The famine fevers did not come back to the Puritans. Under the pretext of possession and evil spirits, they had hung former slaves by the dozens, they had crushed them under rocks, like at Salem on the Massachusetts Bay a little over a century ago. Police decrees these days were needed to prevent the excesses of faith as much as those of vice or corruption.

The marshal examined the WANTED notices pinned to his wall: horse thieves, weapons dealers, murderers. All of them deserved penal servitude or the rope, but one would feel safer among them than in the middle of a crowd of fine people incited by one of these preachers of the apocalypse come from Europe or one of the big cities. On one of the posters, the name William Pill caught his attention in particular. He remembered a swindler named Willie the Faker who had settled on his spur tips in Hydesville, ready to graze from the purse of someone who was more than a weaner of calves. The gambit was only a stopgap for him between two major swindles. One night, after the bar closed, Pill had come to the jail to seek protection: farmers armed with clubs and equipped with a strong rope had more than one account to settle with him. Sheltered behind bars, the man was quick to share confidences, true or false, as a way to pass the time. Big and solid, with a beautiful pockmarked face that a lock of blond hair swept across with every movement of his chin, this William Pill had the gift for shooting the breeze and even a certain spirit about him. He claimed to have been a sentry box officer, a commercial agent, a pharmaceutical representative and several other things in his past lives. He was one of those rather pleasant unscrupulous adventurers who hung around bars and churches. Tonight, while a crowd of parishioners were lighting torches, Marshal McLeann asked himself real questions about his own legitimacy: by comparison, outlaws caused significantly less damage than the public damages of good people. Was a jail good for anything more than to protect the supposedly reprehensible citizens from the supposedly good citizens who might be having a hard time respecting the Sixth Commandment?

But here was John D. Fox coming out of the saloon with bent knees, his wide-brimmed hat pulled down over his nose, with a rubbery neck characteristic of the fourth or fifth glass of whiskey. He staggered and, bumping into a barrel filled with rainwater, soon found himself sprawled on the dusty road. The marshal rushed over, containing his laughter.

"Damn barrel!" the farmer exclaimed, relying on a helping hand to get up. "Oh, it's you, McLeann, many thanks . . ."

"How about I walk you back?"

"Not tonight, I'll be fine. Old Billy knows the way . . . Listen, do you also believe in all that nonsense?"

"Go home and get some sleep, old Fox! And think how it's only a matter of time before Mexico surrenders to the demands: the war is over! That's no small amount of ghosts gone, no?"

He helped the drunken farmer get his foot in the stirrup and untied Old Billy from the drinking trough. The horse snorted and headed off with a confident step in the direction of Long Road.

McLeann studied the blue shadows on the roadside, then a heron flying over bodies of water and over the golden border of the hills. Barely distinct in the obscure night sky, the full moon unfastened itself from the roofs, with an even brighter star strung to it like a necklace. The only error of his life was to have mistaken Venus for a star. His own bright star had faded quickly in a bed of sky and then was extinguished at once, leaving him stupid with a trunk full of dresses. One becomes a marshal by chance, because of love or in spite of it, for having tracked a pair of coyotes or for swearing to oneself to be done with human society.

A holy trembler before God, and a good shot, came out of the saloon, reeling and zigzagging. The road didn't seem big enough for him. It was Isaac Post, a learned man who ended up in Hydesville, an ex-telegraph operator for Western Union, dismissed for having confused the revolutionary system of the Bostonian Samuel Morse with that of a mechanical piano. Headed into the wind, he started to bellow like he had done most nights since his early retirement:

> *Oh my home it was in Kansas*
> *And my past you shall not know*

IV.

Hast Thou Entered into the Treasures of the Snow

The winter that year was particularly bitter. Cold froze still waters. The ground became so hard that the corpse of an old man had to be stored in a communal granary behind the church. Snowstorms and tempests of wind quickly isolated Hydesville and nearby farms. The Rochester stagecoach hadn't enlivened Long Road for at least three days. And no one ventured beyond the isolated barn, on the reservoir side, or the slaves' path once built by blacks and the county convicts that left off at the hills' base between the abandoned slate quarries and conifer forests. One could no longer see even the least convoy of French or Irish immigrants passing by en route to the West Coast: the gold rush was beginning to subside. Wolves and coyotes famished by the seal of ice approached dangerously close to farms, prowling around the sheepfold and barns despite the shots haphazardly fired by farmers numb with cold.

Her pretty blonde head turned toward a window, Miss Pearl was amazed, somewhere between fright and enchantment, by the swirls of snow that came crashing against the windows embroidered at their edges with scallops of frost. By turns it took the docile appearances of a big polar bear, or terrifyingly, of ghouls rising from a mass grave sprinkled with quicklime. But she was even more alarmed by turning back to the thin faces that were watching her, especially Kate in the front row, her owl's eyes fixed on her, a vague smile wandering across her parted lips.

"Forgive me," she said, "let's resume now our lesson in moral instruction. Quickly take out your tablets, those who know how to write will note down all the proper names, the others will make a cross for each one . . ."

The pastor's daughter opened the old King James Bible inherited by her great grandfather. Blistered in places, blackened in others, it looked like bread overbaked by two laundrywomen at sea, or from a trailer fire during the time of emigration.

"There was a man in the land of Uz, whose name was Job; and that man was perfect and upright, and one that feared God, and eschewed evil . . ."

Miss Pearl paused a moment, distracted by all these faces looking up at her. The iron stove was purring in the back of the classroom that had been allocated to the church by the municipality. Three farmers' sons, among the better off, including a new seventeen-year-old boy, almost illiterate, who had registered mostly to learn more about managing the affairs of his widowed mother, seven girls, including the strange Kate and sometimes her sister Margaret, also new, but certainly more gifted than that simpleton Samuel: he was the only child of the High Point widow who had survived consumption, and his hair and clothes were always soaked, even in dry weather. Pearl was rather proud of having convinced so many Hydesville families to enroll their daughters, usually confined all winter to inside chores or at the Presbytery Dame School. Her argument, with its Biblical freshness, frightened the good cowherds suddenly visited by a glimmer of understanding: Those who don't know how to read the Holy Scriptures will remain alienated from God, by the fact that the evil spirit blinds them! To learn to read and write is to guarantee access to His Blessing, without having to claim at the gates of Heaven that one is a happy simpleton. This obvious thesis—that the Puritans had completely gotten wrong—was convincing enough to include even the youngest ones. Why did it make her think of the brilliant Anne Bradstreet whose dear library and manuscripts were lost in a fire in the times of the Pilgrim Fathers, but, by divine grace, whose dear husband and flock of children were spared. What remained on Earth of the smoke released by the too-brilliant Anne Bradstreet's burning poems?

Miss Pearl drove these thoughts away and returned to her Bible: "And the LORD said unto Satan, From whence comest thou? And Satan answered the LORD, and said, From going to and fro in the earth, and from walking up and down in it. And the LORD said unto Satan, Hast thou considered my servant Job?"

Seated at the corner of one of the long kitchen tables the schoolchildren huddled behind, Kate wrote "Job" in pointed letters, after "Satan," "Lord," "God," "Uts or Uz." She wondered if God was a proper name and why Miss Pearl was biting her lips while looking at the window's white specters. So blonde that a sunbeam inflamed her, with eyes like star fruit and cheeks of a soft pink pallor, the pastor's daughter seemed to her more beautiful than the snow covering the angelic curves of the hills.

"What world are you in, Katie?" the teacher asked, finally embarrassed by the fixity of her gaze.

She was aware of the youngest Fox sister's sleepwalker-like absent-mindedness, which sometimes could be easily turned by the least thing into an agitation of the mind. Kate blushed and was smiling now as if to apologize.

"In no world, Miss Pearl, it's the snow . . ."

The other students, having lost their concentration, put down their chalk or their Birmingham metallic pens. Harriett Mansfield, the youngest from the horse ranch, Lily Brown who seemed at sixteen to have already lived several lives, two still innocent little geese-keepers, ten-year-old goat herders let free for a few hours of study, Samuel Redfield in the back of the room, his hair dripping, nodding his head in a silent laugh. That one she suspected of hiding painful secrets. Dressed in a pair of overalls with wide straps and dyed Genoan blue, the adolescent fidgeting oddly in his seat seemed to prefer the warmth of the stove than learning to read and write. She managed never to be alone with him in the classroom and turned her head when his eyes would grow wide while he opened that mouth with lips redder than a calf's heart freshly sliced in two. Sundays at service, dressed in his late father's heavy and broad black clothes, he voluntarily devoted himself to do the collection or pass out hymnbooks. The reverend assigned him even minor tasks with the ringing promise of a silver dollar on his birthday.

Miss Pearl closed her Bible; a little embarrassed, she looked for a way to harness their attention.

"—God had so much confidence in his creature that he abandoned him to the devil. From this testing, Job will emerge the victor. He who had been rich and had integrity will lose everything, he will become frightfully poor and suffer, but in the end, by the sole force of his faith, he will prevail over the powers of evil . . ."

Young Harriett raised her hand and, in the rush of that gesture, knocked off her own wool bonnet. Her copper-colored curls flounced like a fox's tail.

"Excuse me," she said, "but does the devil really exist? Does he walk around, like they say, disguised as a prowler, or an old woman, or a billy goat?"

"Satan would not exist without the Lord! Let's leave him alone and reflect instead on the fate of Job. It was with resignation that the patriarch endured the death of his seven sons and three daughters crushed by the collapse of his house, he endured every calamity without ever denying his master. God also restored his possessions and gave him even more children . . ."

Arms crossed at the end of the table, Kate imagined the house on Long Road so weighted down with snow and ice that all the roof beams gave in, making the walls collapse and in their falling, killing in a single blow her sister Maggie and her dear mother and maybe even her father, kept away from the farm by the inclement weather. Would she ask Heaven for another family to replace them? Could one change families in this way without despair? The memory of Abbey, their little brother who had died in Rapstown—no gift of a good God would be able to heal them of that.

"Class is dismissed for the day," Miss Pearl said wearily. "Bundle up, it looks like it could go on snowing for the next thousand years . . ."

Night fell on the little ice castles born of cold and wind. A farmhand from the Mansfield ranch came on horseback to get young Harriett, as did Mr. Fox, sober for once in his stirrups, to fetch his daughter: Kate raised herself up with an arm and sat sideways on Old Billy's rump. The other students ran along under the awnings of buildings or ventured into the fresh snow to reach their homes in downtown Hydesville.

His face imprinted with a wild exultation, young Samuel Redfield paused momentarily in front of the disappeared roads. He bent down to stir this expensive treasure, eating some snow and spreading it all over his face. Without looking for anyone coming to help, he considered the heights of Long Road, then stepped into the footprints of the last horse with a joyous refrain on his lips:

> *A nice young ma-wa-wan*
> *Lived on a hi-wi-will*
> *A nice young ma-wa-wan*
> *For I knew him we-we-well*

V.

When Heaven and Earth Shall Tremble

Torrents of rain swept by a gusting wind crashed down on Monroe County. It was one of those random nights crossed with omens between two seasons, one just coming to an end before the next has quite begun. In the upstairs bedroom opening onto the staircase, Kate, seated on her bed, watched the glimmers from the woodstove that sporadically revealed three steps of the staircase and the landing. Through the sheer intensity of her concentration on this scene, an immaterial figure began to float in the thick shadow. The clock struck eleven. There were no other lights on and the house was empty: mother and father were keeping watch in the barn over their only cow, a beautiful Devon dairy cow who was certain to calve this night. Maggie, curious about everything, had demanded to assist them at the happy event for educational purposes. Wasn't she now a young woman, after all, with her pointed breasts and all she unreservedly revealed on bath days?

Her younger sister tucked the blanket under her chin. Kate's body had not yet begun to develop, but unusual phenomena were inside her, impatient or annoying sensations all throughout her body, altering her every feeling and mood. Waves of sky beat down against this wooden house like Noah's ark at the time of the Flood, and she relished her solitude even while spiders of fear traveled a long shudder across the skin of her arms and down her thighs. The image of Abbey, their little brother dead in his bed, forcefully came back to her: at that moment, she had found herself just as alone as now, a little before dawn; her parents had gone out to feed the animals. Maggie, also sick, was asleep on the other side of the house in the childhood bed of Leah, who, more than twenty years their elder, had just left their farming life for good and with no regrets. That was in Rapstown, many years ago. Mother had left Kate in charge of taking care of the little one, for just an hour. His fever had risen the night before and now he seemed to be getting better, his skin fresh and eyes closed gently in the consolation of sleep. But he was no longer breathing. She realized it with the breaking daylight, her scream shattering the glass of a portrait of Grandfather Fox drawn in pencil by a starving artist from some day of revelry.

Kate sneezed. The whistling wind rushed down the chimney, the light flickered with more animation on the landing. It was then that she heard a repeated banging; she counted out a dozen strongly hammered knocks followed by three even more powerful and spaced out, exactly like the brigadier's knocks on the floors in old theatres, signaling the Apostles and the Trinity. She thought for an instant that a nocturnal visitor was announcing himself at the door and leapt out of bed, half-naked and panting. Worried, quickly putting on her nightshirt, Kate ventured to the staircase. All the noise had ceased, the winds outside were holding their breath, even the storm had paused its rumbling downpour on the roof. This sudden silence worried her even more. It was in this way, with a wolf's step, that an assassin might worm his way in.

Overtaken by chills, her legs gave way despite herself and she found herself seated in the dark, on one of the winding steps. Those raps, regular, distinct, determined—there was no doubt she'd heard them. If no one was knocking at the door, who or what could she attribute them to? Certainly not the clock or the stove. Taken with the urge to pee, Kate ran toward the landing, bumping against the wall and knocking over a vase that rolled under the bed. The sound of spilling water was almost reassuring. She rubbed her shoulders, thinking of the hostility of strange houses. How it takes time to coax them, to no longer be hurt by their teeth and claws.

Certain long-poisonous houses seem indifferent, bored with human lives, and then one eye half-opens suddenly from the depths of their comatose sleep. Shivering at this thought, Kate had the impression of being thrust inside *the jaws of a wolf*: with its steep steps, didn't the staircase have a toothy look? Maybe it was about to snap shut with a large jerk and grind her ewe's-flesh between its wooden teeth. However the knocks started up again, this time muffled and from under the staircase, from the basement it seemed, she could feel their vibrations all the way into the little bones of her skeleton. Never again would she go down there: basements belong to houses' pasts, all of them are cursed just like the painted crypts of Roman Catholics. It was because of death that the first one was ever excavated—it was to make Abel's grave.

There were nine knocks this time. Tiny in her big nightgown ruffled with lace, one eye on the stove's grate where embers were still glowing, Kate believed herself hostage to one of those hallucinations once attributed to madmen and witches. She shook her head, hands over her ears, and started to recite a prayer. Taken aback, she continued the act of grace in a low voice, invoking in her way Reverend Gascoigne's austere divinity. May it gently come to assist her in that barbaric loneliness of children.

"Turn away from me the demons that don't exist, tell them not to scare me like this, and in exchange I will not go anymore into the woods to visit the Redskin with green glasses, I will no longer go through Miss Pearl's affairs, I will help mother kill the moles in the vegetable garden . . . But I beg you, turn away from my sight these devils even more terrifying than Father after he's been drinking."

There was a loud noise below while the clock struck one: the family was returning from the barn, slamming the door and noisily taking off their boots in the entryway. Maggie laughed, scolded by her mother who was already stoking the fire.

"You're going to wake your sister!"

But when the flame grew high in the oil lamp, the girl appeared before them curled midway up the stairs, her arms around her knees.

"Blood of Christ!" cried the farmwoman. She would catch her death in this drafty air . . .

They led the little girl back to her room, where, feverish, she was forced to submit to the torture of dry cupping, those four or five copper cups inserted with a burning wick and snapping like a balloon on the skin of her back.

It's a little girl cow, a pied-colored heifer, hummed Maggie, nearly asleep.

Mother left the room with her equipment and lamp turned down low. Father's snoring could already be heard in competition with the stove overloaded with charcoal. Little by little calm returned to the house.

Kate, alone, couldn't sleep. Disjointed images were jostling between the surrounding darkness and the unfathomable cavity of her eye sockets. Her eyes undoubtedly open, she was surprised at the subtle changes in her surroundings in the closed room, this sum of impressions overrun by phosphenes and frayed memories, as if everything was about to revolt, inside and out. The sensation of her left hand stiffening a bit consumed her, it felt like it was taking on gigantic proportions while the rest of her body was shrinking. It was so unpleasant that she wanted to change position, but an invisible armor held her in place so firmly that she couldn't move even her pinky. Powerless to extract herself from these stocks, tempted to call out for help, no sound passed through her lips. She wasn't asleep, however, and it was precisely in her room that she was struggling so, changed into a statue of stone. Then by the force of her struggling, Kate suddenly recovered use of her body; she had sprung out of a cement tomb and her voice rang audibly again in this world.

"Now what's wrong with you?" asked her frightened sister as she propped herself up on her elbows.

"I was dreaming . . . no, I wasn't dreaming, how can I explain it, I was dreaming that I wasn't dreaming because I was dead . . ."

"It's the fever! Go back to sleep!" Margaret, annoyed at having lost the thread of her own dreams, turned to the other side and pulled the covers up over her shoulder.

The cold darkness seemed to solidify the way water freezes. It was necessary to open the door to let in the heat from the stove; but Kate no longer had the strength to get up, it even seemed to her that she could get lost in what, similar in almost all ways, was another world. When closing her eyes, the ground of reality grew unsteady inside her. What meaning should she give to this tiny chaos of gestures and feelings? Did there exist, behind that door, something other than a magma of earth, air, and water ready to take on every aspect of fire? The world was out of balance because in it one could die. The image of a hovel of cloth and boards substituted for her little brother's ivory face. There a black wind roared, heaping on confusion. Everything was flying above and below, parents, cows, her sister Maggie, and even the Redskin with forest-green glasses in the middle of battens and sheets unfurling from the armoire, under a beating rain of drops more enormous than the wet kisses of all country women. The dress and flounced petticoat of Miss Pearl fortunately protected her under a bell of pink and black organza. It was necessary to distract herself from the demon singing with a closed mouth:

> *O sister, O sister, come go with me*
> *Go with me down to the sea!*

VI.

In the Abyss Where We Got Lost

Winter lingered in the frosts of March. The glacial wind kept turning from the north to the eastern sea. Uncertain snows of glass and feathers continually swept over the first blooms. But there was always an hour for escaping under a spot of sun before night fell. After having walked half way up Long Road, Maggie and Kate usually parted ways at the fork on the farm's path, each one heading toward her own curiosities.

That day, the presence of Samuel a hundred steps away, also returning home after school, invited them to be more circumspect. He had taken the time to drench himself up to the shoulders in a tub at the public fountain; inundated, he went along like a rain cloud. The adolescent could very well want to take something out on one of them, toss rocks at them, threaten them with the scout knife he'd inherited from his father, or simply pass on his way while throwing them some furtive glances. Despite his size, Kate was not afraid of him; quick to compare him to those prankster coyotes lurking around farms, she didn't hesitate to defy him. As pusillanimous as he was unpredictable, the High Point widow's son would only bite out of necessity or surprise. An intent look alone was enough to disconcert him. As he approached, muzzle down, at least twenty steps behind them, his obscene barking frightened the older girl while the other would've almost been amused if the words he uttered didn't rouse in her a sort of emotion close to disgust. What did this mixture of insults and flattery registering in the hidden parts of their bodies mean? In his blue lumberjack coat, arms too long, and with a pointy head, Samuel grew louder and more worked up, a cruel tone in his voice, until the moment the girls' mother appeared in the middle of the vegetable garden or on the edge of the farm's property. The idea of complaining never occurred to either of them, so impossible did it seem and surely grotesque to repeat such things to an adult. Likewise, the Fox sisters wouldn't tell anyone about Pequot's naughty acts, some nights, as he was leading the goats and ewes back from the high pastures. The difference between him and his dog, a Great Shepherd with red fur, was more in their posture than in their behavior. It was said that he had been taken in as a child by Mohawk Indians after being abandoned by his family, degenerate colonists who left in a caravan for the West, and then that once an adult he'd been chased out of his adopted tribe for unknown reasons. Pequot lived like an animal among animals. No one ever complained about him; he brought the livestock back home and required little. When they heard the cowbell from the hills outside of town, Kate and Maggie quickly turned on their heels to flee from the demon or else climbed up a tree. It was almost a game. The countryside next to their farm was full of natural refuges to share with the martens and squirrels.

Behind the leaning barn, beyond the field of reeds and ferns where wild geese love to fly through, the black pond deeply hidden in the conifer forest was more disturbing than any encounter with Pequot could be. On the alert, Kate paced up and down its edges, attentive to the least trembling. The tall firs packed together on the other side threw down their shadows that were enlarging with the setting sun. That the mother of Miss Pearl had entered these dark waters of her own free will fascinated her to the point of dizziness; she couldn't take her eyes off those ripples of sickeningly floral scents sometimes agitated by gurgling and hiccups of air bubbles. It curled itself up there like an informed intention, ready to expand in tentacles of steam. How could one have existed, and then no longer? Obviously death was hiding a big secret.

Along the bank, Kate entered almost unwittingly into the prodigiously tall conifer forest. Sprung from a tapestry of needles arranged according to a mysterious order, endless colonnades were topped with an immense vault of branches with multiple domes and continuous stellations from which still filtered, by spears and hatches, broken beams of sun. The creaking of a branch, the belated cry of a bird or, more frightening, from the depth of those colossal galleries vaulted by centuries of sap and weather, the sad echo of a moan, the bark of a wild dog or call of a wolf, startled Kate awake with a shudder after the fascinated torpor in which she contemplated the pond—as if the scattered forest spirits were trying to give her a sign. One time, the Redskin with green glasses reported to her the words of a very wise man of the woods: "Nature does not ask questions, neither does she answer the questions of mortals." No need for interrogation, an attentive silence was enough. The myopic Indian was able to learn from a broken twig, a dragonfly's flight, or the shape of a cloud.

Just as Kate reached the stable in the tawny evening light, she bumped into her father who, holding onto Old Billy's reins with one hand, had just stepped out of the stirrups.

"Where are you coming from, you little devil?" he cried in a voice hoarse from alcohol and tobacco. "You should be close to home at this hour!"

"I was out walking not far from here."

"At the edge of that cursed pond? In the forest! There are bears, wild boar, even wolves . . ."

"I'm not afraid . . ."

"You're being foolish! Does the chicken's courage stop the fox? Now go dress the horse and change his bedding!"

Kate took the bridle without saying a word. In the half-light of the loose box, she bustled around his long head. It was an unrivalled relief for Kate to rub down Old Billy, brush his dress, unravel his mane, make him eat and drink, while the darkness streaked with gold from the interstices of boards deepened and the penetrating odors of the night were being exhaled from the beaten earth. Old Billy watched her with one big brown eye, lip hanging. Instead of unsaddling him, she could run away with him, gallop far from Hydesville, reaching bright clearings beyond this world, discovering the coolness of water and the stars when solitude is merged with immensity, to reach large prairies of honey described by the Redskin with glasses, there where memory is torn off like an old coat, forgetting her father and fellow creatures, all bitterly clinging to the stinking air of stables and the land of the dead, with no regard for the trees, mountain crests, the sparkling water of rivers, the hidden fountains of wind. "It's through the murmuring of streams, rivers, and rain that my ancestors speak," the Indian had told her. Where could her own ancestors be, aside from Grandfather in his plot in the Rapstown cemetery where, later on, her family had slid in her little brother to save the money of digging another grave?

Old Billy started to neigh softly while scraping the straw from the tip of his horseshoe. Horse, did you understand me, are you also ready to leave this world so infertile in wonders, this world where even the living seem dead . . .

But who is screaming so bitterly in the moonless night?

> *It's time to go*
> *The soup is getting cold, father's going to get angry*
> *It's time to return*
> *The wolf is keeping vigil, the owl spreads its wings*

Distorted by thick layers of thought, a voice reverberates in echo in the darkened countryside. Her sister is yelling for her from the threshold of the house. The night wind stirs the branches of the ashes and elms. Wrapped in her shawl, Maggie scans every preposterous flickering shadow where disembodied hands and heads are moving. She's surprised when only Old Billy responds to her, but doesn't dare enter the pond of shadows that separates the barn from the house. For several days now, at twilight, an apprehension has made her bristle. An icy reptile of terror sliding between her thighs, on her stomach, enclosing her within its scaly rings, biting her breasts and neck.

Suddenly, a clear and frolicking voice resonates in the open air:

> *Tramp, tramp, tramp, the girls are runnin'*
> *Lie still, sweet comrades, the girls will come soon!*

Little by little the dancing silhouette of an elf or leprechaun emerges from the nothingness beyond. It's Katie, her scrape-kneed little sister, triumphantly returning from chasing after ghosts.

VII.
Some Details About the Meeting

On the last day of March in the year 1848, in the last hour, just before the clock on the first floor chimed midnight, Margaret Fox stifled a fearful cry by biting the end of her pillow.

"Katie, Katie!" she breathed quickly. "Wake up! Something's happening . . ."

"I wasn't sleeping," responded her bedfellow.

"Then you heard it?"

"Of course, and I don't think it's done yet . . ."

No sooner had she spoken than a dry crackling, like bones breaking, resounded from the side of the staircase. Margaret counted seven knocks; the muffled chime of the clock seemed to be giving a musical response.

"Midnight!" she stammered. "Oh, I'm dying of fright! There's someone there, it's certain! A runaway slave maybe, or an Indian from the reservation who's going to take revenge on us with a knife used for skinning buffalo . . ."

While Katie remained silent, her big eyes open like a sleep-walker's shining in the moonlight, Maggie felt an icy blade of terror slide down between her shoulders and, tempted to call for help, was unable to issue any sound but the kind of squeak coming from a chicken being slaughtered. A small hot hand covered her lips.

"Shh," Kate whispered, "our parents are sleeping . . ." Her little otter's nose had such an air of rebellious exultation that their fear immediately turned to bewilderment and a wild, nervous laugh escaped from her. "Hey, listen, now Father is snoring . . ."

"Unless that's Mother!" Maggie corrected, laughing even louder. "But what about the knocking at this hour?"

"It's not the first time."

"What, don't you ever sleep?"

"It seems to me like it's getting louder each night. Maybe someone's trying to get through to us . . ."

"Are you crazy? There's no one here except our parents and you and me! At least . . ." Fear crept between her skin and the cotton sheet all over again. Frozen, mouth dry, breath held, hands clasped around her throat, Margaret shuddered with the feeling that all of her senses were pointing her toward who knows what kind of abyss—her sight, her sense of smell, her hearing, every inch of her skin—perceived the moment with excess intensity. Powerless, however, she felt like a block of plaster inside of which a frantic bird was desperately flapping its wings.

The noises stopped both inside and out. The wind lay quietly down at the feet of tall trees. Even father had stopped snoring. The silence became so total that the thought of nothingness quickly reached a kind of perfection.

"Something's there!" Maggie quavered from the bottom of her terror, her voice collapsed into the register of a very old woman. Through the open shutters, a ray of moonlight slid over a drawn silhouette perfectly motionless just in front of her bed. Her eyes bulging at this apparition, the adolescent let out a howl empty of any substance, convinced that she herself must be dead or unconscious.

"Come on!" said the shadow. "Follow me to the staircase . . ." Recognizing the muffled voice of her little sister, Maggie let out a mouse's squeak. Immediately the catalepsy that had nailed her in place fell away like a lead suit of armor. She threw back the sheets and, unperturbed by that rush of air, walked fearlessly behind Katie.

"It most often comes from right there," she said, pointing to an interior wall. "Other times it rises up from the basement."

"I can't hear anything now," the adolescent noted with a survivor's relief. Kate raised her little mammalian face up to her on which two pupils blacker than night surfaced.

"That's because he's waiting," she said.

"What? And first of all, who are you talking about?"

"I don't know. Maybe he's waiting for us to give him a sign."

With a slow look up and down, Maggie examined the ceiling's beams, the somber wood walls, the worn steps that sank into themselves in the dark, the dying glow of the woodstove, and the surrounding darkness.

"But who? Who are you talking about?" she repeated.

"The spirit!" Kate shot back.

"You mean a . . . a ghost?"

Her sleepy consciousness was filled with the image of a huge coffin, laid out with a huge glowworm inside it. Overtaken by a shapeless sense of panic, Maggie finally swooned and tumbled half-unconscious down to the foot of the stairs from the terror of being devoured by the glowworm. The fall resulted in a house filled with commotion. Their grumbling father, lamp in hand,

and mother, distraught, came to the rescue of the fainted one whose younger sister imagined could be cured by hugs and tickles.

They led her, a big ragdoll with tangled legs, back up to her room. While their mother had already set about trying to revive her with salts and slaps, their father lit a tallow candle at her bedside table.

"What on earth were the two of you doing on the staircase at this hour?

Withdrawn, resolutely silent, Kate smiled at her own thoughts.

"It's impossible to put oneself into such a state!" their mother added. "Smart young girls such as yourselves! What, were you going berry-picking for jam together under the full moon?"

Maggie's eyelids fluttered a few seconds on a shadow silhouetted in the doorframe. Under the candle's dancing flame, Kate's angelic smile took on a bit of a demonic air, while her lips, animated by the golden reflections, seemed to hold back silent, mocking, curses addressed to the company.

"Well, ask her!" Maggie blurted, pointing with an accusatory finger. "Katie was leading me. She claims there's a ghost in the house . . ."

Their mother, disconcerted, threw worried looks at her spouse and at the dark corners of the room. She was a thick and well-groomed woman, eternally dressed in an embroidered bonnet, her black hair gathered at the nape of her neck, with plump and, despite farm labors, very white hands, a copious bosom beneath her blouse, and a strong nose in the center of a rather pleasant face that, with makeup, would have appealed to a horse breeder or a Rochester merchant. Her keen eye landed finally on the younger girl.

"What is this story frightening everyone, hmm, Katie?"

"It's not a story. You must have heard the knocks in the walls and furniture downstairs . . ."

"Goddammit!" their father exclaimed. "So you'd like to make us look haunted to our neighbors? They already mistrust newcomers. I don't want to hear any more of this madness starting from this day on!"

"Don't curse at your daughter," their mother begged, "or it will be you the reverend should punish . . ."

"But," dared Margaret's flowing voice, "it's true that there are noises. And what if the house is trying to harm us? I wish so much that we could just go back to Rapstown!"

"There are no noises!" the man cut her off. "Or let the devil take me to burn! It's an animal, it's the wind, it's creaking wood . . . Now I'm going to turn my eye toward a last bit of sleep . . ."

As her father left, Kate moved quickly toward the window to avoid one of those affectionate slaps marking the end of a minor conflict. It's just that he had the paws of a bear that could tear your head off! She didn't despise him, the poor old man. He was just of country stock. So devoid of mind that he could only believe the pastor's sermons. A descendant of patriots expelled from Canada during the War of Independence, he belonged to the dreary species of farmers, all stubborn bigots and halfway between the slaves, black or white, and the arrogant aristocracy of animal breeders.

As soon as her father left, Kate started to laugh. "It's not an animal, it's not the wind, it's not creaking wood! It's a cloven foot, I'd swear it on the horns of our only cow!"

Their mother feebly bustled about, frightened, her enormous chest undulating under her nightgown.

"Don't be crazy! The devil only comes if called. Go back to bed and not another word! You need to sleep now, for the good sleep of little girls chases away all these wicked inventions . . ."

Kate slipped under the covers, already half-anesthetized by their mother's quavering chant. Recovered from her fall, Margaret sighed at her side. Her long lashes fluttered up, silhouetted by the candle next to the bed, giving the impression that they caught fire with each blink of her eye. Then, from below, three raps were distinctly heard.

"Momma!" Kate murmured. "See, I told you someone was there . . ."

"Shh, shh, it's possible, but sleep, sleep without any fear, your good mother will keep him in line with her fire iron . . ."

"Don't hurt him too badly, please! Don't give Mister Splitfoot too hard a time."

"Mister Splitfoot? Good Lord, now who is that? Well, forget all of this for tonight, I'm blowing out the candle and the moon, as we used to say."

Mrs. Fox, standing in the reconstituted dark, and despite being taken aback herself by the phenomena that appeared to be assailing her daughters, thought then of the faraway past, when she was their age, when she believed in the marvelous phantoms of love and of the future. Softly, right there, at the bedside of her little girls, the farmer's wife began to sing a very old ballad that rose up to her lips from some memory she didn't know . . .

> *Well a hundred years from now*
> *I won't be crying*
> *A hundred years from now*
> *I won't be blue*

VIII.
Polk's War Was Not a Polka

After the arid mountains of the west and the rocky deserts of Arizona, after the perilous canyons all along the Colorado River where he had escaped from the Mescaleros' arrows without much trouble, after the ambush with rifles of a band of Catholic deserters returning to their fold, the plain stretched out, infinitely calm. He was leaving behind him Denver and the memory of a night drenched with whiskey in a smooth featherbed. In the saddle on one of his two horses, for three solid weeks now, William Pill had been making his way on the paths leading north, fixed trails grooved by herds of cattle and settlers' carts in a simmering sea of wild grasses. When the Appaloosa grew tired, he climbed onto the Spanish Barb relieved of his baggage, and so on, from one point of water to the next. The Great Plains were for him the image of a rough paradise without demarcations that left one with complete freedom of movement: all this blondness moving under a sky vaster than the memory of humankind! Step by step or at a gallop, in no hurry, he was returning from the war with a Certificate of Merit in his pocket for having followed

General Zachary Taylor on the Santa Fe trail and later distinguishing himself alongside Old Rough and Ready on the heights of Buena Vista. But his greatest achievement as a free man would have to be enduring life in the barracks for months on end in occupied territories, waiting for the Treaty of Guadalupe Hidalgo, the masterpiece of Manifest Destiny and flying artillery, to be signed: several million dollars of compensation to the vanquished, in return for the reattachment of half of Mexico to the Union, not to mention Texas!

Thanks to the amnesty decree granted to the heroes, William Pill could openly go home. It was just a matter of deciding what home to go back to. All his life he had burned bridges, starting with those rickety ones, his ancestors', leaving Dublin at the age of fifteen on one of those coffin ships that unloaded the white pines from the Ottawa Valley and then left again with a load of immigrants driven from their land by famine, epidemics, and landowners. Five weeks of crossing on the *Brotherhood*—a four-hundred-ton former slave ship bought and renovated by a Quebecois ship owner—a sailing ship with three masts, its holds and decks filled with hostages of misery, this time all white and red, had cured him once and for all of belief in divine mercy, after the dreadful overcrowding, the surliness of the crew, a cyclone that carried away the rowboats from under tarpaulins along with a number of reckless passengers clinging inside, the typhus striking the children first and finally one girl in quarantine at Grosse Île in the company of the dying. Many, well before reaching that hellish haven, had been cast in a bag into the sea with the benediction of a priest there for the occasion. One woman thought to be dead had started screaming as she slid down the tipping plank without the sailors even attempting to catch her. Pill had not forgotten the little girls thrown to the sharks under their mothers' blanched stares. During the crossing, on a mission to Manitoba, an evangelist of the Plymouth Brethren named Edward Blair had by chance befriended him, sharing his victuals and incessantly reading aloud from an oft-consulted Bible even though he already seemed to know each verse by heart. He was the disciple of a German immigrant, the famous George Müller, a former thief and lecher who carried heavy remorse for being drunk during his mother's dying days. Once converted, he devoted himself to orphans, creating schools everywhere, saving them from destitution by the tens of thousands. On the baleful three-masted ship, Edward Blair had all the time in the world to recount his meeting with the German. The reread Bible he ceaselessly consulted was a goodbye gift from the missionary. Having himself in turn become one of the brethren, he had read and reread it every hour of the day without damaging it, then with his hand on the black binding, nourished his own preaching with it. Aboard the *Brotherhood*, in the turbulent sea, the only one who listened to him was an illiterate son of famine. The brethren who left to evangelize America hadn't even succeeded in converting that Irish boy who nonetheless inherited the Bible upon his friend's death. When they threw the cloth-wrapped cadaver overboard, the young immigrant couldn't stop himself from opening the book randomly with the certainty of hearing there the friendly voice of Edward Blair.

And the channels of the sea appeared,
The foundations of the world were discovered,
At the rebuking of the Lord,
At the blast of the breath of his nostrils.

After the required stay on Grosse Île where many other passengers of the three-masted ship perished and where an old prostitute taught him how to dance the polka, William Pill finally disembarked in Quebec, where he promised himself to always keep his head above waves, men, and steeples.

At this hour, with no memory of the Old World, the high plains unfurled before him a finally unpopulated sight, immensely empty, with only the wind, the light, scattered birdcalls, the vacant call of the coyote, and, under the sun's vibrant haze, from a distance, the final foothills of the Rainbow Mountain Range. His Spanish Barb escorting, he was riding the Appaloosa with a shoulder still hurting from the musket shot he suffered during the Battle of Huamantla. After so many days and nights of the sleepy rhythms of horses, Pill had the curious impression of the deterioration of his bearings, of an irreparable loss, as if he were leaving bits of himself on the road, a trail of images flowing down the back of his neck pierced by oblivion. Of his childhood, what still remained today? Not even a face. Sometimes when dusk was holding back its golden wine of shadows, he ruminated over the vague memory of hyacinths in his mother's garden. But he was alone with the sky. His Springfield rifle ready for use—an 1840 flintlock musket converted to percussion lock—he wondered for the moment if he would find enough among the tall grasses to make a fire to cook the coveted rabbit or quail.

The sun was still full above the hills, but the azure was already darkening on the curved horizon. A couple of buzzards circling in flight drew his attention to the carrion of a mustang being swept by the wings of other raptors. The rider was found close to his mount. Burned in areas and across vast distances, probably by bison hunters, the grassland had dried up little by little to the advantage of bare fallow lands where loose gravel rose to the surface. He continued his voyage at a small trot, satisfied despite the hunger that gnawed at him to see the appearance of the evening star that the Mexican Indians at the officers' service identified with Quetzalcoatl, their feathered serpent god. Soon some construction stood out at the bend of the trail leading away from the lands unfarmable at this height. A painted wooden sign indicated Osage City. He rode past a tank perched on a scrap iron frame, past gaping barns, some of them in ruin, their metal roofs collapsed over a heap of wooden planks and old fodder. The agglomeration seemed perfectly deserted, abandoned to the winds. Dust from the road blinded windows and the storefronts of pharmacies. Piles of blackened boards alternated here and there with still inhabitable structures. By the looks of the signs on flaking façades, the enclosed spaces to tie up horses and the numerous saloons, there had once been a life here of hustle and bustle. Pill told himself it would offer him and his horses the best place to stay. Lacking a woodcock, a crust of bread and a can of corned beef would garnish his table instead. At that moment, some sort of wild pig crossed the road. But the gun was in his holster on the other horse, and by the time he could seize it, the creature had turned the corner at a watering trough. In pursuit, this time with his pistol in hand, Pill came across a black albino in a top hat and suit, sitting on a box under the drugstore's awning. The peccary, behaving just like a dog, was lying quietly at his feet.

"Might you be thirsty?" said the stranger, holding up a flask of rum as the rider came to a stop twenty yards away.

Pill jumped off his saddle and holstered his gun. Once his horses were tied to a fence, it didn't take long to share the bottle's contents. The man took off his hat, revealing a bald lily-colored head.

"So you're heading home with a wounded shoulder and a soldier's certificate of merit to New York State? As a former slave can well tell you, that's a free land under Heaven's protection." The starry night stretched out quickly over the ghost town's clandestine day. At the side of the road, under the drugstore awning, the two men shared a dish of lentils.

"I don't miss anything," said the albino, "not even the masters of my youth, papists who taught me how to read with blows of the whip. Look, this whole town is mine. After they saw all the wagons coming from the east and the north going by, the folks of Osage City ended up following them. Horse breeders and farmers who were killing each other here like Cain and Abel over the slightest dispute, left arm in arm as soon as they got wind of the news: tons of gold in the west, on the other side of the Sierra Nevada. All you had to do was stoop down to pick it up. There they went, all of them, leaving anything that didn't move behind. Without any customers, the shops closed, the pastor put away his sermons, the sheriff turned in his badge . . . Now there's nothing left here but me and this pig. Freedom, that's my gold. Nobody picks a fight with me, the Kansas Indians went back to being peaceful once they were allowed to hunt bison again. Once the whites had left, they burned all their empty ranches and farms, wheat fields, to give the grasslands back to the wind, as the Kaws say. They're not called the People of the Wind for nothing. The day the Indians started throwing torches into this village, I jumped out of my hideout and yelled: "Osage City is my house, don't burn it!" I think they took fright of me. A pale Negro materializing out of a ghost town wearing a top hat must surely be a demon. They got back on their horses and, howling like coyotes, off they went!"

William Pill, who had listened to his host for much of the night, thought for no reason of the words to a Mexican song that used to come to him in snatches while in the enemy camp, shortly before dawn, when he was preparing to defend by cylinder cannon a hacienda on a steep pass.

> *Who will rip out my heart's flower*
> *What jaguar of chalk, what eagle of blood*

IX.

The Night of Sleepwalkers
Recounted by Maggie

There's too much craziness right now. My sister Katie must be the devil, or maybe just his wicked little daughter. I've written it out just as I understood it, in this notebook Miss Pearl gave me. It started with knocks on the floor, or rather beneath it, seven and eight times, in clusters, in the exact spot of our bed. That March night and the ones that followed it, Father didn't sleep at home. Squeezed into his venerable black suit, the one for weddings and funerals, he took the stagecoach to Rochester. The poor old man got it in his head that he should open a credit account at the bank, so he gathered his savings in the bottom of his gusseted bag, not a large amount, I imagine. He announced that he would use the opportunity to visit Leah. Our older sister, by coincidence, needed his signature for a right to lease. She gives piano lessons to the daughters of rich flour mill owners in Rochester. Leah despised our way of life. She only loved pretty manners, fancy dresses, and handsome men. The eldest of the Fox sisters dreams of marrying one of the town bourgeois. And at the age of thirty-five, with a few gray hairs, it would be time!

We were alone with Mother last night when the knocks started up again. Katie, who was pretending to sleep, sat straight up as if spring-loaded. I am always just as terrified when she gets up and walks toward the window or staircase with her arms outstretched, eyes rolled upward. But this time it wasn't a case of sleepwalking. In the darkness of the bedroom, I could easily see her crafty look, almost cruel when she smiled. Katie is adorable, all slim, with the pretty figure of a theater actress, but there is a bit of a demonic look to her. It could be said that anywhere she finds herself—in the forest, in the village, in the house—she is looking for the secret behind things.

One autumn day (we had spoken the night before at the dinner table of Joe Charlie-Joe, the former slave of the Mansfield ranch hanged from a big oak in Grand Meadow), I noticed Katie preoccupied with blowing on spider webs in the basement while murmuring a stupid nursery rhyme:

> *Catch me if you can*
> *I'm the spirit of a fly*
> *Devour me if you want*
> *I'm the soul of a hanged man*

Sitting in bed, a little later, she all of sudden started to snap her fingers, thumb against middle finger, like the black day laborers who sing prayers after pulling up the corn. I couldn't stop myself from copying her. We were snapping our fingers in rhythm and then suddenly, Kate called out: "Whoever you are, now do as we do!"

It must be said that the silence of the night overtook us after that command. There is nothing more painful than the silence that follows an incomprehensible phenomenon. Everything was quiet outside, one could distinctly hear the barn owls and the coyotes. Having been spared one night of her husband's snoring, Mother was sleeping, hands curled into fists. There were soft crashes against the windowpane that could only be a moth in the cool air of this end of March. Without Father's help, Mother had been too busy with a thousand other tasks to make our bed and bother with the windows.

"Do as I do!" Kate repeated with authority and loudly cracked the knuckles of her fingers. Suddenly, I write this under oath, we heard the exact same sound echo back. But it was an echo that was so close by! Kate exulted. She was terribly excited. At that moment, I believe she hadn't really imagined the significance of such a phenomenon. Aside from fairies or conjurers, nobody in the world had ever experienced this: we were ordering the invisible to manifest itself and, for the first time since our Lord Jesus Christ, the invisible was answering back! There was my sister who had leapt out of bed and planted herself in the middle of the room, her arms on her hips: a real leprechaun in the dark with her nightgown all tangled mid-thigh.

"Are you a man?" she dared to ask with that hoarseness the voices of girls sometimes have. When there was no response, she continued her line of questions. "Are you a woman? A child? An animal?"

Katie scratched her head and turned toward me. "Help me— do you have any ideas?"

"Maybe we could ask its name and age?"

"That's not easy, if it's nobody! And then how would it tell us? The thing only communicates by noise, or at least little knocks, little purrs of a tiger in hiding . . ."

Kate started to turn slowly in place. She fixed herself, arms spread, like a statue. "Are you a spirit?" she then exclaimed, intimidated by her own question.

We heard two knocks of acquiescence, very clean, same as the blow of a hammer or sweep of a broom. Frightened but radiant, Katie came with a leap to join me in the bed.

"We did it!" she whispered in my ear. "It's a ghost . . ."

With these words, not yet having understood the power such a word could apply, in terms of the invisible, I felt the ice water of terror rise up my throat. Kate firmly clamped both hands over my mouth to stifle the scream swelling up in me.

"Hush!" she said. "Ghosts are shyer than a moon rabbit . . ."

Regaining my breath, I hissed back in panic. "And what if he wants to drink our blood or make us pregnant?" The whites of Katie's eyes and her sharp little teeth sparkled in the dark.

"Shh!" she said without reassuring me in the least. If it was a ghoul or a vampire, we were soon to be dead for good.

It might have been one in the morning. The house became unusually quiet again but I could tell that all sorts of insanity was brewing inside Katie's skull. "One thing is sure," she said finally, "the spirit understands our English, but he seems to have swallowed his tongue, or else Mister Splitfoot has the voice of a mouse, too soft to cross the wall between his world and ours . . ."

Mister Splitfoot! Where did she come up with such a name? Her penchant for mischief is apparently endless.

The exceptional silence of the walls and furniture made her loquacious:

"Imagine a deaf person and a blind person each lost in a thunderstorm. One isn't able to hear the thunder and the other one is unable to see the flash. Neither would be able to escape the lightning . . ."

"What are you trying to say, Katie, putting on those marmoset airs of yours?"

"That the two of us are not in danger of being surprised by the storm . . ."

My little sister likes enigmas. And she likes songs even more. When she began to hum one of her favorite nursery rhymes, I must have fallen asleep, lulled by her voice . . .

What's your name, Mary Jane
What's your number, Cucumber

My dream continued the adventure from earlier in the night. Except that Katie was in my place and I was in hers. In my case I had kept my reserve as opposed to her playful pixie behavior and I was quite surprised to see myself suddenly intrepid, there, across from the body I was occupying, that big carcass of an adolescent who no longer belonged to me. Anyhow, we descended the staircase, one of us bizarrely in the other, me in her and her in me, and I couldn't tell anymore which of us was trembling so much that the entire house felt the tremors. "Let's not be afraid," I said to Katie in my body, "there is always a step after the last step." Through the open door of the woodstove, tongues of fire shot up while it roared all the way up its thick iron stovepipe. Leaning over to shut it, despite the intense heat, I saw in this aquarium of embers the skeletons of children the color of molten iron. They were moving slowly like long delicate fish, sea needles, or seahorses. My mirror-faced sister tugged at my sleeve.

"Come on, come," she said in unknown words, "the fire will go out all by itself." We let ourselves flow immediately into the swirl of a staircase of whitewater that seemed familiar to me, even if I had not forgotten that a sort of riveted wooden ladder was what led down to the basement. We slipped at full speed down those step-shaped wavelets until soon underground, in the middle of the roots of cedars and tall pines. Green glowworms were performing the service of streetlamps in these depths.

At another moment, I had the sensation of myself being buried in an old rock salt mine or in one of those caves all vaulted with the ribs of branches in full sun. Katie, my little Katie transformed into Maggie (what an unpleasant impression of stiffening!), already below me exclaimed, "It's Mister Splitfoot! Here he is in his manor house! Mister Splitfoot in person . . ." And singing out loud at the top of her voice without my being able to see who it was, aside from a wicked will-o'-the-wisp climbing up from the entrails of the earth:

> *Where do you live?*
> *In the grave!*
> *What is your favorite song?*
> *Hello maggot!*

Waking with a start, I realized that my bedfellow had hardly finished her nursery rhyme, also perceived with strange deformities, and that my dream had lasted the length of a yawn. But either from precaution or superstition, I felt first for my breasts, rather developed for my age, then for my sister's almost nonexistent ones.

"What's gotten into you?" Katie was irritated.

"Oh nothing, really!" I said without laughing. "I just wanted to assure myself that you weren't me . . ."

Timidly, with one arm numb, I asked if she would repeat the end of her little song.

"What song?" she asked with surprise.

"You know, '*Where do you live . . . ?*'"

"Oh, Mister Splitfoot's nursery rhyme! I don't remember it very well anymore. Wait, it's coming back to me:

> *What is your name? Horn of the chin*
> *What is your number? Zero plus zero*
> *What is your country? Far from paradise*
> *What is your address? Street of Two She-devils*
> *Where do you live? In the black house that kills*

X.

First Conversation with Mister Splitfoot

Over the course of March nights, these phenomena took on an unprecedented magnitude. The floor shaking in the rooms made the beds tremble and one couldn't remain standing without feeling, at each blow, a long vibration straight up the spinal column. At the approach of midnight, the sounds—by turns muffled or clashing, far away or close, like an axe chopping into a log or a load of cast iron crashing against some cleanly broken board— grew more frequent and continuous, so that the sleep of the entire family was interrupted by the mysterious tantrums of their home. Only John D. Fox, a man of certainty who would swear only by the beliefs and theories of the Methodist Episcopal Church, quite disinclined to superstition and always skillful at attributing commonplace causes to the unusual, wanted under no circumstances to renounce his stertorous sleep. Faced with the increasing worrying of his wife, he displayed the stubborn countenance of a headstrong convict stupefied by alcohol. According to him the house suffered from age, the wood was tired and worn, the ground had shifted. Those ghost stories were just nonsense. The only thing to fear was being swept away to the bottom of the pond by a land-slide. But by the grace of the Lord and several shots of an honest whiskey, his dignified repose was not seen as that of a disturbed person's.

One night, the last in the month of March, 1848, with Mr. Fox still being away on business in Rochester, the three inhabitants of the farm on Long Road, absolutely exhausted by the previous night's disorder, all went to bed in the parents' bedroom in the hope of escaping insomnia's throes. Margaret and her mother had long been dozing when, just before midnight, the knocks started up again.

Kate always slept with one eye open. Like the night before, she watched for the first signs of the phenomenon, impassive to her core, penetrated by the great miracle of being alive in the heart of these shadows. She could very well have disappeared unexpectedly or metamorphosed into a cat, or a pitcher, which wouldn't have changed by a hair or a world this strangeness that ticked along with the clock on the very end of each second. To be herself, an insignificant little girl, and to feel with a mad keenness the interlacing of the night's mysteries was an experience she wanted to relish so as not to die of terror. Mister Splitfoot, once and for all, brought her fantasy together with the enigmas of closed and dusty places, whereas the Redskin with green glasses had accompanied her in open spaces, forests, and high plains, as a messenger of the People of Wind and Light.

Even so, the knocks grew more violent, enough to wake up Maggie lying on the right side of the bed, in the same spot where their father usually snored, whereas their mother softly sighed on the left. Maggie saw her sister busy snapping her fingers, thumbs against middle fingers. To her amazement, the sounds answered back in echo, just after the finger snapping. A knock for a snap, two knocks for two, and so on. Mister Splitfoot was playing the game of give-and-take.

Kate took on the mischievous tone that worked so well with grown-ups, who were simultaneously won over and perplexed by it.

"If you know how to count to seven, prove it!" Seven knocks followed, perfectly spaced one after the other from an alarming proximity.

"Now count to ten."

While the knocking continued, their mother, awakened by the racket, exchanged a long look of astonishment mingled with circumspection with Margaret, sitting up now on her side of the bed. The whole thing was so outlandish, in this solitude without recourse out in the countryside, that the emotional rush of assailing thoughts must have suddenly opened in both of them, a simple woman given to superstition and a young girl hurt by friendship, the subtle and radiating channels of the psyche. Without any warning, because of the imagination of an insomniac girl, another world was knocking on the walls and floorboards. This sort of spontaneous communication took on such an uncontrollable vehemence that their mother lost all her reserve and ventured to ask the entity a personal question.

"Hey there, how many children have I had?" Seven knocks thundered in response.

"That's false!" she cried, suspecting with a secret desolation an artificial and mechanical cause for the phenomenon. "How many, how many do I have in my only life?"

Seven knocks followed once again.

"Let's see," she said, suddenly very weary, "I only had you two and Leah, and my eldest David who is so brave, and poor Big Bill, who we had to put in an institution . . ."

"And Abbey, are you forgetting?" Kate whispered, still in her bed, eyes fixed straight ahead of her.

"That's true, God forgive me! With little Abbey, that makes six . . ."

The farmwoman, absorbed in a painful memory, let out a brief moan.

"The stillborn counts as well? May it be spared from hell! At least it lived happy in my heart . . . That would make one more, then. One plus six . . ."

There was a silence barely disturbed by the creaking of a huge branch of the cedar behind the barn. Through the disjointed slats of the shutters, the entire night threw splinters of light across their sheets and faces like ember-colored insects born in the oblique refraction of stars in the pond's dark mirror.

Kate and Margaret too were listening to the night's breathing, infinitely relieved for no clear reason that their mother had entered into their confidence. A large person with wide hips would escort them from now on in these questionable vicinities possibly laid with traps. Katie remembered her farewell visit to the Rapstown cemetery a few days before their move. It was the end of one of the most beautiful autumn days, and the scattered graves of notable people were casting their gloomy shadows into the red grass. Springing out from a freshly dug pit, a squawking band of crows seemed to cast a pall over the azure sky. In a remote corner, away from the stone monuments, the Fox family's square of grass, with its granite gravestone, had been invaded with a mixture of brambles and passionflower. Grandfather and Abbey were resting there, one on top of the other. By what absent-mindedness had they forgotten her in the twilight, alone among the dead? She held on to the mental image of a field empurpled at the setting sun, with all those stones askew, wooden crosses, inscriptions. Shadows bickered in a violent contrast of light. She would not have been surprised to see Beelzebub's horns emerge. "Are you waiting for me, little brother, way below, are you waiting for me?" "Don't leave me all alone, in the night, in the ground." "Are you waiting for me way below?" "My sister, don't leave me, I'm cold, the ground is burning me . . ."

At least a meter's width apart, Mother and Maggie exchanged a complicit glance. They mustn't wake her up. It's dangerous to wake sleepwalkers. Katie, pupils wide, got out of bed and began to walk in the dark room. She was leaving the cemetery. She's looking for the source of those tears, melodious as the song of a woman weaving baskets. In these unexplored plains, big animals with paws of smoke flee at her approach. What is that noise of cymbals high up in the mountain and these hordes around the final blazing flames? Abbey's face stays with her, a fine mist heading toward a night more blinding than the gates to paradise.

"God, we're sleeping!" she suddenly realized. And then she awoke, wavering, just at the foot of the staircase. Rushing over, the farmwoman and the adolescent led her back to her own bed as she asked. No, she would not be afraid to be alone with the spirit. Their mother had heard it said that one must not disturb a sleep-walker. Even when he looks quiet under the quilt, he's traveling, arms stretched in front of him, toward the other world.

Once Katie was tucked into bed, unable to hear the anguished calls of Maggie, who stayed in her parents' bedroom, Mrs. Fox began to murmur through closed lips a nursery rhyme so gay that

her own dying mother had sung it to her to console her for having
to continue alone on the restless path.

>*Good night little girl, sleep tight*
>*Keep this ring on your finger, so bright!*
>*In your sweet rosebud bed, good night*

XI.

Reverend Gascoigne and family

Between two clouds wherein all of memory's tombstones seemed to be knocked over, the April sun suddenly inundated the fields and meadows with a light more delicious than a sip of pure water. Sitting at his old oak desk, his sermon board as he called it, Reverend Gascoigne was considering Pearl's movements. She had come to a halt at the window she'd just opened, slightly bent over, surely captured by the clearing after the storm. One could hear the quiet step of a horse ridden by some cowboy. Was he going to stop in Hydesville or continue on his route toward Rochester? Pearl had closed the window again and lightly, eloquent of beauty and grace in her chiffon dress with its inlaid belt, she pivoted in a turn to the right, exactly like in a waltz, but with a slowness that gave each of her gestures a simple domestic necessity: picking up a jar of sulfide, rearranging a bouquet of forget-me-nots and blue lilies of the valley, a quick blowing away of some pretext of dust . . .

"Pearl! Pearl!" the pastor was impatient. "Do you have something to ask of me to be circling around like a pitiful top?"

"Oh, no, Father, I was just thinking about those events. The Fox sisters weren't at school yesterday. Can you believe . . ."

"There is nothing to believe or to think about from this point of view!"

"It's said that even Mr. Fox, who has a solid head, is telling stories in the village . . ."

The reverend had a moment of weariness. His face, paled from sleepless nights, turned a little more gaunt. But wanting to appear kind, he corrected the seated posture of his poorly stacked vertebra.

"That Christian man communes more fervently at the saloon than at the church. Alcohol and dominos will end up disorienting everyone, him as well as his peers. When they're not busy fulfilling their blessed need, sinners have only one eagerness: to distance themselves from the divine light . . ."

Pearl, with the delicacy of an egret, was leaning with the tips of her fingers against the study table, casting the old man one of those heavenly blue stares beneath the shadow of her eyelashes.

"You are probably being too harsh on those poor farmers . . ."

Reverend Gascoigne considered his daughter with an inextricable feeling of annoyance, limitless affection, and profound melancholy: at a few years difference in age, Pearl so resembled Violet when she was a young mother, certainly in thought as well, her form of reasoning was more like protest, almost a reproach, a manner of systematic petition. He admitted without thinking it, deep down, that the mourning of his wife had burned away all true charity in him and hardened the cardiac tissue of his compassion, leaving only a bit of scar tissue for the potentialities of grace. Since his wife's suicide, his status as a pastor flirted with imposture, yet he never departed from any of his priestly or civic duties. Pearl meanwhile carried on as if morality were still intact. Hadn't her mother drowned by accident? She understood nothing of the insinuations and other derogatory claims around her. All the battles for freedom and equality written in the Gospel were hers. He suspected her participation in the network helping fugitive slaves, for she had never hidden her radical beliefs in emancipation, as much for blacks as for women. Pearl had a flawless energy and certainly the appearance of those beautiful slender angels papists like to paint. To whom would he marry such a phenomenon as herself in this land of swine? Before the cult of liberty, in the Ancient World, she would've ranked among the obstinate being dragged to execution on the racks of infamy . . . The reverend was annoyed by these absurd associations that kept bombarding the mind's emptiness.

"Could you leave me to work on my sermon, I have to readjust the brains of a bunch of renegades gaining strength . . ."

"Why is it that you don't believe them?" the mocking young woman confronted him, her eye of infinite blue landing on the knife of his mouth.

"In those stupid stories of knocking spirits? I adhere only to the Blessing of Jesus Christ!"

The reverend watched the outline of his daughter vanish in the shadow of the landing. She didn't close the door behind her, and her laugh, turned toward invisible presences—undoubtedly her old long-haired Yorkshire tumbling down the staircase or the Mynah bird holding forth in the pulpit of his cage in the vestibule—reverberated back up to him, rendered almost unreal, like another time, long before unhappy Violet's first attack of neurasthenia.

Forehead lowered over the Bible, he placed his head between his fists to hear no more of the world's noises. Meditating on a sermon the night before delivering it was a respite for him, a break from his prosaic duty, which was either to entertain a mass of dolts and simpletons or to frighten children. A single ray of true light in these narrow minds could do more harm than a loaded revolver. How to grant them glimpses of the Lord's ways? Since Luther, the Moravians, and the Holy Club, there was no other way to announce the Good News than by making the church thunder with horrors and curses. Outside or in the coalmines, mortals understand only the thunder of God, all of them blind to his lightning. Back in the day, John Wesley, founder of the Church, ran like Attila through the moors of England, reading and writing his sermons on horseback, the conquest of souls his exclusive ambition. In the haunted high plains of America, it was better to have to deal with masses of unbelievers or papists in favor of slavery than with a single necromancer.

Reverend Gascoigne leafed through his Bible. With the dexterity of a Monte card player, he flipped from the Pentateuch to the Book of Nahum, from Leviticus to the Proverbs. His finger rested without hesitation on the useful verse, echoing from countless homilies. And so the Eternal God said to Moses: "Regard not them that have familiar spirits, neither seek after wizards, to be defiled by them." And so the king of Manasseh offending the Eternal God placed Baal and Astarte in the Temple and immolated his own son; like the Philistines, he surrounded himself with sorcerers and false prophets.

"O house of Jacob, come you, and let us walk in the light of the Lord!" the pastor whispered.

Then, without reading anything more than folds of his memory:

"May you never find among you anyone who would put his son or daughter in the fire, no one who exercises the trade of diviner, astrologer, augur, magician . . . Enter into the rocks, and hide thee in the dust, so as to avoid God's terror and the brightness of his majesty."

Abruptly stopped short, he told himself that if the Prophets, great and minor, were all firmly diverted away from this funereal form of prostitution, it must be because they thought the gift of prophecy was wrong. Ending his arbitration, he exclaimed:

"And the soul that turneth after such as have familiar spirits and after wizards, to go a whoring with them, I will set my face against that soul, and will cut him off from among his people."

But what persons, falling into weakness, could be so demonic to have at heart the desire to rekindle the flames of hell? Closing his eyes, he took on a more assured voice:

"Rejoice in being alive and without sin, give to the Lord all authority and power over impure spirits!"

The reverend remembered King Saul in quest of a necromancer capable of intervening in God's fierce deafness toward him. His servants found him a woman in Endor. In disguise, the king went to visit her and commanded: "Conjure someone from the dead in order to tell me the future." The woman replied that it would be risking her life, for a royal decree forbade it, but Saul swore to protect her if she obeyed and asked her to make Samuel, the last Judge, come up from the kingdom of the dead. And the terrified woman said that she recognized Saul as her king, then: "I see a divine being, he comes back up from the earth!" But the old man wrapped in a cloak, the very man who during his life put

Saul on the throne, did not want to respond to the king's distress. Why wouldn't a prophet no longer prophesize once deceased?

In a voice vibrant with indignation, the reverend exclaimed: "The horseman lifteth up both the bright sword and the glittering spear: and there is a multitude of slain, and a great number of carcasses; and there is no end of their corpses; they stumble upon their corpses . . ."

Then, more quietly, coming out of a daze: "No, the dead never answer the pleas of the living, except to announce the destruction of their kingdom! The dead are without memory and without love . . ."

The reverend lowered his voice again, confused. Orating up to this point in the Tower of Babel of his own thoughts, mingling Kings and Prophets, he now turned back on himself in vain exhortation, against his loneliness as a dried up widower, these verses of Ecclesiastes:

"Also their love, and their hatred, and their envy, is now perished; neither have they any more a portion for ever in anything that is done under the sun."

XII.

If You Forget Me in the Desert

On Long Road since dawn, William Pill suspected that he'd crossed the Monroe County limits without there being anything yet to recognize: fields of wheat and other fodder for animals or humans frequently extended to where prairie grass once had alternated with lakes and forests. Those last few days in Ohio, then in Pennsylvania, leisurely riding toward an idea, he'd had the time to turn his memory in every direction. He had a few dollars left of his severance pay to which was added a sterling silver watch won through poker in Cleveland. Not far from Philadelphia, on the banks of the Delaware River, the Appaloosa had started grumbling awfully while the Spanish Barb, encouraged toward mutiny, had decided to lie down like a cow at the slightest halt.

And so at great cost he would have to change horses, for his own, having lost all stamina, would bring him nothing but the price of their carcasses. With most of his luggage piled on his solid new Quarter Horse, 1.6 meters tall at its withers, bought from a wheelchair-bound cowboy who claimed he'd broken his back in a rodeo—which he pretended to believe as much as that the queenly mare appeared to be easy-going—Pill started back up again on Long Road, reassured by his star and at the end of both a war and perilous journey. Despite some fickle Iroquois tribes and some bloody disputes between clans of breeders and families of farmers, New York State was a haven of peace in comparison to the West and the Great Plains at the borders of the Colorado River and the Rocky Mountains. His shoulder healed, the Mexican bullet in his pocket as a good luck charm, he owned nothing, aside from his double-cased pocket watch engraved with an eagle, a Springfield rifle, and the old Bible of his late friend Edward Blair—no inheritance, no family, not even a close friend. The only thing he had was the future, which belongs to no one.

In the late afternoon, still at a light trot on Her Highness, his boisterous mare with a flaming mane, he finally seemed able to recognize, like a face coming closer, the panorama of landscape. He had no more doubts when, on the left, mists parted to reveal the dense hills of the Iroquois, with their steep rocks here and there, markers between the cultivated plains and the break of high valleys where herdsmen lead their flocks on sunny days. Dividing these two was a river whose appearances varied, sometimes impetuous, sometimes sinuous and calm. Massive expanses of aspens and conifers with huge trunks brought a sort of meditative interiority to the landscape, a shiver of worry populated by bird song and indefinable echoes, as if silence itself were breathing. Two eagles circled in flight, high up, in the bruise of the setting sun.

Once again, with such an insidious fire in the heaths, the river sparkled at the bend of a shadowy valley. Pill finally caught sight of the big windmill-like reservoir and, posted on the lower side, a signboard with the inscription HYDESVILLE painted in black. A little farther off, in the middle of a pasture surrounded by low chalk cliffs where the black roots of pines burst up in places like the crooked fingers of the devil, stood one monumental tree, solitary, *dans son immensité d'ombre.* He recognized the Grand Meadow oak, which, by chance of a random fallen seed, had taken over a third of the sky with its branches, and with its roots doubtlessly explored the depths of Hell. From its low boughs was once hung high and taut, after many other summary executions, a certain Joe Charlie-Joe, son of a slave made white as snow before the Lord by the Mansfield ranchers because of a stolen kiss with the beautiful Emily, the sole heiress of her clan. This fifteen-year-old story had been repeatedly told to him at the saloon. The one who had denounced the unfortunate boy, a mother now with a necklace of the Virgin hanging above her admirable breasts, had been from then on the reigning mistress of the ranch one could see beyond the winter pastures: a large wooden house in the old style with white painted columns. Even further, a little below Long Road, the slate and metal roofs of downtown Hydesville blinked in the sun's last rays. Apart from a few exhausted barks and the transparent noise of birds, no sound rose from the village.

William Pill pulled the bridle in the direction of these habitations, curious by their silence. Quick to change course, with one ear back, Her Highness ascended onto the main street. Her hooves rang in quarter-time rhythm, raising a white dust. The man had started to have a doubt in this desert; he had seen more of it in the south, where entire villages were empty of inhabitants. People around here had held on to their own good land, but California gold had driven many others mad. However, two young Mohawks crouching on the church steps gave him pause: Indians don't like abandoned houses. He greeted them by raising a finger to his hat and continued his distracted visit of the place. An old man in suspenders smoking on his doorstep, some toddlers hanging from the skirts of a black nurse, a horse hitched to the gate of a grain counter, a band of cats around a tanner blind in one eye: these fragments of life in the flying dust were part of a community still intact, probably gathered together elsewhere, by the attraction of a healer come from Boston or Rochester, some itinerant preacher or the lynching of someone who'd been stealing chickens. At the window of a rather nice building that he recognized to be the home of Reverend Gascoigne, the tulle curtains parted to reveal a woman's face, so luminous with her blonde hair let down, that he froze on his saddle to the point that his surprised Quarter Horse turned her neck and flinched.

Piqued by a sensation of unspeakable emptiness somewhere between his diaphragm and throat, William Pill took his reins in hand. He signaled a trot, eager to get back to Long Road, and his horse, mane in the wind, started to pick up speed. That's when the click of a gun barrel engaged nearby.

"Stop there or I'll shoot!" yelled a man, rushing over without losing sight of his target in the middle of the road.

The newcomer obeyed in good faith. He had recognized the marshal despite his heaviness and wrinkles. Was it possible that Robert McLeann would have remembered him?

"Get off your horse and approach with your hands up, *Willie the Faker*! We've got a lot to catch up on, the two of us . . ."

Knowing the unreliable trigger of the type of firearm being pointed at him, he did as he was asked. This McLeann, with his migraine-inducing integrity and respect for procedure, had always amused him.

Seated behind the office desk, gun lowered, the marshal had to admit his blunder while unrolling the Certificate of Merit personally signed by General Zachary Taylor.

"If it weren't for your name and birth date written out, I might believe that you won this in a poker game from some other heroic fellow!"

"I won it with my own blood!" Pill replied with a certain emphasis, exposing the nasty scar on his shoulder. "And if you were only equipped with a telegraph, like all respectable sheriffs are, you could avoid these unfortunate mistakes . . ."

"That's not going to prevent me from sending a request for information on your record first thing tomorrow by post!"

Pill laughed, one eye on the closed saloon door through the window, the other across the road.

"So what's going on around here, Marshal? An outbreak of dysentery?"

"I would have preferred that. Or even yellow fever . . ."

And with these enigmatic words, the Sergeant of the Army Reserve left the former Jefferson County Sheriff, downgraded now to Monroe County police officer because of an inconstant woman or, if one prefers, a woman constant to her own instinct alone.

Night started to fall without resurrecting any more of the Hydesville population. Stray dogs and a lone escaped cow occupied the main street in the false light of dusk. One could easily distinguish lights in the windows, and sometimes the hanging faces of ancestors, but everything with legs seemed to have vanished on a secret pilgrimage. Her Highness took up again the path to Long Road, between the shadowy profiles of groves and the evanescent flight of hills that one could confuse with the malleable contours of dream. Imbued with the mystery of spaces transfigured by the inversion of light, hidden and intensified at once, the spring evenings had a surprising freshness that fell down from the stars. These moments of approaching darkness, between the dog and the wolf, reminded William Pill of a background of exaggerated images and feelings gaping like wounds. But all that was from a different world, now claimed to be old, that on reflection had its cruel youthfulness, with its share of disasters striking children first. And it was his brothers and sisters brought here to escape the cholera that were, beyond all logic, keeping the youthfulness of this continent intact.

Sailing thus between hill and valley, riding now into the night, his mind taken next by the continuous shipwreck that was his Atlantic crossing on that skiff of bitter discord baptized in derision as the *Brotherhood*, William Pill thought he could perceive, surrounded by darkness, an entire array of floating lanterns glittering on the sea of tall grasses and boughs.

XIII.
Evening Visitors to the Haunted House

Curiosity pushed to its fever pitch often turns into a riot, but for the moment the crowd was huddled in an avid silence around the Fox family farm, lanterns and lamps in hand, most of them outside, while inside the house, the first-comers pressed against the walls listened with an air of studious fright to Mrs. Fox's injunctions:

"Don't move, my dear neighbors, don't make a sound, that was how we were last night when the knocking occurred against the floor and under our beds, which honestly made us jump. We heard footsteps in the pantry, and right here, at the foot of the staircase. It was impossible to close our eyes: an unhappy spirit was prowling around my daughters and me, looking for any means to make itself known to us . . ."

Crossed with conflicted feelings, from joviality to the most incomprehensible of terrors, the faces of the villagers wrinkled like curtains in the wind beneath the dangerous flames of an oil lamp. More and more assured, the voice of Mrs. Fox was identified with a wave of amazement changing their faces with each moment.

"So I said, 'Is this a human being who is ready to answer in an honest manner?' But then, nothing, not even the rattle of a key. I added: 'Is this a spirit? If that's the case, knock twice.' Two knocks, I swear it, immediately followed. I added again: 'If you are an injured spirit, knock three times.' The house was entirely shaken by the count. Then I asked, not at all reassured: 'Were you wounded, then, under this roof?' The answer came without delay. 'Could it be that you might have once been attacked?' It was yes, inarguably! By this same process, I was able to discern that the spirit of the deceased who was giving me all this information had been a peddler and the head of his family when he was alive, and that he'd been killed for his money fifteen years ago in the age of our Lord in this house, that his body is in fact buried in the basement . . ."

At that exact moment, a dry and unusually violent rapping sound translated into the bursting of a white vase filled with cornflowers, bluebells, and gentians, which scattered all over the table and the floor. With round eyes, Mrs. Fox pointed at the broken glass.

"That's the second time!" she exclaimed. "Are you going to break all my dishes like this?"

In the living room full of people, there was a general movement of stepping back accompanied by a stifled groan of rising fear in everyone's throats. This panic contrasted with the beginnings of jubilation that had overtaken the crowd gathered outside, for it is true that, even at the worst moments, a few lamps in the hands of good people on a clear night can suffice to put everyone in a festive mood.

Standing on a step in the threadbare dress suit that he never seemed to take off, Mr. Fox considered his world from a certain height, arms crossed beneath his beard like an easily offended Mormon. Significant events were taking place under his roof, and the idea had gradually occurred to him to take some pride in it. A poor Methodist farmer unknown by his contemporaries and made fun of by his daughters could well, for once in his life, imagine himself chosen for mysterious purposes. For he had been persuaded that a great curse had struck them. Wasn't he for a long time the sole person in the household refusing to accept all this madness? But a demonic will had imposed itself from another world. There was nothing he could do. A simple man who's only been taught about God couldn't know how to fight against such phenomena. And how could he have anticipated the madam his wife would become in a matter of days, more loquacious than Reverend Gascoigne? The spirit had touched her tongue, without reaching her brain! It was she who had sent him to find their closest neighbor, the widow of High Point. Mrs. Redfield, handkerchief trembling, almost fainted when Mrs. Fox finished describing the peddler's slit throat, especially when at that precise moment a vase that little Katie had just filled with wildflowers shattered into a thousand pieces.

Mrs. Redfield and all the others turned their batrachian eyes to the floor and the table. First in line was Isaac Post, the only one in the group knowledgeable about transmission. Almost sober, mustache quivering, this good Philadelphian shook his head like a contrary mule. The Dueslers, former breeders who turned to farming after a ruinous epidemic of equine rhino-pneumonia, were only too willing to rush over. It was Mrs. Duesler who gathered all in the area who were still dragging their heels. A respected woman of independent means, the austere Mrs. Hyde—now a septuagenarian and daughter of the founder of Hydesville, an enterprising pastor who had a giant sawmill built in the middle of the valley with the hopes of profiting from the agriculture and its foresters—ascended by foot up Long Road, her servant at her side, a dim lamp in her hand. Mr. and Mrs. Jewell wouldn't have missed the opportunity, the two of them trembling with a mad hope. And George Willets, the solitary bear the village only just tolerated ever since he instigated his own quest for an inner light and separated from the Society of Friends. Stephen B. Smith, big hunter and lover of guns, was counted there, and his wife Louise who claimed to be a distant relative of Mrs. Fox. As well as the eldest of the siblings, David S. Fox and his wife, farmers three miles from here in the district of Pittsford. The mistress of the event was trying to take it all in, this whole group here on the lookout. Never, not even at church on public confession days, had she found herself to be in the center of such an assembly. Without really planning it, she had invited the village community over to put an end to rumors and in order to share a wonder. Wasn't it amazing that for the first time since the resurrection of our Lord, the afterlife was making itself known to poor mortals!

"I asked: 'Are you going to continue to sound your responses if I gather the neighbors so that they can benefit from this too?' The spirit answered in the affirmative . . ."

"In that case, would you allow us to interrogate him ourselves?" interrupted Isaac Post, weary of this woman's homily.

"I would like to ask him questions about my dear son," Mrs. Jewell cried out.

A good head taller than the circle of farmers, standing firmly in his dusty boots, a solid man with a pockmarked face called mischievously from his corner: "And how can you prove to us that your daughters aren't both in a closet fooling us with a broomstick!"

Eavesdropping on the landing since the invasion had begun, Kate and Margaret descended the stairs in a dignified manner to counter the mean laughs bursting forth.

Isaac Post intervened with his cavernous voice, exhorting his hosts and the public not to disturb communication by unwanted interference. He discoursed to everyone's boredom on the encrypted codes of the electric telegraph of Morse and Vail.

"What are you getting at?" Stephen B. Smith interrupted.

"It's simple. Because we can now transmit and receive messages from considerable distances, between Washington and Baltimore for example, by the means of electrical pulses, it seems like we could do the same thing with the other world . . ."

"But because he answers only with yes or no, why would we annoy him with your codes," grumbled a second Quaker. "A ghost isn't a little telegraphist . . ."

A restless murmur ran through the group. The woodstove had been relit because of the cool nights, its acrid fumes emitting an odor of sulfur to the nostrils of the Dueslers and Mrs. Hyde.

Isaac Post went over to the table and with the knuckles of his fist, clearly explained his system: each letter was assigned a number of knocks, from one to five for the vowels A, E, I, O, U, from six to twenty-six for the consonants B, C, D, F, G, H, J, K, L, M, N, P, Q, R, S, T, V, W, X, Y, Z. Two quick knocks to agree, three spaced knocks to reply no.

"*Spirit, are you there?*" he drummed out, letter by letter, without forgetting to translate orally in good English as assistance.

The coded response, one of the loudest, emanating indistinctly from the wooden floor and walls, subdued even the most skeptical.

"*What is your surname and first name?*" Isaac Post telegraphed with dexterity.

"*7-11-1-19-14-2-20 . . . 11-1-25-16-2-20*," the entity immediately responded.

Isaac Post continued his investigations without worrying about interjections from the group. A religious silence followed this long sequence of knocks. The man turned finally toward those witnessing like a judge before the jury: "C-h-a-r-l-e-s . . . H-a-y-n-e-s . . . the Spirit is named Charles Haynes! This is a historic moment that we're witnessing, fellow citizens. For the first time in the world, on this night in April 1848, we've entered in direct contact with the dead, which is to say that the doors of the other world have opened for us with the assistance of our Savior. Do any of you realize for a single moment the consequences of such an event?"

In an eruption of inner light, Mr. Willets suddenly stood tall, saying in a single breath: "I still have many things to say, but none of you would be able to bear it right now. When he comes, he, the Spirit of truth, he will guide you in the whole Truth."

His spurs tintinnabulating with impatience, the pockmarked stranger in the leather vest ventured to express some doubts about the mental equilibrium of Isaac Post. Laughing aside, he suggested that each person present ask the knocking spirit a question of a more personal nature that only concerned himself as a way to thwart any possibilities of fraud. More simple than the ex-telegraphist's coding method, he proposed to the questioner to recite the alphabet in its traditional order and as many times as necessary, the entity being ordered to respond with a knock after each letter as a way to give a response. A volunteer to recite, pen in hand, would transcribe as they went along. The devout colossus George Willets accepted with grace this role of secretary.

Everything in place, the widow Mrs. Redfield, holding back a breath, spoke hastily: "What sickness is my son Samuel suffering from?" The knocks started to rain down while Willets uttered the alphabet more and more quickly, all while making his pen spit. Reported finally with a certain reserve at the edge of his lips, the laconic one-word response provoked in the room a hilarious fright and filled the widow with confusion.

"What is the first name of my oldest son," asked Mrs. Jewell, very pale, in her turn.

"*John*," Willets transcribed.

"And what happened to him?"

"*Scalped by the Hurons*," he recited in a dull voice at the conclusion of the drumming knocks and their ritornelle.

Mrs. Jewell let out a piercing cry and fainted in the arms of her husband. The stranger, in compassion, offered his flask. After Mr. Jewell's disdained response, he took a gulp for himself instead and declared: "We believe we possess the science of a thing . . . when it is only possible that the thing is something other than what it is, that's what good old Aristotle said. I propose therefore that the residents of this house sleep at their neighbors' tonight and that a search committee take over the quarters to verify the constancy of these phenomena . . ."

Impressed by the eloquence of the newcomer, several approved the idea. Having free rein since his wife was living in Rochester, Isaac Post offered himself straight away to be on guard. The colossus George Willet and Mr. Smith also volunteered themselves as starters for this new kind of vigil.

"But not you, whom no one knows from Adam!" the ex-telegraphist announced to reserve sergeant William Pill.

XIV.
Maggie's Diary

My sister Katie is definitely crazy. Or else she's possessed like the Salem witches. If it wasn't for her, none of this would have happened. With these dangerous games, she set in motion a strange machine that makes some kind of goat: scapegoat or demon. None of us is going to escape from it however, I can already tell. As if invisible forces were holding us all captive, animals, children, and adults. I'm only fifteen, but I know how to see what hides behind faces, and beneath the polite words of others. Things took an unimaginable turn once Mother had the idea of stirring up the neighborhood, starting with the widow of High Point. Until that moment, everything was happening just between us. Even if we were very afraid, Kate and I were making a kind of game out of these exchanges with Mister Splitfoot, as she calls him. And that Quaker currently far from his wife's surveillance—everything he believes he invented to communicate with the rapping spirit, we had been doing since the first signs of understanding. At first, we were unaware that a peddler had had his throat slit with a butcher knife in our bedroom about fifteen years ago, at midnight on a Tuesday, before being buried in the basement on the following night. Did we need to know that? Now Kate keeps waking up with a start in the dark, stammering that she sees the murderer, that he's raising his bloody knife right in front of our bed. What scares me the most is not the murderer who lived in this house, but the ghost with his horrible pains. Luckily he remains invisible to me. It's plenty to bear all the pandemonium, all of his impatient rapping from the depths of death, and to suddenly see chairs lifting one foot then another, doors slamming shut for no reason, glasses shattering. Sometimes I'm so afraid this is all going to end badly that an icy sweat runs down between my breasts. To top it all off, there's some kind of infernal carnival around the house, while the inside swarms with a bunch of neighbors I only recognize from having seen in church. From the window, tonight, Katie and I counted dozens and dozens of lanterns. Most of the people assembled kept their calm, but sometimes there were hostile yells. We watched it all in dismay, my sister and I. And whether by spite or anger, is this crowd going to throw their oil lamps through our windows before they go off? You hear of these kinds of stories in the country. It was less than twenty years ago, not far from here, that an old woman was burned alive with her twelve cats under the pretext of witchcraft. There's a saying that goes something like: There will always remain more ashes than remorse.

For the moment, we're in the flames. Not a single day goes by without all sorts of individuals knocking on our door or parading around the house like those people from Asia who get carried away around priceless relics. That famous night in April, my sister and I were separated, one of us at our older brother David's house and the other with the Dueslers, an impossible couple always making a scene, while Mother went to stay with the elderly Mrs.

Hyde, a funny woman who night and day irons the dresses of her deceased mother. The men of the village stayed to keep vigil with Father. Their admitted goal was to inspect the facts and to catch an evil prankster were they to find one. Bizarrely, the knocks didn't stop that whole night, despite Kate's absence. Whether he's called Charles Haynes or Mister Splitfoot, the rapping spirit detached himself from her. In the early morning, unable to hold back, those keeping watch for the ghost went down to the basement with shovels and began to dig, unearthing small bones and tufts of fur, going all the way down until they hit water without finding the cadaver among that debris. It wouldn't surprise me if those gravediggers were also looking for treasure.

We all returned the next day a little shaken, Mother and us, we had to tend to the barnyard and our cow, so sullen ever since the butcher had come to take away her little one.

But another life began for us in Hydesville. Children without much status, we had now ascended to the level of prodigies. The power to communicate with the dead isn't bestowed to common mortals. Especially since our raucous host was having a field day, to speak frankly. Never had he been so talkative. Kate provokes him mischievously. I don't dare report all her questions: even a pirate with a wooden leg would be offended by what comes out of the mouth of that naughty little girl. She's come up with more ideas for a system of conversation than our austere fellows: we snap our fingers, even our toes, to prime the pump. And then we ask our questions in good English.

"So Mister Splitfoot, are you looking at me when I'm completely naked?"

"Nudity," he replied a little sharply, "has no meaning for a spirit who can see inside beings!"

"Hey, Mister Splitfoot, do you want us to go looking for your wife?" In the hell of a cacophony that followed, we learned that his wife was no longer in this world. A dead person not being able to be a widow, it would have been silly to present him with our condolences.

Ever since the whole town assembled in front of our farm, the visits haven't stopped. Father and Mother, acting as if they've won a fortune at blackjack, dress properly to receive people, offering them drinks in such a mannered way that one would think they're bartenders. On holidays, an unending herd of the curious march by in procession, hands in their pockets, laughing or walking solemnly. There are families of geese, the male leading, frightened groups of snooping hares, angrily snorting buffalos, rings in their nostrils, and then more and more, the ladies and gentlemen of the town with their escorts. They park their carriages and wagons up and down Long Road. Everyone wanted to see the haunted house. There was even a sorcerer who'd escaped from Virginia, a black exorcist covered with charms and amulets who claimed to be a pastor, whom we allowed in because of his face and arms, scarred by barbed wire from slave drivers. To make him leave, Father pointed his flintlock at some bats and fired in the air, trying to kill two birds with one stone. The man, driven even crazier than my sister Kate, started to call out to Lazarus and Saint Peter in loud cries:

> *Protect us, Voodoo spirit!*
> *Open the gates of the two worlds to us!*

They say that former slaves keep alive inside them the spirit of their deceased ones deprived of burial. In Hydesville, we lost count of the lunatics on a pilgrimage to replenish themselves. Thanks to Mister Splitfoot, we were keeping a small business alive.

At the house, everything changed after Leah's arrival from Rochester by stagecoach five days ago. Leah knows what she wants. "I've passed the age of childishness!" she likes to say in response to everything. Bursting into the living room late one morning with her beautiful trunk deposited by a valet, she didn't take long to get a handle of the situation. "We'll see what truth there is to your stories," she immediately declared. My big sister is a fashionably dressed lady from New York. Once she removed her cloak, which was big enough to hide five lovers inside, her chest flat as a chicken's wishbone in her traveling outfit, she revealed a long skirt swelling with crinoline in the back and little boots of yellow leather that allow her ankles to show. And above all that, placed on the jackdaw wings of her hair, was a pretty turban made of costume pearls and lace. Our eldest sister has religious beliefs and a piercing gaze. She understands everything not through investigation, but by nitpicking. The Lord judges us, she says, with a yes or a no. When she's around, Mother is never at ease.

After that night in March, poor Mother had suddenly aged. Her hair had become whiter than refined flour. She and our old father were convinced in their mission: to reveal to all the key to the other world. The two of them, who'd never even left the county! Our good mother usually so modest now takes herself as Anne the Prophetess. Leah, who knows everything, says that she should get some rest instead, leave the farm, settle down in town. The countryside is worthless for farmers. In Rochester, Leah gives piano lessons and appreciates beautiful linen. Despite a personality more cutting than a knife sharpened on a rock, she must not be lacking in suitors with such a corset and those yellow-leather ankle boots. In town, luckily, bigots are like bees calmed with smoke, they sting less often. But I think that Leah is waiting for that rare bird, one with solid gold feathers that prevent it from flying off.

What a commotion at home when she decided to dictate how we spent our time! First of all, she wanted to sit in on this spirit act. That was the first night. The eagle owl was ululating high in the cedar. Coyotes called after the moon on the hills. At the first crack, Katie began the invocation in her way: "Do like I do, Mister Splitfoot!" And then snapped her fingers to encourage him. Suddenly there was a hellish racket, as if the entire skeleton of Goliath was cracking. And then it was decided that the spirit must find Leah attractive. He revealed to her, in little counted blows, details that even she was unaware of, the little beauty mark on the back of her neck, hidden by her hair, and a birthmark on her lower back. And it was up to me to confirm the one completely out of view: right in the crease of her large buttocks was a wine-colored mark the width of an index finger. Mother swore, befuddled, that she had forgotten these details since forever.

The night before her departure, after several hours of sleep on a mattress unrolled in the living room, Leah had a magnificent idea: why don't we all come live closer to her in Rochester! Our parents treated the idea as extravagant. They didn't consider it for a second. Kate and I of course liked the idea, but who would look after the farm? Today, while reading the letters she's sent since leaving, we're starting to understand what she has in the back of her mind.

Troubles began for us right after her departure. Most people live in haunted houses without even realizing it. Some in harmony, others causing worry or up to some other devilry. What was upsetting in our house was that the spirit had broken the ice. All because of Katie, I believe, because of her way of sleepwalking from one world into the other.

XU.
The Columns of Duality

That sunny Sunday, the Hydesville church was stormed the moment it opened by everyone the district counted in its more or less zealous flock; added to that were a number of Protestants from other parishes, all wildly curious about the event, including local personalities, politicians, men of law, doctors, officers in uniform. And even, arriving that morning from Rochester in a convertible pulled by four horses, Henry Maur, the rich trader of furs and opium, flanked by Miss Charlene Obo, the famous actress and curious specimen with a beautiful waxy face, dressed all in black under her vicuña cloak.

Reverend Gascoigne did not go up to the pulpit alone. Alexander Cruik, a brilliant preacher in the Methodist Church formed at the University of Oxford, came expressly for the occasion from the Adirondack mountains, the barren territories of the adjacent Hamilton County, where he was trying to convert surviving Indian tribes: Cruik, who claimed to descend from George Whitefield and the Great Itinerants, had called in reinforcements with a choir of young black women that the public received in a mixed uproar of delight and fury. After the reverend's sermon on excommunication, which his own sermon would have to follow under the banner of the Great Awakening, the evangelist intended to pay a visit as discreetly as possible to the seditious family. An annunciator of the return of Christ would not be able to misjudge the unceasing gift of His Blessing. Alexander Cruik considered the crowd assembled between the brick walls, under the nave ceiling. Never at church had he seen such a diverse landscape. There was, beyond a majority of Methodists, all species of Puritans come from the neighboring villages, Sunday Baptists, Adventists, Lutherans, and even a sampling of dumbfounded Quakers, with some Negroes sitting in the back released from the corn plantations for church.

The reverend swiftly defied heresy: "There is no obstacle between God and his faithful, no border, no customs, and the New Jerusalem is open to all Christians keeping faith and good will. Each of us draws conscientiously from his own reading of the Scriptures. However, didn't Christ declare to the Apostle Peter that what binds us and what unties us on Earth will bind us and untie equally in Heaven? That is why we condemn without appeal dialogue with the dead as senseless and heretical. The occultists are all imposters who are ill-advisedly seizing and using the memory of the departed in order to feed the demons of evil and resentment with a putrid blood. These misguided ones conjure the dead from out of their own terrors and ramblings. But necromancy is the opposite of spiritual experience. There is no place for our dust and ashes in the afterlife! Yesterday again, without success, we warned the incriminated loud and clear, we have implored them to abandon their nefarious practices. As it is taught by the Apostle Matthew:

'Moreover if thy brother shall trespass against thee, go and tell him his fault between thee and him alone: if he shall hear thee, thou hast gained thy brother. But if he will not hear thee, then take with thee one or two more, that in the mouth of two or three witnesses every word may be established. And if he shall neglect to hear them, tell it unto the church: but if he neglect to hear the church, let him be unto thee as a heathen man and a publican.'

Therefore, by ecclesiastical decision, we find ourselves solemnly obliged to put the fate of the family of John D. Fox back in the hands of God; from this day forward they will be considered as banished from the Episcopal Methodist Church. They will no longer take part in our brotherhood! Whoever would follow their example or be tempted to accompany their erring will swiftly suffer a similar ostracism . . ."

The crowd of farmers and stable boys gathered at the back of the room could not restrain an animal grunt of satisfaction that made Pearl, seated in the first row, turn back to look. In this worried gesture, after staring down several faces with low foreheads and thick jaws, she crossed glances with William Pill seated five rows back in the span of men. Embarrassed, she blinked her eyelashes and gave a vague polite smile that she immediately regretted. That man had an unpleasant way of fixing his steel-blue eyes on her, as if with his silence he was speaking crudely and in his full right. Pearl turned back around and hunched her shoulders. Her neck was burning. She had no doubt that he was studying the back of her head and each stray hair that had fallen loose.

At the pulpit, the minister of the Holy Gospel was finishing his curse. His daughter, her throat tightening, was already frightened of the consequences of this strictness on the Fox sisters, their elderly mother, and that ignorant farmer who, with the help of alcohol, believed himself to be invested in a supreme mission: consoling all the mourners on Earth by opening up the secrets of the other world.

At the signal of Alexander Cruik, anxious to appease everyone's spirit, the choir of young black girls started to sing:

> *I am free*
> *I am free, my Lord*
> *I am free*
> *I'm washed by the blood of the Lamb*
> *You may knock me down*
> *I'll rise again*
> *I'm washed by the blood of the Lamb*
> *I fight you with my sword and shield*
> *I'm washed by the blood of the Lamb*

The guest speaker experienced slight vertigo at the moment he stood to approach the pulpit. Those hymns of incorruptible faith born in the cotton fields had risen viscerally, with mouths closed, among the millions of slaves evangelized by his church, who on the horizon of their martyrdom aspired to nothing other than freedom. And what then were the impecunious white farmers aspiring to who were whispering into the ears of the dead? Thinner than a rail and with the lividity of a revenant, the preacher was amused by the fright that ordinarily occasioned his appearance amid a crowd of believers. If, by an exception in the Methodist Church Council inclined to sobriety in all things, his outspokenness and inspired wise-man fantasies had been allowed for services rendered, he knew from experience that there was almost nothing held in balance among these crazed settlers, who were pioneers and sons of pioneers with barbaric inclinations and, notwithstanding, were sworn opponents of superstition carried out with the candor of crusaders. With these people—the severe Gascoigne seemed to have forgotten for the moment—a single word too much could make things worse.

Intuition more than reason guided Alexander Cruik in situations like these, and he let himself go off in a loud voice about numerous parables of his own creation, which his listeners imagined were taken from the Bible and that the wisest took accurately as apocryphal. But both the illiterate and the learned were under his spell. Under the fur trader's wide shoulder, a dark figure decked out like a Byronian privateer had the frustrated outburst of a scholar confronted with an undateable document. If Charlene and Harry Maur had rushed to these fields, allured by the story, he, Lucian Nephtali, had agreed to go along with them as a way to find out more about whatever rarified process of excommunication was fomenting under the leadership of a district pastor and a visionary who'd risked his scalp with the Nagarragansetts or the Oregon Indians. Since the young Quaker Mary Dyer had been tried and hung in Boston now almost two centuries ago, trial by opinion was no longer acknowledged in the Union. But where did this strange bird of a preacher find this story of a corpse brought back to life in the bottom of a cave containing jars filled with scrolls of Hebraic manuscripts?

Now he was quoting the book of Psalms with the same casual fervor:

"I was nothing more than a lunatic made of water and clay and your eyes saw me!"

Alexander Cruik heard his own voice resonate under the vaulted ceiling. For nearly an hour he preached to the perfect silence, with no direct allusion made to the case at hand. An anesthetized audience was listening to him, ready for eternal sleep in the cave of Elohim. For what other reason than terror do sinners seek refuge in the church? Exhausted by his own performance and thinking to himself that he still wasn't done, the preacher started in on the parable from the Gospel of Mark:

"And when he was come out of the ship, immediately there met him out of the tombs a man with an unclean spirit, Who had his dwelling among the tombs; and no man could bind him, no, not with chains: Because that he had been often bound with fetters and chains, and the chains had been plucked asunder by him, and the fetters broken in pieces: neither could any man tame him. And always, night and day, he was in the mountains, and in the tombs, crying, and cutting himself with stones. But when he saw Jesus afar off, he ran and worshipped him, And cried with a loud voice, and said, What have I to do with thee, Jesus, thou Son of the most high God? I adjure thee by God, that thou torment me not. For he said unto him, Come out of the man, thou unclean spirit. And he asked him, What is thy name? And he answered, saying, My name is Legion: for we are many."

Plagued by the many expressions his eyes met in the audience, Alexander rushed to conclude:

"If every mistake distances us a little more from the Lord, could a truly righteous man create a world? And if this man existed, could he be anyone other than our Lord?"

While the gathered crowds had started thinking about how to get back home without mingling any further, the choir took up again its antiphony with a celestial intonation.

I am free
I am free, my Lord
I am free
I'm washed by the blood of the Lamb

XVI.
In the Waves of Boiling Blood

Head on fire, tormented by a nagging stomachache, Kate was still contemplating escaping through a basement window from the house, which for three days now had been transformed into a tribunal at the heart of which the inculpated were none other than the entire Fox family. Doctors, priests, and judges arriving in succession wouldn't stop examining every last thing, the furniture, the least object, and even the bodies of the Fox sisters, inside their mouths, the conformation of their organs, the joints of their feet and hands, and submitted further bombardments of questions as if they were seeking a confession from the throat-cutters of Charles Haynes, peddler of his estate. Luckily George Willets and Isaac Post, both Quakers, came as honest witnesses to counter these charges. These two had attended the séances of invocation and could swear on any Bible about the veracity of these phenomena.

Among the investigators and those faking curiosity, the most unusual was certainly that likeable Mr. Cruik, who didn't ask a single question, but penetratingly observed the people present, whether they be family members or self-imposed hosts. Quite gaunt, with a hollow face and long hands like a sorcerer's, the depths of his eyes sparkling with embers, he evoked some kind of convalescent on leave, one of those cursed consumptives to whom one would benignly allow a little breath of fresh air. That didn't prevent the preacher from catching Margaret's every word; once so shy, she had become quite talkative in the presence of gentlemen with ascot ties and top hats. He paid particular attention to Kate, deferential, strangely intense, and thought that Mary and Martha, the sisters of Lazarus in the tomb, must have resembled these two.

Outside, the waning sun was forging the most beautiful gold. The blue shadows of trees grew long. A marvelous light haloed each leaf. Kate, unable to bear it any longer, had climbed out the window and withdrawn to the side of the pond while clutching her stomach. This crushing heaviness, could it be because of all the clashing inside her, all along her legs and in her insides? Last week, Lily Brown, the oldest student in Miss Pearl's class, had told her, reenacting with energetic gestures, that some kind of suffocating demon would leap at her throat some nights during her sleep. She also recounted how a water snake had slithered one time into her bed and that she still had its trace on her belly, close to her navel. Kate too had been having awful nightmares, especially since Mister Splitfoot had entered into her life. A horned and hairy little being with the hooves of a goat and huge white eyes would come and sit on her chest, so heavy that she found herself completely paralyzed. After a minute or a century, she'd manage to escape and, as if ejected from a waffle iron, she would immediately recover use of all her vital functions. None of the disgusting details Lily Brown described—a demon's long, hardened fingers, or mice brains smacking down on you through holes—had happened to her, but she felt the paralysis of a great terror in those nightmares. They were going to think she was dead and put her in a coffin, while she would be squirming and crying out in vain, a prisoner under a spell, which hadn't happened to anyone else, not even Maggie busy with her daydreams or babbling on at her bedside . . .

This time it wasn't a nightmare that she wanted to flee, but a pain quite real beneath her navel. One doesn't talk to her mother about girl parts, so instead she ran under the big trees, biting her lip. The black pond sparkled in the glow of sunset. Kate made her way to the stream of bubbles and foam, hanging over above on the aspens' side; it flowed down in cascades from a rock, tumbling between mossy stones before disappearing without a trace into a plane of water where the nascent brilliance of the full moon combined its silver spokes with the golden sequins of the sun. There, in the misty countryside little lights were scattered as if on the prow of a night fishing skiff. A rider in the distance was going in stride, emerging like a strong-chested centaur.

Under the branches of a willow, on her knees before the stream, Kate rolled her dress up above her thighs and, legs parted, cried out in horror. Blood with an acrid odor was flowing from an unknown wound; it spread in tiny beads on a rock flat as the granite block where her mother decapitated chickens. Then she remembered that one morning last winter, before the stained sheets under her, her sister had claimed a nosebleed, and that she'd asked herself, perplexed, how her sister's nose could have bled under her buttocks. Soon to be twelve years old, Kate wasn't entirely ignorant of those mysteries that transform girls little by little into mother pelicans good at laying big, soft, milky eggs ready to hatch. Frenzied, she began to splash her belly with that still sparkling, bracing water while pinkish threads spread out across the rock like veins in a hand. Could this be what old women called the lunar cycle? It seemed to her like her blood was dyeing the whole river. At that moment, on the other bank, she thought she perceived two fiery eyes scrutinizing her between branches. Frightened, she quickly pulled down her dress. Was it an animal from the forest, an otter or a fox attracted by the scent of blood? Or that man-goat of the hills always on the lookout for a hare or flycatcher? But Pequot and his flock had gone camping off into the mountains along with the beautiful season. Other entities, more elusive than bestiality or lust, were roaming these edges in the dark.

Running alongside the pond, Kate hurried back toward the farm. A pale light stretched over the hills to the edges of the high forest while the blue light turned to purple. She perceived litanies of some sort, screams, like someone calling out. Out of breath, madly worried about her family, she reproached herself for this escapade. Soon she saw wandering lanterns and made out the silhouettes of many people. Even more than these unwelcome strangers who'd come to investigate every draft of air, she feared their neighbors, all the farmers of placid temperament who, gripping their elbows in fear, were capable of transforming into a mob the moment one of them let loose a curse. They were who prowled and howled like a bunch of wolves around their farm.

Finally getting close, in a darkness swept by torchlight, a feeling of shame to be coming back in such a poor state overcame her, her dress stained with dirt and blood. Farmers gathered outside their windows were shaking their fists while waving their lanterns. One of them threw a rock at the front door.

"Death to the witches!" he bellowed.

Those most excited went one better: "Let them hang!"

Then there was a commotion. A rain of pebbles rang across the wooden walls. A window on the ground floor broke, adding to the tumult.

"Stop! Stop!" cried Kate, rushing to the doorstep.

There was a furious movement toward her, a tempest ready to carry her away, but at that moment the door opened and Pearl Gascoigne, undoubtedly the final visitor of the day, pushed the girl behind her back and threw herself in front of the crowd, stunning in her Amazon behavior, wearing a linen jacket and English skirt, with lace collars and sleeves. Defiant, without the least hesitation, she took them head on.

"Have you lost your minds? Leave these people alone!"

"Let them hang!" some in the back cried out again, quite giddy at her appearance.

A large decapitated body gone running in its own blood, the crowd had already begun lunging when a gunshot added confusion, cutting short its momentum. Each person looked around for a possible victim. A second shot froze that little world for good.

His Springfield gun held up in one hand, William Pill dug his knees into the saddle, spurs back, and pulled the reins so his monumental mare sprang from the dark, rearing up with a whinny at the shocked villagers.

"You all can kindly go home now," he said in a tone both cheerful and firm, his gun lowered to the right height. "Go back to your wives! What a shame it would be for them to end their days with nothing but a poor rapping spirit for company . . ."

Relieved, with a radiant pout on her lips, Pearl had rejoined the Fox family inside. For his part, Mr. Fox was encamped with his shotgun behind the broken window, determined to hold his ground. His wife and two daughters were huddled in the hall at the foot of the stairs.

"Everything's safe for now," said the pastor's daughter. "They're dispersing. But they will come back more numerous, tomorrow or in a month if nothing changes here."

"What can we do?" declared Mrs. Fox with the aplomb of the elect.

Pearl noticed Kate's small hands who, in the background, was entertaining herself by snapping her fingers. Even despite the biggest frights, she allowed, nothing stops the appetite for play in children.

In the silence that had returned, the youngest of the Fox sisters cried out in a raucous little voice:

"All right, Mister Splitfoot! Do as I do! One, two, three, four . . ."

The parquet floor took back up noisily in echo, leaving Pearl seized with disbelief.

At that precise moment, the hinges of the front door seemed to let out a meow. Paralyzed, the farmer took aim into a haze of mist bathed in moonlight. A figure on its guard stayed without advancing further. The voice was quickly recognized as the stranger with the pockmarked face.

"Your horse is getting impatient, Miss Pearl! It would be best if I accompanied you back home on this troubled night . . ."

Part Two

Rochester

One need not be a Chamber—to be Haunted—
One need not be a House—
The Brain has Corridors—surpassing
Material Place—

—Emily Dickinson

I.

I Want Only a Long Drunkenness

At this time of the year, all the mills of Rochester, which alone furnished more flour than the whole of New York state, were busily grinding grain both upstream and downstream of High Falls, the three powerful waterfalls of the Genesee thundering for eternity in the heart of town, echoing other falls just as powerful along the course of the river between Canandaigua Lake—where several Seneca and Onondaga tribes still lived—and this sea of freshwater that was called Lake Ontario, at the southern point of four others that were even vaster. Thanks to hydraulic energy, several industries had rather quickly established themselves along the river in the capital of Monroe County: textile mills, paper mills, manufacturers of clothing, and various tools, all of which, ever since the Erie Canal linked the city to Albany and also to New York via the Hudson, were able to export quantities of merchandise aboard houseboats, barges, and steamboats whose paddle wheels evoked water mills. The increasing prosperity of Rochester—the first American boomtown, founded a half-century earlier by industrious landowners—accommodated more than ever before an influx of miserable immigrants freshly disembarked.

The center of Flour City, as this mill city was nicknamed, had recently been developed with imposing stone buildings, while on the peripheries new neighborhoods of log houses were being constructed, crammed with workers' families, Germans or Irish escaped from typhus or cholera, wandering pioneers, African-Americans in the delicate status of free men without civil rights, who at any time could arbitrarily be chained up again, farmers ruined by drought or the Indian wars. Between the shores of the Great Lake, the docks of the Erie Canal and the winding banks of the Genesee, in the beautiful avenues around Midtown Place or the dirt roads beyond Mount Hope Avenue, a diverse world evolved of dock workers and sailors, scrawny beggars looking for work, preachers of the apocalypse and street vendors, transportation workers of all kinds, artisans working in their booths, fortune seekers in waiting—not to mention the blind mendicants and street orphans, pieceworkers, inventive traders, and finally, the recent bourgeois. The latter keeping their distance much more than they or their fathers had previously, who, with a Bible in hand, extracted themselves without regard or remorse from the marshes of survival, while from their dry footing still giving orders to managers, procurers, and other intermediaries, who along with government workers and the liberal professions constituted the middle class that made the town habitable and even commendable to all pious souls, young girls from institutions, and congregation members of various denominations continually on the move toward universal salvation. In Rochester more than in most states in the North or South, the spirit of enterprise was opening to the ultraliberal aspirations of abolitionists and pacifist democrats, women's rights movements, preachers of the Second

Coming, or anarchist federationists in clandestine work for refugees from four continents.

Strolling a little drunk at dusk between the aqueduct and the old cemetery, Lucian Nephtali thought about the strangeness of these multiple existences in this city, of all the inundations that he'd practically seen be born, like at the end of the world. To look deep into the heart of things, the cascades of adventures carrying along this not particularly scrupulous, but neither exceedingly wicked individual were somewhat explained by credulity. It was in his temperament to believe everything suggested to him, even the impossible. His profession of lawyer, left behind for that matter, couldn't have been the cause: a promoter of justice does not prejudge any truth and coldly puts into doubt everything, including the surveyor's calculations. Lucian Nephtali on the contrary sought the enchantment in every circumstance, even if it meant marveling at a blade of straw in the hollow of his palm after a river had just washed over him.

Surreptitiously, between two buildings off an empty street, he entered into a dark courtyard feebly indicated by the flicker of a lantern. A series of winding staircases, each designated by a candle sconce, led him to a landing lit this time by an oil lamp, and then, after showing his credentials, into a vestibule with no distinct feature apart from a bronze knocker in the shape of a Chinese dragon. The colossal man at the entrance dressed in Western clothes merely bowed to let him pass by. Through mixed vapors, Lucian followed the padding step of a young servant to a room where two or three clients sprawled on ottomans quietly smoked their water pipes behind curtains. The manager of the establishment, a Chinese man from Hong Kong with an exemplary British accent, who'd recently arrived with a large staff from the forest-town of Cleveland, came over personally to set three trays on the adjoining coffee table.

"Not many people tonight at the Golden Dream?" the visitor inquired while taking off his boots and cape.

"Not many. Your friend the coroner is sleeping like an angel in the corner. You didn't bring the missus?"

"It's not good for her. She's playing tonight at the Eastman Theatre . . ."

Stretched out, head propped on a cushion and an ivory-tipped cigarette holder between his lips, Lucian watched the manager go off while inhaling his first puff. Propriety demanded that Charlene Obo, who was barely his mistress, be viewed as his wife in such a place. Besides raw opium or the chandoo imported in brass boxes, they also served absinthe, among other alcohols, and black tea. Lucian could very well settle for a hot drink, like this automaton of a police officer, during the times he needed to keep his faculties alert. But tonight would require a descent from the cross into hell. The funeral of Nat, so young and such an old ally, at the Buffalo Street cemetery marked his entry with no return into a grand canyon of loneliness—he'd known it intuitively when looking down at Nat's coffin earlier and then up at the suddenly indifferent faces hovering above the graves of a few other close friends. Giant cranes swiveled on Pinnacle Hill in the back-ground, where the last building of a large and still vacant hospital was being constructed. Nat Astor had lain at the bottom of his hole for barely three hours, but from now on he would be a con-temporary of all the disappeared who'd ever haunted this Earth, a thousand eternities of lived lives. Lucian thought of Harry Maur's awful words before the still-warm cadaver of his friend, in the winter greenhouse where the servants had moved him: "This is worse than revenge—one doesn't go kill himself like that in his host's home." In his right hand, as if he were going to empty the barrel into the dead man, he grabbed the Colt Paterson with which Nat had shot himself right in the heart. The day before, or two days before his death, last week, they had all three found themselves outside of a reception in the new villa of Leah Fish, on South Avenue. The music teacher and rather mediocre pianist was becoming a celebrity ever since the Hydesville affair. It was Harry, the most superstitious of millionaires, who'd been taken with the oldest of the Fox sisters, a divorcée envious of her maiden name and full of ambition for her little family.

The faint bubbling of the pipe and the snoring of a neighbor lost in illusions mixed with the sounds from outside, the river's waterfalls and a sudden rain shower falling on the slate or zinc-tiled roofs. On one of the trays, the wick from an oil lamp was opening a golden fan aged by the fire of centuries; within it very ancient and translucent figures were coming to life, an inexhaustible wildlife where memory silently dispensed its effigies, immediately unfurling in endless floral hybridizations with an exuberance at least equaling nature. The visions of an opium smoker are more entrancing than any siren song. There where a member of the Temperance Society or of the Anti-Saloon League might discern a face or shape in the background, between other inept rebuses, there universes were opening up for him, bringing their demonic engineering to the surface, pulled from unfathomable equations. A pinch of opium was enough to melt the wax of the seven seals. For a few hours, a freedom more elusive than the dream of dying would cease altering all feeling in him. His wells and fountains were now dry; his only friend in the ground, where would he find a semblance of intimacy again in this world? Charlene Obo only expected a bit of fun out of him. And if Harry Maur, whom courtesans and other fawners mobbed incessantly, had gladly paid the lawyer to advocate for clouds or the roses in his park, it was only from the cruel lack of interlocutors.

A filiform servant filed between the smokers' compartments, which were similar to tiny theatre boxes. A regular, solid man with a bull's neck and sloping shoulders painfully stood up and staggered in the bronzed half-light of the room, undoubtedly just informed of the time. His sluggish steps managed to keep plantigrade: a bear coming out of hibernation. Lucian didn't try to hide from him. The coroner knew all the customers of the Golden Dream, most of them lawyers and functionaries. They constituted in all casualness, through a tacit agreement of discretion, a sort of the extrasensory vision club.

Which didn't prevent the coroner for better or worse from conducting his investigations between two divinatory lethargies. In a state of absolute detachment, he made an excruciatingly slow gesture toward the lawyer.

"A car is waiting for me in front of the old cemetery. I'll take you along?"

"I prefer to stay until dawn," Lucian murmured.

The coroner nodded with the simple drooping of the face, eyelids, cheeks, and lips. He had hesitated to say something about the suicide of that wealthy old woman's young hypnotist. Although his self-sabotaging seemed to leave no doubt, this Nat Astor fellow left quite a riddle engraved on his tombstone: who could have been camouflaging himself so long behind such a name! Wide open to invasions, America was a paradise for truncated, concocted, usurped identities. With the kindness of a judge and a few dollars, one could invent a gilt-edged civil status for oneself without a lot of trouble. Nobody would go verify your qualifications or aptitudes in the archives of the Old World. The graduates of not to be found learned societies, officers of Napoleon, international financiers and English or Russian aristocrats abounded in the city as well as the countryside, not to mention the acknowledged charlatans parading on the village squares or in conference rooms.

The coroner came close several times to falling down those damned labyrinthine stairs that echoed like piles of empty coffins. He told himself that the tea was giving him indigestion. He never should have drunk that tea, blacker than bile. Finally somewhat satisfied to be alone in the night, he began to hum, hand on his pocket revolver:

A house without love
Is an empty homestead
But wherever love lives
Is home indeed

II.
Maggie's Diary

What a whirlwind since our hurried departure from Hydesville! The most bizarre events have followed one after the other with Kate and myself, admittedly the origins of all this disorder, not being able or knowing how to stop any of it beforehand. Spurred on by Reverend Gascoigne, who banished us from his church, the farmers harass us a little more each day, some of them gathering in front of our house with torches. Once, when just the two of us were coming back from the village, a band of cowherds followed us on Long Road screaming horrors. Instead of heading for the farm, Kate ran toward the pond, leaving me no choice but to follow her in that absurd flight. They were throwing pebbles and clods of dirt, treating us like witches or imps of the devil. At the edge of the forest, a dripping figure stood half-naked, holding a white veil like a flag in one hand and in the other, the other . . . It was Samuel, the High Point widow's son. He buttoned up his pants and with a funny smile signaled to us while the pack kept approaching. Without thinking, lacking any other choice, we followed him into a cave hidden by the river, which at that spot falls in a cascade. Inside, there was lingerie hanging from stakes. My sister guessed it immediately: the rags were Violet Gascoigne's, the drowned woman of the pond. And below that, items stolen from the laundry lines of young farm girls. When the horde had passed, Samuel hid his face in a flannel pajama bottom. Despite his demented air and curious forms of entertainment, he probably saved our lives.

The next day we left Hydesville forever.

So there we were, our dear mother, Katie, and I setting out in a stagecoach for Rochester. Before joining us, our father had to work alone for a little longer at the farm. Our older brother David, whom my little sister and I hardly know because of the many years' difference in age, was willing to take over the operations of the farm, which brought in a better yield than his. Obviously it was Leah who had organized all of it. We look up to her for her discernment and her resourcefulness. With her corsets and satin dresses, she doesn't look a thing like the farmwomen of Hydesville! Our big sister is also a piano virtuoso who can play sonatas by Bach and Mozart without missing a note. At thirty-seven years of age, she could easily be our mother. It is so much more chic to have an elegant mother.

Kate and I have had a hard time making sense of our new life. It's crazy, all that's happened to us thanks to Mister Splitfoot! A real fairy tale, even if the Puritans treated us like witches. Our mother, who only knows how to read out loud, received dozens of letters a day, often anonymous. Hearing them, there was a lot to be afraid of!

But this is too emotional, I'm mixing everything together, I no longer know the purpose in even telling this. Leah found us a big furnished house on Central Avenue, even more beautiful than her own, a palace compared to our Hydesville dump, with at least a dozen doors, not to mention closets, and ceilings as high as those in churches. We each have our own room, with beautiful new linens acquired at Fashion Park folded in our dressers and chests. Leah of course took care of everything. Even our mother now has the air of a member of the English bourgeoisie. In her fine clothes, she no longer talks such nonsense. At the recommendation of her eldest daughter, she makes herself heard as little as possible.

Leah promised to attend to our education. She's teaching us how to sing correctly and not to swear about everything like country people. We try to make her happy by being accomplished young girls and no longer crying about goblins under the pretext that Old Billy's mane is all in fairy knots. But Old Billy died of old age this winter! Katie cried about it just like she'd recently cried about our dog Irondequoit, and, sempiternally, our little brother in Rapstown.

Katie hasn't changed too much, despite having the waist of a dragonfly and small, pointed breasts. So weird, a little coquettish, she has in her such a damned naïveté and a sadness that comes from far away. We've remained accomplices so that people could imagine she and I shared the same powers. From my end, I learned plenty of tricks from our nights in Hydesville, as opposed to Katie, who, like all awake dreamers, never lacked resources (they say that sleepwalkers are born with one eye too many). The secret that must remain in this journal is that Mister Splitfoot hasn't left us. Like cats, ghosts choose their masters. They're not homebodies so much. Now the spirit accompanies Katie wherever she goes. It was him who asked us to reveal his story to the whole world, on one of the last nights at Hydesville. We know almost everything about his past life, when he was a peddler weighed down by a heavy briefcase full of haberdashery. A spirit, if I've understood correctly, is an inkling from infinity struggling with past feelings, or else the shadow of a soul full of regret, still captive either way to our pettiness as living creatures. All because of a violent death, a suicide or assassination, or an immense sorrow or some terrible disappointment at the moment of entering the door to the afterlife.

When her eyes mist over and fix into a stare, Kate sometimes starts to say terrifying things. She claims for example that the drowned woman in the Hydesville pond follows our former teacher Miss Pearl around everywhere with abominable intentions, and that she should run away, far away, otherwise she will depart this world or go mad. How could a mother want to harm her daughter? She also says that there are thousands of shadows watching us, everywhere, but that only some of them try to break their silence. And then her eyes get cheerful again and she invites me to a game of hearts or dominoes. I get the feeling that she is unaware of what happens to her in those moments, like when she gets up at night, all disheveled, arms stretched out, her white nightgown dragging behind her.

When I invoke the spirit, since that is what is expected of us here, there is so much tension around me, such an attention in all the people that surround me, that by the end it makes a noticeable sound of creaking in the furniture and in my skeleton, at the ends of my hands and feet, in the joints of my knees. Even my teeth are involved. Kate, on the contrary, is not contracted, tensed-up like a bow; it seems more like she abandons herself entirely to the mystery, imperturbable and quite sad. Even at the brink of fainting, she smiles absently. Mister Splitfoot is surely goading her from the other side of appearances so that she doesn't turn her eye away.

We don't lack for visitors in our sumptuous lodgings. Worldly people, as Leah says. Rich businessmen, the middle class from all the professions. And then there are the journalists who file in, insolent, mocking, or conversely so attentive that they put their fat paws on my arms or brush a finger against my thigh or blouse. Their questions are sometimes surprising: what are your tricks? Do you believe in animal magnetism? Do ghosts remain good Americans? Have they ever been abusive toward you?

Without wasting her time with that hullabaloo, our big sister solicited a very fashionable decorator from downtown who came to install what she called "a cabinet for spiritualist consultations," with rosewood panels and bronze chandeliers with nine branches, and thick curtains of crimson velvet. Also called in by Leah was a bald coppersmith wearing spats, who soon installed on our front façade a copper plaque with the inscription:

FOX & FISH
SPIRITUALIST INSTITUTE

Our role consists in putting visitors in contact with their dear departed ones. Even Leah gives consultations. Our mother, meanwhile, is responsible for collecting payments and keeping the accounts up to date. She applies herself to this with joy. In just a few sessions, it seems, each of us brings in several months' worth of rent.

On some nights, Rochester personalities come to talk with us. Among them scholars of I don't know what talk seriously about expert commissions and inspections. Not all of them are benevolent. Even the police and churches get involved, sometimes claiming that we are hiding vile deeds. Fortunately we have our supporters, like the Quakers Amy and Isaac Post, or that large sequoia of a man of the same denomination whose name I forget. And so Leah, to put an end to all these slanders, has rented the biggest room in Rochester. We are going there soon to make a public demonstration monitored by a group of experts. Kate is terrified. I'm ill at ease about it myself. Girls like us aren't used to self-exhibition. We don't know anything, we're just intermediaries to the other world. Kate comes out of her divination séances as if from a dream, with no memories. For me, it's worse, I have the feeling that I'm stepping out on a bridge that's collapsing, or steering an enormous boat into a black abyss where everything is creaking and streaming with water. And in those conditions, I still have to maintain the look of being tranquilly seated in a salon, awaiting the deluge! So, when nothing comes, it's true, I crack my toes. What charitable person would expect someone dying not to cheat with death?

III.

Exploration of a Mining Field

After getting rid of a lusterless husband who left her a nice pension, Leah Fish went on to leave the Irondequoit Music School, where she had for so long taught piano and music theory to inept damsels of the new middle-class. The Spiritualist Institute, her creation, demanded her full attention. She seemed to have taken on all the responsibilities of running a theater: administration, directing the actors, budget, props, stage setting, all the way down to costumes and makeup. Not to mention diction instructor, one of her most thankless tasks with a family that chews their English like cud! It was a mystery to her, and doubtless to any number of her fellow citizens of second, third, or umpteenth generations, this indigent extraction she'd managed to wrench herself free from thanks to a childless marriage. And where had they all come from themselves, those wretched Puritans, all branded with Sin, if not the putrefactions of the Old World and abysses of misfortune? But good blood wouldn't know how to lie—and everyone around here armed his heart, kept a rifle behind the door, ready to play double or quits in order to obtain prosperity and his due share of salvation.

While arranging bouquets of callas and lilies on the dressers and coffee tables in the room, the eldest of the Fox sisters wondered with a hint of anxiety if she wasn't asking for a little trouble by renting Corinthian Hall from the manager of the Lecture Society, after the talks given in this high place by some of the most prestigious orators in the country like Oliver Wendell Holmes, a famous man of letters, the director of the *New-York Tribune*, Horace Greeley, the great theologian Charles Finney, author of the so subtle *Heart of Truth*, the very boring Ralph Waldo Emerson whom she could have heard last year, or even the preacher Alexander Cruik, who needs no introduction. Leah sighed with pride at the thought that he had agreed to be in their company at her soirée. The invitation of a divorced woman, a musician certainly and actually quite literate, can only be accepted by great minds. There would be other singles there this evening, like the superb Wanda Jedna, who campaigned for women's liberation, that priceless Lucian Nephtali with his fake Manfred airs, as well as frightfully old men who were always useful for finances and promotion.

The bell from the nearby Presbyterian Church rang seven o'clock.

Nervous, Leah called out to the youngest of her two servants: she had forgotten the cinnabar lamps and incense to burn!

"No need to light the chandeliers," she added. Ambiance is really just a matter of scents and shadows.

She went to close the lid of her baby grand piano, certain that she would be begged to reopen it after dessert. Overtaken that moment by light-headedness, she leaned against the corner of the piano and saw the days and nights marching on the ivory keys. All the events since she had taken charge of the family's destiny for its own good resembled a series of favorable tarot cards. This sudden celebrity almost worried her though: it was happening as an omen, a probationary period of sorts. The other world—its angels or its demons—had visited Katie and Maggie, incontestably. But it was she who, as shrewd proselyte, upheld the communication to her own spiritual level. Neither her sisters nor her poor mother were any good at doctrine. They had only understood the most trivial or absurd aspects of what had happened to them in Hydesville, that invisible neighbor beating against the door from the other world. As if holy Nature gave its place over to fantasy! As the granddaughter of a pastor, even if her father was just an uprooted drunkard, she immediately understood the quasi-liturgical dimension of this telegraphy of souls, notwithstanding that such a process could be laborious in comparison to the Eucharist. Leah stifled a little laugh. She'd liberated two useful sacraments to Rochester, out of the grasp of priestly ministers. She had long leaned toward the natural religion of her sister deists, those rational lovers of God who made fun of prophets and miracles. The Hydesville revelation had managed to restore her childhood faith in mystery, but no longer being a child, she envisioned a mystery that was a real object of study and devotion. Couldn't we arrive one day at a kind of practical science of the beyond?

The macadam road was soon clanging with iron harnesses. Convertible and sedan coaches followed one after the other on South Avenue. Upstairs the panoramic rooms pulsated with bursts of voices mixed with intelligent laughter. Couples greeted each other according to custom. More circumspect, the single guests distractedly examined the scene. A monocle screwed into his left eye, Lucian Nephtali silently raved to himself about the hostess's bad taste. There was, however, poorly hung, an acceptable watercolor of a small master of the Hudson River School. The tulle curtains of the plate glass windows let in a view of the Genesee River, wine-colored in the evening twilight, and of the three partly illuminated waterfalls. Wanda Jedna, nicknamed by her fans The Only One, serenely contemplated the view while wondering what it was Leah Fish wanted from her now. In the back of the room, the industrial clothing manufacturer Freeman and his spouse were already talking about investments and capitals with the nurseryman, Barry Nursery, who owned all the forests along Braddock Bay and Mendon Ponds.

"We are seriously considering a bridge for the railroad on Upper Falls. A huge wooden bridge, the biggest ever constructed, around fifty thousand cubic meters of wood is already on its way!"

"Perhaps we should build a train station first!" Mrs. Freeman dared.

"But why? Bridges, first we need bridges!"

An old retired soldier, displaying all his medals, imposed himself into the conversation; his eye was on the new aqueduct.

"I myself was present in 1829 on the right bank, a young and dashing officer, when Sam Patch, a real daredevil, made his leap of death from the top of the waterfalls before all of Rochester. Bah! The unhappy man broke his neck there . . ."

Leah pretended to be helping behind the bar where a black servant in livery was in charge of aperitifs.

"You don't have anything stronger?" drolly grumbled a blond financier with a little moustache maintained in the fashion of an Alta Italia aristocrat.

Knowing for a fact that Sylvester Silvestri, in addition to being the nephew by marriage of Colonel William Fitzhugh, Junior—cofounder of the city with his counterpart, Colonel Nathaniel

Rochester—had been the local vice president of the Independent Order of Good Templars, one of the more active temperance societies, it was with a wink of complicity that Leah served him his lemonade.

"There will be French wine at the dinner table, my dear!"

The arrival of the preacher, followed by Harry Maur puffing on his cigar, and the actress Charlene Obo dressed as queen of the night, provoked a bustle of curiosity that visibly offended the latter. Among the first to arrive, the Post couple stood side by side, stiff in their Puritan outfits, looking bored, wondering if there had been some kind of mistake. The former telegraphist—rendered temperate by the proximity of his wife—missed Hydesville and its saloon more than ever. The two of them were astonished not to see a single other member of the Fox family or its entourage in the group.

But the guests all found their assigned seats around the Arthurian table. Amy and Isaac Post were relieved not to have neighbors who were too awful, like that effusive actress or the somber character dressed like a buccaneer, who had fallen into each others' arms with a shocking affectation. Framed by the young Andrew Jackson Davis on her right—a brilliant supporter of mesmerism with thin glasses and a patriarch's beard—and the Milanese banker on the left, the mistress of the house did not expect that the preacher placed across the table would exclaim loudly enough to turn a dozen heads.

"But where are your dear sisters, Mrs. Fish? I was so hoping . . ."

"They are too young!" Leah responded defensively while throwing embarrassed glances at her nearest guests. "And soon you will be able to applaud them at Corinthian Hall . . ."

The two servants back-to-back served a boiling soup until, bowl by bowl, the steam had formed a circle.

"Yes, of course, at their age!" added the booming voice of the gaunt Alexander Cruik. "But it would have been so pleasant to talk with them. Especially the youngest . . ."

"With Kate? Is that so?" was the only way Mrs. Fish knew to respond to hide her confusion, seeing that the evangelist of the Redskins, with a voice accustomed to outside gatherings, was the kind who would pursue his idea without fail.

"Your Kate is gifted with an exceptional sensitivity, she captures psychic waves not perceptible to the common man. It's an acute form of intuition of beings and situations without being able to actually deduce anything herself. I've known Cherokee Indians capable of a similar extrasensory perception, one of them above all, a sorcerer with a mustang's mane who could read the future in the wrinkles of the dead. In his trances, he pointed out without fail warriors who would be condemned, women soon to be pregnant, children struck by our maladies . . ."

"May the Lord preserve our sorcerers!" cried out Mrs. Freeman, a fat woman with a hairdo in the form of a crow's nest.

"So natural and so candid," the preacher continued in the same tone, "little Kate is a sort of shaman who is unaware of it which, however, grants her the powers that the first apostles must have had. She is an intercessor between two spaces of perception and comprehension usually hermetically separated, a kind of . . . of *medium*, if you will allow me the neologism . . ."

"Medium, medium . . . ?" Leah exclaimed. That's the word they were missing! "But allow me to explain that modern spiritualism, if I may use your expression, is as much the business of

Margaret Fox and of myself, not to exclude our dear Kate, nor my mother or my old father . . ."

"It's a family business!" joked the corpulent Barry Nursery from a distance.

"Do you consider yourself to belong to the current Religious Revival?" her neighbor on the right, the magnetizer Andrew Jackson Davis, asked more cautiously.

"Assuredly," stammered Leah, a little sorry to see her soup growing cold. "We are, my sisters and I, passionately enflamed in our faith, and this mystical fire spreads especially today, waking in each of us our piety for the afterlife where our dear lost ones continue to exist. The dead are our angels, believe it. Wasn't the resurrection of our Lord the first manifestation of spiritualism?"

"There have been plenty of others since Osiris, Dionysus, or Orpheus," sighed Lucian Nephtali wearily, mopping his brow.

"And the prophet Elijah!" boomed the preacher with an amused zest. "Remember the widow of Sarepta in the time of Ahab, the idolatrous king: 'And it came to pass after these things, that the son of the woman, the mistress of the house, fell sick; and his sickness was so sore, that there was no breath left in him . . .' Housed in a room above the widow, Elijah brought the little corpse up to his room, stretched himself three times over him, and cried to the Lord: 'Yahweh, my Lord, will thou also hurt the widow hosting me, for that you make her son die?' Immediately, the soul of the little boy was returned to his body by divine will. Elijah brought him down to his mother and declared: 'See, thy son liveth.'"

"But this isn't about reviving the dead! We have, God willing, much humbler ambitions than prophesying the Messiah. Our mission is simply to put mourners in the presence of spirits, thus enabling consolation, opening the world finally to hope . . ."

The women present, wives and celebrities, loudly applauded Leah.

After dinner, Wanda Jedna, charmed by this new cause, prioritized it now in her mind just after those of Negros and women—for didn't our virtuous dead participate in the full rights of the great human family?—and caught the hostess off guard, who pushed passed in surprise on her way to open the baby grand to perform a recent air from Paris. The martial harmonies were so stirring that Charlene Obo and the banker with the fine moustache started to clap their hands.

> *L'homme, ce despote sauvage*
> *Eut soin de proclaimer ses droits*
> *Créons des droits à notre usage*
> *À notre usage, ayons des lois!*

IV.
Oneida! Oneida!

No one asked any explanation of Pearl Gascoigne when she pre-sented herself one summer night at the doors of the commune. On the way back from haying, tools over their shoulders, the Per-fect Ones stared with amazement at this sublime mare and her thoroughbred, still intertwined in the same energy, both of their manes flowing, the woman and her horse visibly out of breath. It seemed like this girl was fleeing a fire, the lightning of God, and some band of Algonquin cannibals all at the same time. While the frightened horse raced back and forth between the fences and log cabins, several young women wearing short dresses for evening service appeared.

Pearl found herself staggering in the middle of a strange assem-bly of bearded farmers looking like magi, of farmwomen looking like old queen regents draped in dark colors, an indefinable smile on their lips, in their lightweight dresses or frocks with straps, and very young children suddenly frozen in their games. Pearl had immediately noticed the short hair of the teenage girls, their cheerful and at the same time defiant air, and a type of hierar-chy belonging to animal herds in the physical appearance of the males, according to age, but also a sort of relaxed quiet on their faces. This pastoral tableau, worthy of a genre painting of the epoch from the thirteen colonies, inscribed itself upon her, a little unreal, after that entire day of galloping aimlessly in the dust of the roads.

She had left Hydesville without explanation, mind on fire, on a stormy night. Suddenly following a clash with her father on the question of her clothing and the expense of lace ribbons, she had turned away in silence. Running to his stable after putting on her riding clothes, Pearl didn't have the least concern about the following day, like someone anesthetized, abandoning without the least regret both her little treasures and large responsibilities. The thoroughbred, an extremely rare White Beauty bequeathed by a farmer of the county, was the sole luxury of Reverend Gascoigne. Submerged in anger, having decided impetuously to flee as far as possible, she didn't think twice about whether to instead seize the ordinary horse hitched to an English wagon. And it was with a worn out bridle, in the sweltering midsummer night, dizzied by the scents of the thatch and the bland exhalations of stagnant waters, that she'd traveled half of Monroe County and all of Wayne, before galloping erratically the days that followed between mountains and forests, then through the endless plains, in Oswego and Oneida territories where, thinking she was lost in an Indian reservation, Pearl had unwittingly found herself hostage to a most curious tribe of pale faces.

She will remember for a long time the welcome given by the women her age under the hungry eyes of the men, once over the general amazement upon her arrival—a beautiful equestrian archangel filthy with sweat and dust but dazzling in the twilight. Several of them grabbed hold of her after a few words. Pearl was hungry and thirsty, she wanted a deep sleep after her hypnotic ride. Once she slid off the saddle, the women, almost carrying her, led her to the bottom of a narrow valley where a river flowed. Laughing, they took off her boots and completely undressed her while the patriarchs stood above at a proper distance. Then they immersed her like those statues of Durga, inaccessible goddess in the waters of the Ganges, half-naked themselves, soaping and scrubbing her down from head to foot, kissing her hair and her mouth, saving her from nearly drowning. Dripping wet with her long hair plastered to her hips, there was a murmur of almost religious admiration around her. Washed, the statue had the beauty of seraphim and demons, a mortifying perfection, marble sculpted in the fire of a desire that blinds the overexcited. Even children pale with emotion came to the hillside.

At that moment, more than ever, with one hand on his heart, John Humphrey Noyes must have thought about the humanity, pure in blood and soul, that his community had the mission to create, by *passionate attraction*, beyond the abominable sacrament of marriage. Her glorious anatomy, exempt from the tortures of procreation, reminded him painfully of his former wife, with a body deformed by successive aborted pregnancies.

But there was in this improvised baptism an intolerable bacchanalian release. With the title of spiritual guide, he severely inquired about the disorder caused by the intruder, then summoned her into the reflection room. After these water games, dressed now in a short, sleeveless frock furnished by the laundry women, Pearl, her eyelids heavy, had to face a curious interrogation of a paternal firmness, close to a sermon. The man reminded her of the reverend with his austere bearing, his grave voice, and thin face with strong jaws poorly concealed beneath a beard. But John Humphrey Noyes took on a whole other tone when it came to the question of the Celestial Free Spirit and Universal Love, of the sanctity of work and voluntary confession. There was in his eyes then a great persuasive sweetness. Pearl, helpless, accepted the protection and the lessons of the mentor.

That is how she became his primary companion in bed before agreeing, as was customary at Oneida, on a weekly change of partners. A recruit by chance or by fate, her days were devoted in part to picking fruit, weeding the garden, or in making preserves, and in part in graduated book study. A devoted child of God, she shared by privilege the enlightened appetite of the oldest pioneers of this brotherhood of complex marriage, who initiated her at length in the technique of sexual continence—while the eldest women were in charge of educating novices in the matter with a maternal patience. To prevent unwanted pregnancies and to increase female orgasm, the officiants were forced to master the act, here there was no question of abstinence like in numerous other competing sects, but of dry perpetual copulation: each member of Oneida, once his or her share of tasks were completed, indulged with modest joy in the simultaneous sharing of carnal love and property. Spiritual freedom and contraception being inseparable, the community never ceased to expand by the arrival of new followers rather than by the rare selective births.

The Edenic dream of the austere father Noyes, derived in part by his reading of an imaginative French philosopher and the discovery of Robert Owen's cooperative societies, floated paradoxically over these heads who had forgotten nothing of the Puritan propriety but an evangelical permission that delivered them from the miasmas and necrosis of sin. Hymns and canticles were sung on all occasions. At night, at evensong, the most beautiful voices raised toward the stars:

> *Let us go, brothers, go*
> *To the Eden of heart-love*
> *Where the fruits of life grow*
> *And no death e'er can part love*

What Pearl had felt during those long months of the abdication of her integrity resulting from her rash revolt was unlike anything she could imagine. To give up a resolute virginity in a graceful commerce of skin had annihilated in her once and for all that constriction in her virtuous reticences, and all those duplicities of public morality that eventually paralyze bodies and souls. Subject to the Family and its discipline, Pearl nearly forgot about the world—and her father even more. Had she ever had another permanent home, all-powerful and of a tenderness as transgressive as it was strangely respectful?

But this place, where the quest for perfection took unusual paths, had its setbacks that in the end became intolerable to her. Noyes and his council of elders summoned the tribe of God's children two or three times a week, disturbing it from its generous instincts for inquisitorial meetings of mutual criticism. Under the big trees on beautiful days, or in the only stone building—a vast warehouse that in addition to storing grain and fodder was a place of rejoicing, and in other seasons a space for meditation and meals—they stood in silence waiting the call of their name before the council of Perfect Ones. It was everyone's duty to point out each person's lacks and crimes, his most intimate failings. These sessions of *criticism*, according to the expression used, were intended to be purgative, cleansing one of his pride and selfishness by the sheer force of mutual love and in the apprehension of divine truth. Called to the tribunal in session, in the guise of pardoning, the collective sharing of faults, Pearl was persistently vilified by a majority of female accusers: they accused her of coquetry, reproached her too long hair, her repeated offenses in bewitching the males, her casualness in the children's education, her lack of enthusiasm for household chores. The Perfect Ones nodded meekly. In order to satisfy the biblical communism instituted at Oneida—and to appease the umbrage of the offended women—they would without fail choose her time after time to serve as surrogate mother.

When she started to miss her White Beauty, sold by the community leaders in compensation for their hospitality to neighboring farmers, who never missed a chance to trade with their brood of Christian mongrels, Pearl knew she didn't belong with them any longer. The hymns at night around the large bonfire saddened her with the memory of her orderly life in Hydesville. But there was no question of her going back.

Every night on beautiful days, the Perfect Ones intoned their hymn under the stars.

> *Let's go, brothers, let's go!*
> *Soon the true love will live*
> *In peace and joy forever*

It was through the woods that she left Oneida one night in the middle of evensong without waiting for dawn—her hair short, wearing the clothes of her poor sisters paid for in *coitus reservatus*, and more impoverished than when she arrived, but with, throbbing, deep inside her, the exquisite violence of freedom.

U.

Like Galloping Carriage Horses

Two strong teams of horses were quietly lined up behind Charlene Obo's cabriolet in front of the Central Avenue house. The Fox family and its entourage were getting ready to leave after a rehearsal nervously led by Leah under the expert eye of the actress. In the main room, which was transformed into a theater dressing room, she was bullying her two young sisters in the middle of piles of clothes and sewing notions.

"Look at me with that oafish face of yours!" she exclaimed under the nose of their exhausted and worried mother. "You'll never be anything but little peasants . . ."

She pinned ribbons to collars, tightened waists, removed ridiculous fake jewelry.

"And you, Mother," she added in a categorical tone, "you can keep that brooch and necklace on. We will not be seeing you on stage . . ."

"But I would have really liked all the same to say a word . . ."

"With your accent and your royal magus naïveté? You must be joking. Our enemies would turn away in derision . . ."

"Your daughter is certainly right," Isaac Post allowed himself to say, with his wife's consent. "It's first and foremost about convincing these people, and believe me that in this good city of Rochester, the unbelievers can be fierce . . ."

Discreetly facing a window, his enormous body folded in thirds on the piano bench, George Willets reacted fierily:

"But there will also be a crowd of people committed to your cause! Those of our church in particular, you know well that our Quaker friends are devoted to you! And the Mormons whose going astray I cannot agree with. And Adventists! I would bet that the marvelous Ellen White will be in the room . . ."

"You read the newspaper?" Amy Post was alarmed.

"The *Rochester Herald* is nothing but a sanctuary for pathological conservatives!" quipped Charlene Obo. "Tomorrow we will have a panegyric in the *New-York Tribune*!"

Being the professional entertainer, the young woman rushed their departure for Corinthian Hall. One never faces the public without having first inspected the stage and regained one's breath and color backstage. Especially since this was a premier!, and with novices! As for her, Charlene Obo no longer doubted the amazing gifts of the Fox sisters. She had participated with a poignant joy in a performance of retrospective divination: all of her wishes had been granted. Her twin sister Jane, dead of typhus at seventeen, had responded mercifully through the innocent mind of Kate. In the other world, her twin was keeping watch over her, she couldn't doubt it any longer after so many years of horrific nightmares where the same red and black gnomes were incessantly tearing her half apart, an arm, a leg, an eye, and that unspeakable bloody part in her belly. Thanks to her friend Leah, thanks to the singular power of Kate and Margaret, she had been delivered from these dwarfs she'd so long identified with theater boxes and orchestras, while she no longer knew, in her confusion, who was acting on stage beneath the rafters, her twin sister or herself, whether Jane or Charlene Obo.

"The horses are stamping their hooves!" she finally cried out on the porch. "They sense our impatience . . ."

The three cars filed through the wide avenues of the city center. On a corner seat in the second coach, forehead against the glass, Kate isolated herself from the talkative agitation that surrounded her. This adventure was taking an ominous turn. Disguised as a model young girl, she had the feeling of being driven to the gallows in the old days like that class of English schoolgirls accused of petty larceny. Across from her, Mother had the stunned face of a large freshwater fish, pale and purplish, which seemed to be coming off and falling at her feet. Kate was astonished at how removed she felt at that moment, those near her unexpectedly revealing their secret aquatic natures inside the passenger compartment, a sort of aquarium of sloshing water. An inappropriate thought made her smile: maybe there were spirits from the other world above baiting the fish down here with invisible lines . . .

Outside, a fine rain illuminated the gray asphalt roads that alternated with the paved esplanades. The gas lamplighters began their rounds, from one sidewalk to the other, and sequined halos followed their quiet steps. Department stores had just closed their doors on the nose of indecisive flâneurs. A number of shadow puppets filed by in front of the backlight of shop windows—clerks, beggars, hawkers, families, prostitutes—swept away each moment by the teams of horses' manes. Kate scrutinized these shooting stars and felt a sense of displacement. Everything was going too fast, nothing resembled yesterday. The adults around her all wanted to play a game of cat and ghost. They all had a lot of victims on their conscience. Who is ever able to swear that he is not responsible for the suicide of one, the fatal illness of another? Kate was quite certain of her own responsibility in the death of her little brother. She had clearly noticed his lack of appetite and burning cheeks during his first sleep. She should have helped him eat and held him tight against her each night to absorb his fever. But death is unexpected like every other moment down here below. In his final delirium, Abbey was giving her defensive smiles, stammering long words, while pointing with a frightened finger at a tiny crack in the wall. A child knows everything because his fear is not of any world.

Kate looked over at the sleeping expression on her mother's face. The jolting of the carriage shook her cheeks and tufts of her white hair. An old woman filled with dreams while facing a precipice, that was the excruciating feeling each second had for her. What differentiated the two, really, the living and the dead? She rested her forehead on the glass, eyes open, sensitive to how the vibrations changed her view of objects, themselves become shaky, undecided. Among all those shadows scattering in all directions, how many were wandering spirits or corpses reanimated by a magician's breath? To help her sleep as much as to complete her education, Leah had on many nights told, with a witchy pout, stories of the living dead and dark prophecies drawn from English authors, such as the capricious Horace Walpole who loved to wear a wooden necktie, Ann Radcliffe in her fatal castle, Mary Shelley's seam-riddled monster, or of a certain Polidori, so frightfully pale. Whispering at her bedside, eyes wide and teeth sharp, her older sister would lean in to say: "At the side of the bloodless beauty the lord was thirsty for fresh blood." While enriching her vocabulary somewhat, she was undoubtedly trying to maintain in her, through fright, the black fire of what was called Modern Spiritualism . . .

Kate listened to the hooves of the three carriages thunder across the stony ground; she thought she saw women's heads flying in the middle of a dance of knives. When Leah would narrate these selected horrors to her, she made a habit of reciting nonsensical counter-spells from the foot of her bed, to keep her from dying of fright:

> *I give my elephant*
> *Against its weight in ladybugs*
> *Oh, what happiness! what happiness!*

Huddled against the carriage door, she wasn't far from using the same strategy to exorcise her anguish at the approach of their destination. They were about to be released to the tigers, she and her sister. Oh Maggie, Maggie let's find a magic formula fast to escape them!

> *The king's page from neck to sole*
> *Swims flat on his belly all the way to the North Pole*

"What gibberish are you saying now, Katie?" asked the skinny Amy Post, sandwiched in the middle.

Without answering, suddenly perfectly consoled, she thought back to the elf with scraped knees from the woods and streams of Hydesville. But childhood had swallowed those days like spun sugar. A young woman should find her strength in the folds of her gray dress rather than on the swirling flimsy checkerboard of her dreams. However, speak of the devil! She squeezed up close against her noisy old ally. Right, Mister Splitfoot?

Big dry knocks resonated in the cramped lodging of wood and leather, provoking a burst of anxiety among the passengers.

"Oh!" their mother exclaimed. "That's the announcement that we'll be arriving soon!"

Kate wasn't the only one noticing the quantity of beautiful coaches, carriages with inlaid mahogany, curricles, and horse-drawn vehicles of every kind being slowed down by a mixed crowd, where groups of bony and bearded Puritans lurked menacingly next to great ladies in hats and rather cheerful old men dressed like dead trees. But where were these multitudes headed? Isaac Post stuck his long narrow head outside the coach.

"What could we have as competition? A well-known choir, surely, or a preacher of the Second Coming . . ."

"Giddy up, old girl!" Amy Post exclaimed, crazy with exalta-tion. "This beautiful crowd is here for us, for our cause! O sweet Lord! It's hope that brings them!"

VI.

Assembly at Corinthian Hall

It had been a long time since the high walls of Corinthian Hall had been the scene of a mob: the place was overtaken and conquered beyond all expectations and the organizers, starting with the director of the hall, were already envisioning future events. People crowded in through every entrance to save a numbered seat or to claim ones for themselves. Public rumor, amplified by the telegraph and the press, had brought together everyone the state of New York and its environs could call *amateurs*—the erudite or the merely curious—nonconformists or the rebellious enticed by the sulfurous scent of a new Reformation, astrologists and itinerant hypnotists passing through Flour City, most of them fervent followers of Franz Anton Mesmer, credentialed scholars, men of letters, and academics envious of their merits—all these people in tandem with the Puritans who were swarming like ants, not yet knowing if they should applaud or boo.

In the first rows, protected by guards from the invasion, important personages were taking their seats after entrusting canes, top hats, and furs to the cloakroom. Students and preceptors gathered in the aisles of the balcony waited patiently by putting names to faces of the more or less elite who, one by one, slid like playing cards behind the backs of velvet armchairs. The wealthy cart manufacturer James Cunningham could be made out, as well as the banker Sylvester Silvestri, and the businessman Henry Maur, joined by a famous actress dressed in perpetual mourning. Also in attendance were the very influential director of the *New-York Tribune*, Horace Greeley, and Alexander Cruik, the famous evangelist suspected of occult collusion with the Redskins, worshippers of the Great Spirit. Political luminaries campaigning in Monroe Country preferred to keep their anonymity by hiding in the corners of back boxes. In this way, the presence in a personal capacity of the old lion of the Whig party Henry Clay, current Speaker of the House of Representatives, went unnoticed by journalists. The solemn entry of Judge Edmonds, eminent lawyer, of the chemist James J. Mapes, a professor at the National Academy, or of his colleague Robert Hare, aroused less interest than the arrival of local owners of mills and textile factories. The town mayor, grandson of Colonel Rochester, and his lymphatic wife, received applause and whistles . . . Nobody noticed the numerous figures of spiritual renewal scattered throughout the room, some accompanied by their disciples: the Adventist visionary Ellen White, all dressed in white and wearing a headband; the publisher of the deist Thomas Paine, author of *Age of Reason*, which threw the baby Jesus out with the baptismal bath water of the Gospels; the withering Andrew Jackson Davis, already devoted to the picturesque Leah Fish; and many others who had no celebrity yet—not to mention a host of merrymakers interested in various illusions, and dubious fortune hunters focused on finding the deal of the century or at least of the evening.

Among the latter, settled down now in his seat after being rudely jostled, William Pill was smoking a foul-smelling cigar while meditating on his immediate prospects. Thanks to the amnesty of good soldiers and his military certificate, done with the High Plains, he had nearly repaired his reputation in the Rochester gambling houses. But those fine winnings from time to time only allowed him a modest lifestyle, easy women, and a whiskey that was just drinkable. During his escapades in Texas, returning home from pacified Mexico, he'd had some more extravagant days. But now here as elsewhere, luck taunted him. Money, that wind in his hands, only brushed through his fingers until his next ruin. The only thing still in his possession was a Bible recovered from a shipwreck, aside from the smallpox that had hailed down on his face. Reading the *Rochester Herald* announcement of the spiritualist demonstration that day while in the barbershop, he had hardly suspected the connection to the mischievous Hydesville girls until the journalist's acerbic comments had refreshed his memory. This "buffoonery of knocking spirits" was an ingenious idea: he estimated eight or nine hundred people had crowded under the columns of Corinthian Hall, the largest auditorium in town, which must have brought in around a thousand dollars, minus the fare-dodgers like him and free entries granted to those in the first rows. William Pill knew how to appreciate mystifications. In Ontario he had known a conjurer in a cabaret capable of swapping the heads of his subjects, chosen among those who'd imbibed the most alcohol. In Philadelphia, he'd had the privilege of observing a ventriloquist up close, the fallen disciple of the Utopian William Abbey, very clever at stripping the bourgeois of their pocket watches while declaiming, with mouth closed, the *Declaration of Mental Independence.*

Between two Puritan women pale with nausea, his cigarillo stuck to his lip, Pill yawned to unhook his jawbones. The evening running behind, he let himself grow sleepy in the good warmth of the place. Immediately, the gallop of a horse carried him off to an immense dreamed prairie. He too was visited by a ghost, always the same one. Met in the street corner or viewed in an interior, it was a young, very blonde woman, too beautiful to be described. The only thing for certain was that he didn't know her from Eve and yet loved her madly. Nothing, nothing made sense on this Earth where anything happens except what one expects. *A stranger before me who once was me in another time, before an unknown young woman tells me: who are you, faceless man, and what do you want of me with your empty hands, your hands like two corpses . . .*

A voice thundered now from somewhere unplaceable. Eyes half-closed, he perceived on the illuminated stage a character dressed in a swallow-tailed coat, with an olive face and raven black hair, who had the formal appearance as master of ceremony. Pill pulled himself out of his somnolent paralysis with a start. The show was finally beginning.

"I have the honor to present to you tonight Corinthian Hall's invited guests . . ."

With these words, Lucian Nephtali discerned the plump face of the coroner in the third row. He hadn't seen him since that night of oblivion at the Golden Dream, after the funeral of his friend. The shudder of surprise that suspended his voice for a second was perceived, he thought, in the fleeting ironic grin of the police officer. But he pulled himself together the second after, while imagining a grave veiled in opium smoke.

"Listen to the prophet Ezekiel! It's on Spring Hill that he was summoned to call back to life the many Spirits of the dead: 'The hand of the Lord was upon me, and carried me out in the spirit of the Lord, and set me down in the midst of the valley which was full of bones . . . and He said to me: "Son of man, can these bones live? . . . Prophecy upon these bones, and say unto them: O ye dry bones, hear the word of the Lord" . . . Thus saith the Lord God unto these bones; "Behold, I will cause breath to enter into you, and ye shall live." So I prophesied as I was commanded: and as I prophesied, there was a noise, and behold a shaking, and the bones came together. And when I beheld, lo, the sinews and the flesh came up upon them, and the skin covered them above: but there was no breath in them. And Yahweh ordered me: "Prophesy unto the wind . . ." And the breath came into them, and they lived, and stood up upon their feet, an exceeding great army.' Like Ezekiel, like Ulysses or Hamlet, we have all been in contact with the soul of a lost one, that of a little child or of a beloved spouse, or of a very dear friend . . . It is now possible to provoke at will this gratification of Providence."

"If only someone would make the undertaker shut up!" a mill-worker shouted unexpectedly.

"Cormorant!" added a sailor, while imitating the bird's cry.

"Dead body packer!" cried a slaughterhouse butcher, for the sake of balance.

From the back of the room, jeers and laughter continued.

Undaunted, thinking about the challenge thrown down by Leah and her friends in search of a speaker, a challenge that he had accepted with some cynicism but in the manner of a perfect gentleman, Lucian raised his voice:

"The integrity of the Fox sisters has unnecessarily been called into dispute under the pretext that one could counterfeit certain phenomena or attribute them to physical or even psychic causes. But beware! The Fox sisters are championing no sectarian fantasy. With modern spiritualism, we are witnessing the collapse of a wall of silence that separated us from our precious lost ones. This is about a moral revolution that is going to change the face of the planet . . ."

Boos redoubling by this time in all the rows, Lucian Nephtali told himself that he could stop there, that the damn service requested by Leah and her accomplice Charlene had largely been rendered.

One arm stretched toward the wings, he almost danced his gesture of retreat.

"Present here tonight, the Fox sisters will now perform for you according to the rules an authentic demonstration of spiritual telegraphy . . ."

Gaslight lanterns and Fresnel lenses were dimmed, leaving the stage lit only by two astral lamps with bluish globes. Assistants lugged a beautiful oval walnut table, tall chairs, as well as an imposing armoire onto the middle of the stage as if some theatrical drama were about to begin.

There was a sudden spell of calm in the room. The bursts of laughter had stopped; the disruptive ones were themselves taken by surprise at the sight of the three sisters in somber and austere dress making their way from backstage at a mesmerizing pace. Leah, whom many took to be the mother of the other two, separated from the group and broke the silence.

"The world of Spirits pre-exists us. Spirits surround us, they are your dead children, they are your fathers and mothers! Most of them are willing to respond to our call. There are some that are caring, so close to being angels; others, tortured by their terrestrial sins, come back to haunt the scene of the crime. Some of those who suffer most don't even understand they have died. But all, without exception, journey toward perfection. After their many wanderings the Spirits will reach deliverance at the breast of the Supreme Being. All of them will be saved . . ."

Muffled mutterings and sobs rose up from the crowd. Kate and Margaret, withdrawn in the chiaroscuro of the lamps, waited for the signal from their older sister. The youngest considered the abyss of the auditorium with the same fright she'd had discovering Lake Ontario shaken by a violent gust of wind. An elementary power was at her feet, blind despite its thousand eye-sockets, ready to swallow her up. Who was she to risk such a confrontation? And what more did she know than other girls her age? The surrounding tension was so intense, her skull received such a nervous influx that she thought about fleeing by any means, fainting or hypnotic crisis. However she clenched her fists and invoked Mister Splitfoot with all her might.

Next to her, Margaret, noting her sister's pallor, discreetly pressed her shoulder. She was also uneasy but despite everything was still amused by the enormity of the phenomenon: an even greater wonder than their story of the knocking spirit was this crowd who had paid just to see them! She told herself, knees shaking, that secrets would abound under her pen as soon as she opened up her diary. Wasn't she, a silly girl, living a pure moment of History?

After a solemn warning to the skeptics who risked scaring off the Spirits, or even of making them dangerous, Leah returned as rehearsed to their side.

"Margaret and Kate Fox will sit at this table under your inspection. In the name of God who has granted them this holy gift among us, do not disturb the mediums in their channeling of extra-sensory powers . . ."

On the brink of panic, Kate and Margaret glanced furtively at one another. The mischievous smile of one behind the shelter of her palm recovered the other's serenity, while electrical vibrations were already traveling from the depths of their bowels to the ends of their hair, hands, and feet. "Oh oh! Mister Splitfoot, don't leave me!" Kate begged. For she had no doubt that the peddler's spirit had followed her all the way from Hydesville. She imagined his cloven foot as being incredibly swift, able to leap in a single bound the distance between the Earth and Moon. In the blink of an eye, Mister Splitfoot could save her from the bottom of a well or from the mouth of a brown bear. Moreover, here he was now leaping without anyone's knowledge on the table as if to say: "But what do you want from me now, naughty little girl!" "Wow! Did you see that band of ogres and mean crows out there? Here we are, Maggie and me, in a terrible position . . ." "You sought it out, I swear it on the slit of my throat! So let's talk! What are you waiting for?"

"Spirit, are you there?" Kate exclaimed out loud in direct response to Mister Splitfoot. "If you are there, knock twice . . ."

The table was immediately the instrument for two powerful knocks that had the dryness of actual bullet shots or of a hatchet thrown at a hollow tree.

There was revolt in the room, and one woman let out a sinister howl. Shaken with convulsions, Charlene Obo frantically applauded. Camped behind the backstage exit after his buffoonish performance, invisible to the public and protagonists that he could now observe at leisure, Lucian Nephtali was smoking a cigarillo while pondering the degree of fantasy the Great Watchmaker placed in his work. Quite curious phenomena surrounded these young girls. The furniture seemed to respond to them as feeling persons, like paralytics in fervent skeletons. And why the devil did the dead act so turbulently at the least invocation? Leah monitored her sisters with the eye of a night owl: white moon rabbits, surrounded in a gloomy forest of Puritans, they were frolicking between two coffins of old wood, one in the shape of an armoire and the other a table.

The dry knocks turned into a rain, more regular than the clangor of a gallows, and the afflicted crowd roared in anger and dismay. Were they afraid under the livid light of the astral lamps of the apparition of a vast population of numb souls, with scythes and fangs, such as Breughel had depicted in his *Triumph of Death*, coming by the thousands of millions to put an end to the scandal of the separation of the beyond from here? If little girls had the power to abolish such borders, logically an apocalypse should follow. Lucian burst out laughing at the prospect. He himself would be ready to give credit to all this nonsense to see his friend again, to ask his forgiveness and press him once more against his chest. But Nat Astor was without a doubt still in the old cemetery on Buffalo Street. And what could answer to the mystery of the abyss? O you who do not enter, *or not yet*, abandon here all hope!

VII.

Fox & Fish Spiritualist Institute

From then on the house on Central Avenue with its *Fox & Fish Spiritualist Institute* sign was frequented by all the polite Rochester society. They even came from New York City and Boston, from Illinois and Pennsylvania in order to consult one or the other of the Fox sisters. Leah managed the business with determination and rigor, selecting the clientele, taking care of the ritual of welcome, and the staging in each of the three rooms decorated without ornamental overload in a neo-Gothic style. The most difficult for her was banning any semblance of a desire for independence in the two sisters, who were certainly both of marrying age—Margaret especially. The little farm girls were growing refined thanks to her lessons and now knew how to appreciate beautiful corseted dresses, taffetas or black satin, tasteful jewelry, and smart hairstyles with hairbands and chignons at the neck that looked so nice with thick hair. They'd become so beautified that contenders flocked, even among the widowers coming with the hope of corresponding with their deceased wives. Why bother with a husband, that's what she, a divorcée and happy to be so, repeated to them at leisure. Thanks to the paid séances and the donations from their wealthy followers, they lacked neither the ordinary nor the extravagant—even if the bank accounts remained hidden to them. A fortune acquired outside of marriage has for a woman the exquisite taste of revenge.

Leah held bitter memories of the tests they'd had to pass before actually establishing themselves and building their reputation beyond Monroe County, the state of New York, and then in the whole Union! The episode in Corinthian Hall, however decisive for their careers, fed her worst nightmares, where an anonymous voice suddenly destabilizes the precarious equilibrium of the believing public. "Witches!" the crowd had cried at the moment when a randomly chosen spectator was learning from the counting of knocks a shameful secret. Then there was a battle of insults carried out in full force by the Puritans, ready to take action. The demonstration happened to be coming to its end, but the released audience congregated outside, unleashing their animosity. The most virulent of them had stolen thick ropes from the storefront of a saddle shop that they were brandishing in the half-light of the evening. Perched on a horse cart, a sententious pastor named Ryan excited the lynch mob. "Whoever plays with Satan will not take delight in God!" he started to proclaim, among other cookie-cutter slogans.

Press correspondents gave considerable coverage to the event, though their reports contrasted wildly. Whereas the papers of the South and Midwest spoke of the shameful deception of abolitionist clans and women's rights movements, the *New-York Tribune*, under the pen of a young follower of transcendentalism, in fashion with progressives in the North, announced it a fundamental discovery proving nothing less than the immortality of the soul. The article ended with a quote from Ralph Waldo Emerson: "There are persons, from whom we always expect fairy tokens; let us not cease to expect them." The Quakers on their end were heavily engaged in the spiritualist path, in competition with the Mormons who had the aim to recall, by their lawful baptized name or with good reason, all the souls that ever lived on Earth since Adam and Eve, without neglecting anyone.

The lawyers and scientists present at Corinthian Hall, however, suspecting a hoax, joined together to assemble a commission of experts. Seeing this merely as a ploy and case of bribery, the populace threatened to hang the three girls and their protectors in the case of favorable findings. It was at their risk and peril that they presented themselves at those meetings in the form of a public hearing at Corinthian Hall. Neither the first commission nor the second could detect the least stigma of fraud. All sorts of tests, however, were conducted by a clerk of the court. They listened inside the armoire and the table with a stethoscope. They placed felt pads under the chair legs. After having inspected under all their garments and up to their private parts, they bound the young women's hands and legs during the invocations. The court doctor Brinley Simmons restricted each girl's diaphragm with straps to thwart any attempt at ventriloquism. Nothing suspicious could be detected in the course of these extravagances. The experts confined themselves to stating the absence of mechanical causality between the mediums' action and the various means by which the knocks were produced. An Episcopalian commission headed by an itinerant bishop of the Evangelical Association even concluded the entire good faith of the two youngest sisters without explaining or endorsing the phenomenon.

After the lynch mob, the fortune attached to the fame didn't fail to attract predators. A certain Norman Culver, distant cousin by marriage, had tried in vain to blackmail them. He ended by declaring loud and clear that Margaret had revealed to him her method of cracking the bones in her toes. With a little practice, he claimed, anyone could deceive the simpletons recruited among the public at fairs. Dealers in bankruptcy were not far behind; one of them, of Irish stock, wanted to sell them the handwritten map of a gold mine in the Rockies bequeathed by an illiterate father, certain that the animal magnetism contained on that flimsy piece of paper would serve as compass. But these vagaries were only the ransom of a glory that promised to be universal.

Leah herself had learned a lot by adversity; although deprived of the natural grace of her sisters, as a medium of some consequence in her own right she felt protected by her great piety from the random charlatans that kept up fertile if inept competition. But who was she to complain? The money deposited each week in the Silvestri bank was fructifying nicely. Reliable friends surrounded and advised her, starting with the devoted Sylvester, as well as George Willets, that good giant who had saved them from lynching after the favorable verdict of the Episcopalian commission, not to mention dear Charlene Obo and that singular Wanda Jedna, figurehead of all great egalitarian causes. Supporters and followers flocked to the private meetings of the Spiritualist Institute, such as the enthusiast Andrew Jackson Davis come from Blooming Grove, the quite amazing Anna Blackwell who carried the spiritual grief of a Luciferian poet from Baltimore, the cloth merchant Freeman, Jonathan Koons, a farmer from Ohio who promised to build a sanctuary for Spirits, and those dozens of war widows, weeping mothers, or theology students all trembling at the invocations like willow leaves when the night wind blows. To such a point that she no longer knew how to differentiate a patient from an affiliate or a courtier from a possible rival.

Also not without influence on Leah's mood was the languor of their mother, affected all along by all the dramas that had come rushing upon her daughters as much as by the strangers rushing in from endless funerals, and the increasing hostility of Margaret, always a nervous wreck and ready to repay her devotion with tantrums. The Fox & Fish Institute's success was at its zenith however, since her younger sisters' latest ingenious discovery. One idle Sunday in the South Avenue villa, they had seized upon a small round table with tripod legs flaring out from a base inlaid with a ring of palmettes, with the idea of card reading in the manner of the Marquise de Fortia. But the table being too narrow, the cards were instead spread on the floor, some on their back, others face-up. Margaret had then claimed that this couldn't be a coincidence. While she knelt to read the future, her sister, hands flat on the mahogany tabletop, started to invoke the chosen knocking spirit, who seemed to find this new mode of communication very convenient: the delicate little table, literally possessed, started to tap from one foot to the other and spin around like a Bavarian dancer. Alerted by chance about this wonder that she had readily attributed to animal magnetism, Leah knew to draw on it as an immediate option during her private séances. With her most loyal spiritualist friends—all as unaware as she of the ancient *mensa divinatoriae*—the handling of turning tables was deliberately developed according to many codes and variants, a repercussion that delighted her, and a profound reflection on Science and Progress revealed through spirits by heavenly Intelligence.

Whenever she could, on evenings without obligations, Leah took refuge in her haven on South Avenue and tried to forget the madness for which she didn't want to believe herself solely responsible. Wasn't divine will invincible? In these moments, released from the anxieties of the strictest vigilance, she dreamed of gliding over the surface of things, a soap bubble on bare skin.

In her tulle negligee, after taking a bath in a tub her Virginian servant filled by kettle, running between the well in the basement and the coal stove, Leah smoked one of those long cigarettes given to her by Sylvester, her banker friend, thinking of the path she'd traveled since her lousy childhood on some farm in Rapstown. Facing the lights of High Falls that overhung the enormous construction site of the new viaduct, which would allow trains to pass through to New York, Cleveland, or Buffalo, she had the sense of losing her bearings. What kind of life was turned so absolutely toward the incorporeal? A bright blood flowed through her veins. What she felt could be compared to homesickness, but the lost country was that of the flesh, of great rivers and showers of stars. Cracking open the windows, she breathed in the air permeated with spray. She could hear the roaring cascades of the Genesee River between gusts of wind. Leah was taken by a long shiver. There was too much madness mixed into her line of business. Her sisters and her mother, her father taking refuge with their brother David—the entire family was going to disperse in the winter wind and she would remain solitary and sterile amid all the disembodied, like an abandoned garden. The words of a *lied* came back to her in her head:

The autumn wind,
Will it cry over my ashes
Before blowing them away?

She opened the bay window wide. The sails of her robe floated up to the piano. A jewelry of tears on her lashes, she stroked both hands across the low keys. It was her ruse to overcome melancholy with more melancholy.

VIII.
Farewell Dear Mother

The death of their dear mother happened unexpectedly, on a December night. Deeply ingrained for years now, her depression finally started to seem to those around her like a temperament that the damage to her health had come to accuse. Having become loyal to the household, the court doctor Brinley Simmons, always encumbered with his surgery bag, had amenably followed the evolution of her languor, which he had treated primarily with mercury, as with syphilis.

But in the end their good mother gave up the ghost without having complained of any other torments except for an irrepressible fear for her children's future. It was the youngest that, one fleecy morning, found her in her bed, believing she was asleep, but so still, so identical to herself, the perfect sleeping statue of a life. Kate had just dreamed of her and, happy to keep the memory intact, was eager to go tell her about it at daybreak. "Dear Mother, I dreamed that you were cured of all your pains. It was snowing. You were so happy to be leaving on a trip alone and without luggage . . ."

Kate had crossed the cold hands atop the covers and leaned over to brush her lips on that marble cheek. Back in her room, she'd waited more than an hour for either Janet, the maid, or Margaret to make the discovery. Margaret's agonizing cries were inimitable. Still in the unreality of the present moment, it was with an exalted air that she entered her room crying, "Mother is dead!" Speechless, Kate looked at her without reacting, paralyzed by a terrible sense of déjà-vu.

"Yes, I know," she said finally.

"But how could you know?" Margaret immediately asked with alarm.

"I must have dreamt it," she replied in a faint voice, as if she were still dreaming.

Paradoxically, the death of their mother was a welcome interlude for the Fox sisters in their trying activity as mediums. On leave *due to a death in the family*, they didn't want to hear talk of spirits and the beyond any more than circumstances required. Leah busied herself with the various tasks and the usual formalities. An announcement notified the family and a few close contacts. Among the first to hear were witnesses of the Institute's increasing renown: some Shakers on pilgrimage, Baptists of the Millerist strain, a couple of Seventh-Day Adventists, and an old Mormon escaped from prison all presented themselves at the Central Avenue address in order to pay respects to the remains laid out between four candlesticks.

On the day of the funeral, hiding in her room, all ready to go, Kate considered the comings and goings on the avenue. A hearse hitched to four white horses was waiting for the end of the casket-closing ritual. Her sisters and Janet were calling her from across the house to come for the farewell kiss. Were they unaware that for her there was no farewell? Dear Mother lived always in her dreams, busy, worrying over the least snail wandering across her thin arms, but she no longer wanted to approach, all of a sudden passed through to the other side of the big glass wall that prevents hands from holding, breaths from caressing the eyelids, and scents from reminding you.

That night, from her bed, an outline had appeared to her behind the glass windows, between the curtains. There had been so many of these in her dreams, these wanderers from the void. Solitary, they came and went from one world to the other and often, in town, they were recognizable by their hunched-over gait and by the steam on their too-smooth faces.

"What are you waiting for, come down!" Margaret cried out, forcing open the door. "It's the farewell! It's the farewell!"

Kate, unpredictable, ran into the warm room without saying a word. An undertaker from the funeral home was about to seal the lid of varnished wood. Using both hands as he lifted the plank, she pushed it back down like the god of doors.

"I forbid you!" she screamed, furious, before practically lying down in the coffin, blanketing the dead woman under her flowing hair.

But the box was screwed closed and the convoy reached the Buffalo Street cemetery undelayed. Other cars were waiting in front of the entrance. It was on foot that the Fox family and their friends followed the hearse along a road lined with yews. Placid after her outburst of desperation, Kate walked in a distracted step behind her sisters who, from time to time, threw worried glances back at her. She was astonished by their extraordinary resemblance: the same outfits, black taffeta dresses and bonnets, even the same complicated hairstyle of a bun with raven wings.

Despite the age difference, their features seemed copies, with their narrow mouths and those huge eyes of Hindu deities on large faces wide as two hands. It did not escape her that Maggie was fighting in vain against her older sister's influence, so obvious was the mimicry. Similarly, Kate studied the details of the little formal crowd as they advanced along. Her brother David, whom she hardly knew, was going in the heavy step of a farmer in the company of their father, an old man indifferent to the world. How was it that her father and mother had conceived two distinct generations of offspring, nearly twenty years apart? Had they been separated from one another, the time for each of them to rebuild their lives, or were they hiding some hecatomb of miscarriages and childhood diseases?

The convoy was now walking on the slopes of a vast park planted with stone slabs upright or lying down, crosses carved in granite, steles and truncated columns. The scattered stones seemed to drift like little urban islands on a grassy sea of lawn out of which small areas of chapels and mausoleums emerged, isolated by cypress trees, the sinister enclosure of the common grave.

Each person in his own thoughts, Kate perceived the regulars from one house or the other, their first supporters Amy and Isaac Post, so scrawny on their patch of yellowed grass, George Willets, carrying his dignified colossal head askew above a giant body, Mr. and Mrs. Jewell also, and Charlene Obo under her veil beaded with obsidian pearls. Lucian Nephtali, dressed more somberly than usual, leaned into the tip of an ivory-handled cane and seemed to follow her eyes with the strange fixity of a painted portrait. Was he trying to hypnotize her? The court doctor Brinley Simmons, who was one of the experts in the Episcopalian commission before getting involved in the game of spiritualism and, on occasion, treating mediums, somberly observed the rudimentary work of the gravediggers. Could a specialist in violent death who cut up the cadavers of suicides and murder victims, like a farmer would his chickens, have any feelings about the afterlife?

But now they were tipping the coffin down by means of leather straps and thick ropes. Above the heads of the gravediggers, as if emerging himself from the tomb, Alexander Cruik pronounced a few words about the remission of sins, the resurrection of the flesh, and of life everlasting.

"It's the living who must be consoled," he added in his message to the audience. "Come into Salvation free of charge! No salary exists for the soul. God alone is responsible for those gone . . ."

Kate, frightened by that glaring pit, crept backward away from the assembly and fled toward the slopes. While wandering among the stones, she looked here and there at the epitaphs: "Here lie my chains," "No tears for the sinner," "Your Word is Truth." One quotation from the apostle John stopped her the longest: *Whoever believes in me, though he die, shall live.* Raising her head, she saw a few dozen meters away a waxy specter in a top hat emerge from the misty gloom. What else could she do but go over to meet it?

Having also escaped from the group, Lucian Nephtali stood affected on a mound in the middle of which was placed a slab of pink granite engraved with two names, one encrusted with lichens, the other biting cleanly into the stone.

"Is that you, Kate?" he said, folding up in a quick gesture the handkerchief that until then, he'd kept in between his palm and the handle of the cane.

"Ah," she whispered. "I'm sorry . . ."

"It's all right, come here . . ."

Kate yielded to that persuasive tone and was soon in front of the grave. She read a single name: Astor, Nat Astor, but could only decipher the last syllable of the other name taken over by a leprosy, and imagined with no trouble a family connection between the two, surely a son and his mother.

"It's me who owes you the apology," said the man. "I snuck out a little early to visit my friend."

"Yes, I know . . ." stammered the young girl.

"You know?" Lucian Nephtali murmured with a bit of amused disbelief. "You know who rests in this grave . . ."

"I meant that it's probably a young man and his mother who died when he was still a child . . ."

"That's exactly right," Lucian observed without much surprise. "Nat lost his mother when he was much younger than you: tuberculosis. He would never stop mentioning her, talking about her. He had very few images to hold on to, but that doesn't change anything. Forgetting, on the contrary, clarifies the principle of love. The less one is encumbered with memories, the more whole memory is and the more partiality is definitive . . . He swore only by her, his mother was his only true love. The pension that he received from a father who'd gone back to England left him free, too free undoubtedly, entirely abandoned to this holy absence. He lived in a state of mourning that had no recourse, do you understand? He bullied, drank, gave himself over to the worst excesses, and at the same time devoured with an always-flawless intuition the best American and British writers of today. Have you read Elizabeth Browning? And the great Nathaniel Hawthorne? Herman Melville, he too, is guaranteed to surprise you. As would the extraordinary Emily Brontë who died unnoticed, so young, just one year before that unhappy Edgar Allan Poe, gifted with double vision, stricken by every curse . . ."

Lucian paused, aware of the impropriety of this panegyric in a cemetery. Pensively, he stabbed the tip of his cane into the frozen ground with increasingly pointed blows.

"When they were children," he continued in a more playful tone, "Emily and her brother and sisters imagined an extraordinary universe, the *Glass Town Confederacy*, which they made come alive taking turns with all sorts of writings, geographical maps, newspaper articles, dramas, poems, and all this in a sort of always frenzied ever-expanded fiction by all available means . . ."

Kate thought she could sense some irony behind this digression—was it an allusion to the Fox & Fish Spiritualist Institute? More glaring in her eyes was the moral desolation at heart that this man seemed to be struggling with. And then she knew none of the authors he mentioned, but on the other hand had read Longfellow's *Voices of the Night* and followed for months Harriet Beecher Stowe's series, so moving, in the *National Era*, that abolitionist newspaper Wanda had loaned her.

"What do you think my friend died of?" Lucian abruptly asked the adolescent.

"He was murdered," she responded in a lost voice.

"You're mad! What allows you to say such a thing?" he said, losing his temper, before recovering: "Nat Astor, my only friend, my soul mate, killed himself with a bullet straight to his heart on Harry Maur's property, I know it, I was there . . ."

Some snowflakes flew over the graves without Kate allowing herself, pupils fluttering at the milky pulsation, to openly marvel as was her usual custom on the first snowfalls in winter. Lucian noticed this delightful burst of childlike surprise and couldn't help but smile. This girl just-become woman was as alive and distracted as the snow, everything in her mind surged thrillingly only to be erased in an opaque mirror. A reflection of Edgar Poe rose to his lips: "This terrible way of life nervous people suffer, when the senses are cruelly sharp and the faculties of the mind dull and drowsy."

"What are you saying? What people are you talking about?" Uncomfortable, Kate considered in turns this hypnotizer's smile and the swirls of snow now so prodigious that they were erasing the inscriptions on the tilted stones. Turning back toward where her family was just assembled, she could see only the same curtain of whiteness swaying between the occasional cypress, and was suddenly frightened of being absolutely alone with this man in the wax mask whose gaze insinuated itself within her.

IX.
The Aspiring Medium

Across the territory—from the Champlain Valley to the Great Plains, from the mountain states to the Gulf Coast, or from New England to Main Street America—the new doctrine that wasn't yet a religion, but rather a credo combining devotion and an aspiration toward the scientific, spread with the quickness of a brushfire that, like a thousand voices in the wind, gave greater credence to the Messianism of the Quakers, Seventh-Day Adventists, or the Mormon pioneers in the West fleeing persecution. They all denounced hell, that pagan invention, and likewise rejected the purgatory of the Catholics, longing for an intimate communication with God and his angels, without counsel or arbitrator of good and evil. Under the clear-sighted protection of the Spirit, spirits could very well populate spaces and worlds.

This providence of Modern Spiritualism very quickly touched hundreds of thousands, millions of Americans rich and poor in an age when the Grim Reaper spared no one in his vast harvests, let alone children of all ages, who were more likely to disappear than to one day follow their parents' path. One thus saw the emergence of countless mediums, like so many frogs born in the rain, a new species of preachers with their props, a number of whom discovered themselves: pastors at odds with their congregations, itinerant apothecaries, hypnotists dragging along Mesmer tubs in their wagons, retrained street peddlers, rodeo jugglers, professional cheats, and other conjurers. They officiated in every imaginable place after a media campaign or a circus parade, in churches, private homes, convention halls, covered markets, public spaces. Each in his or her manner promised a variety of shivers to gullible crowds for a dollar or a cent per head. These post-mortem communications became so popular in town, where turning tables was the fashion, that it was common among the bourgeois to gather in the evenings around a pedestal table, and anyone could improvise being mediator of the other world, provided that the rest didn't die laughing.

Encouraged by the aura of the Fox sisters led by Leah and their most fervent disciples, including the poetess Anna Blackwell, the actress Charlene Obo, the miraculously healed rheumatic Achsa W. Sprague, or the enigmatic Wanda Jedna, American women finally held a new way to take their turn speaking without being booed at like those feminists in municipal assemblies advocating the right to vote, or else persecuted and threatened with death, in the wake of intrepid abolitionists like Lucy Stone, Elizabeth Cady Stanton, or Susan B. Anthony, who were running from hills to valleys preaching a holy war against supporters of slavery and males, those predators of a similar breed.

In order for Modern Spiritualism not to be taken over by charlatans and to remain pure of any commercial alloy, as well as to keep away conspiracies and virulent charges from universities and scientific institutions as much as from the leagues of orthodox Puritans with figureheads like Ellen White, a sworn opponent of irrationalism, the sensible followers of the Fox sisters introduced missions of mediums in charge of enlightening the masses. Following the first Spiritualist Congress that took place in Cleveland in 1852, several independent societies were established, financed by wealthy philanthropists, which founded propagandist newspapers and dispatched missionaries with proven psychic skills across the Atlantic to conquer the Old World.

At the initiative of Leah who had hired a manager answering to the name of Franck Strechen, a Scotsman of apparently common strain, the Fox sisters traveled through the great cities of the Northeast: Newark, Philadelphia, Boston, Baltimore, Pittsburgh, Washington, Buffalo . . . Often hosted by local spiritualist societies, they multiplied demonstrations of mediumship with uninterrupted success, inspiring vocations everywhere and giving rise to emulators.

In Boston as in New York, Paschal Beverly Randolph, having returned still young from a tour of the world as the self-proclaimed Prince of Madagascar, alchemist, and Grand Master of the Fraternity of the Rosy Cross, had acquired an unusual glory thanks to his mixture of genres. Egalitarian and abolitionist, struggling for universal rights including those of sexual freedom, this child of slaves had founded a Bureau of Freedmen and made a reputation as comforter to the poor by invoking spirits specifically chosen to provide the best advice to all the oppressed. He took advantage of his powerful magnetism to connect bereaved widows with their dead companions, giving women access to interesting nervous sensations. Rushing in from all over, his public listened devotedly to his invective: "Remember, oh neophyte, that Goodness is power, Silence is strength, Will reigns the Spirit, and that Love holds the root of the All-Mighty . . ."

A little by chance, William Pill found himself one day listening to him while chewing his cigarillo and, by an even bigger chance, later shared the same carriage and fraternized with him along the ride. Now at Paschal Beverly Randolph's service for the past several weeks under the title of bodyguard, he'd had the time to assimilate certain aspects of his art of persuasion as well as several beautiful phrases. Like, "The only aristocracy is the aristocracy of the mind," which rang pretty true. However, Pill was not the kind of man to wear a collar for long, even a solid gold one.

Taking refuge in Rochester following a flagrant offence of fraud in a Boston gambling room where he thankfully escaped with his life, William Pill—who had learned unbeknownst to the black medium several mechanisms of suggestion to abolish the will or simply to put an entire assembly to sleep—then launched a new career, after several failed attempts in the realm of clairvoyance, as a merry necromancer.

It was to the Fox sisters, however, ever since that famous night in Corinthian Hall, that he unequivocally attributed his brand new vocation. For the last several months, he'd been able to improve his concepts as a tutor of Chinese wisdom or of the hierarchy of angels among the Catholics and Muslims. Easily convinced of the Great Spirit's love, the values of progress and the telegraphic function of the pineal gland (that antenna to the cosmos), it remained only for him to deck himself out in mourning clothes like any respectable commissioner of the beyond. Something achieved not without elegance, he amassed for himself a complete set of conjuring equipment thanks to his poker winnings: smoke bombs, a pulley system, cardboard heads, bulb syringes, magnetite rollers, fake hands made of resin, silk scarves, trick shoes, a couple of small tables covered in papier-mâché, some miniature shelves on wheels for automatic writing, screens, and a supply of candles acquired honestly in a Catholic church.

His very first demonstration took place in the private room of a brothel in Rochester before an audience consisting mostly of girls from the establishment and married men of good society. Madame Tripistine, the manager of Cevennes origin who had received him in her room and appreciated his urbanity as well as his way of opening bottles with his teeth, hired him for awhile as a bouncer, then remained friends with him after having made it understood that he was too bellicose for employment. It was she who had offered to let him make his debut at the brothel. "My girls will adore spirits," Madame Tripistine had assured him, "because of all the sorrows they lug around." Thus they lined up over thirty chairs in five or six rows, for the pimps and big shots of the area who wanted to be there, alongside the regular clientele slumming it. The stage set up between two screens was hardly bigger than a Guignol puppet theatre, but the apprentice medium found himself at ease and, showing a rare ability to make tables talk, provoked happy swoons among the ladies. Finding the use of mechanical transcriptions rather tedious, Pill even improvised by letting the spirit speak through his voice. A lout with a battered nose and ears shouted out to him at the same moment a cleverly placed fan blew forth a ghost made of silicate powder:

"And what does your spirit think of what I'm carrying under my jacket?"

William Pill, who remembered from his time as a security guard throwing this individual, then dead drunk, out one night after the precautionary confiscation of his weapon, had not forgotten what the collector's object was.

"A Colt 1851 Navy revolver, serial number 27139 . . . Is that right?"

"That's the truth! But as for the number . . . let's see now," said the man, taking out his weapon in front of everyone.

When he had called out the numbers in the right order, the audience clapped and whistled in amazement. But it wasn't until after having put Madame Tripistine in communication with her dead father—a disturbed and rigid man who, between his daughter's twelfth and eighteenth birthdays, on certain Sundays, had the crazed idea of whipping her half-naked while her arms were tied around a freshly-killed pig whose blood she had to drink to heal her lungs—that Pill knew his reputation as medium was official. In a big city, prostitutes spread rumors faster than syphilis, which competed with the johns who warred with each other, endlessly unaware that they were ushering in their own violent deaths.

Since that inaugural night, Pill multiplied his demonstrations in Rochester and its environs. He hung his own printed posters modeled after a search notice for a fugitive black slave nicknamed Moses, who had become an energetic abolitionist activist:

WANTED DEAD OR ALIVE
HARRIET "MOSES" TUBMAN
For Stealing Slaves
$40,000 Reward

Instead of "Dead or Alive," he had asked the printer to compose "Death Is Alive," followed by the smaller headline with his pseudonym, "William Mac Orpheus," then "Famous Medium."

This led to his debuts in numerous fortune parlors, a home for Irish and German immigrants run by religious Catholics who thought they were dealing with a buffoon, a theater out of use since the ceiling had collapsed on its actors during the performance of a romantic drama, and a Baptist church in a black community that was an actual station of the Underground Railroad and which protected itself from the intrusion of slave hunters by encoded hymns and songs:

> *Come follow the wind*
> *To my father's house*
> *We shall all live free*
> *In my father's house*

William Pill collected contributions himself after his demonstrations. The poorest would go in together to garnish his hat, the richest would invite him to dinner with the idea of solving the mystery of his powers or his science. This was how a blind man of a certain age came to request a private interview with him at his home, in a house outside of Rochester. Of a rare and natural beauty, his short-haired companion was dressed in a sort of uniform of unbleached linen, faded blue like the kind worn by Chinese railroad workers. Pill dreamily accepted the invitation with an acute sensation of déjà-vu. He remembered for no real reason an ancient Mexican fable where a jealous prince inebriates his young brother so that he breaks his vow of chastity, thereby causing him to lose the coveted virgin. The prince will not be rewarded for it in return for, she, the dishonored one, will go rip her heart out on the altar of the sun, condemning the trio to reproduce the quarrel for eternity.

X.

When to Burn Her Diary?

Have I already written this? It's amazing what's happening. It feels like our star is spinning so quickly on itself that from now on all the events it promised will follow one after the other in an insane acceleration, for better and for worse. Leah's marriage to a very rich man is going to change our existence. Instead of her banker lover Sylvester Silvestri like we all supposed, she gave in to the advances of a Wall Street broker, a cigar-man with crocodile shoes who seems to crumple wads of bills just to blow his nose. Everything happened very quickly after our return home from Manhattan Island. Leah, Kate, and I had been invited there by Horace Greeley, editor in chief of the *New-York Tribune*, an important person it seems. Influential enough in any case to host us for three months in a sumptuous hotel near the Barnum Museum, in Times Square, in the heart of Midtown, in exchange for some public sessions of our turning tables. We were received at his home, a huge apartment on 59th Street overlooking the city and harbor lights, at the top of a building at least ten stories high with a curious elevator that operated with a steam-powered motor.

Nowadays we can build mountains. If this continues, the spirits in the sky will be able to open our windows all by themselves.

For us, who had been living in the middle of cows and chickens, such luxury had something magical about it. The furniture and the walls, everything was covered in leather and precious woods, with marble and bronze statues in the corners, gilded clocks, impressive mirrors, painted vases, and very somber paintings everywhere. Leah taught us this lesson: it's important to keep one's composure and to appear to find these palaces perfectly commonplace. The child of a poor farmer like us, without any education other than what he taught himself, this Mr. Greeley is now the boss of the biggest newspaper in America, the voice of the Whig Party and the publisher of that H. D. Thoreau, a defender of the Spirit and of liberty. And all that by starting as a simple printer's apprentice! In any case, the reception given at his residence in our honor was a fabulous moment, unforgettable, which left me speechless. Imagine all these ladies sparkling with jewels, gentlemen with white collars and jackets with satin lapels, while mute jugglers called butlers go back and forth. Bald with long grey hair at his temples, with fine glasses that slightly veiled his kind face, Mr. Greeley went from person to person, presenting us as prodigies. Even his political enemies had been invited, starting with the terrible Isaiah Rynders, king of the Irish gangs of Tammany Hall, who in the past, they say, was attacked with a knife on the Mississippi River. This ogre supported with all his might the young president Franklin Pierce whereas Mr. Greeley, who's a vegetarian and friend to Negros, defended the unhappy Whig candidate. And there they both were reunited in a truce of minds! Mary Cheney Greeley, our dazzling hostess marked however by grief, took me aside while the guests reported on the drama of the presidential couple, who had just lost their son Bennie in a railway accident. "We ourselves have lost five of our children," she confided to me that evening. "It's the Massacre of the Innocents! We have two daughters left not far from your age and I struggle for them to be free women. But what will become of our dead children?" I read in Mrs. Greeley's face the same pathetic plea as all those other mothers and grieving spouses.

That's the kind of mediums we are, universal consolers! I'm not proud to admit my insufficiency at it here on this page. Reading these words over my shoulder, a spirit would surely be amused. The same people who forgive the setbacks of the boxing champion William Thompson still expect us to always be in our best form, though we're only receiving the blows. When an uproarious room, half filled with lynchers, is expecting the Spirit to manifest itself, how should one react if one would like to keep her skin? At the Empire Club and in other places, all three of us impressed the public, especially Leah, who is such an eloquent speaker and so adept at diverting attention. It was in the conference room of the Barnum Museum that our most difficult demonstration took place. Under the patronage of the *New-York Tribune*, journalists, scholars, and men of letters were invited, quite courteous besides, but who observed us without blinking, like poker players, from the beginning to the end of the séance. There was James Fenimore Cooper, Nathaniel Parker Willis, William Cullen Bryant, who I remember very well, and also Mr. George Ripley. The Wall Street magnate, a certain Mr. Underhill whom Kate had nicknamed "the man with a skeleton of gold" ever since the night at our benefactor's home, installed himself in the front row and devoured Leah with his eyes. Silencing the skeptics, she proved herself with stunning craftsmanship. I haven't forgotten her audacious gibberish:

"Spirits are freed from the physical laws that govern our world. The medium who serves both as a receiving antenna and a transmission relay requires great concentration to establish a magnetic area permitting communication to be established. By their presence alone, skeptics and the irreligious provoke disturbances in this perimeter that make our work difficult . . ." This was devilishly sneaky. The skeptics felt obliged to cut their whiskey. Kate, just to my right, stuck her tongue out at me while closing one eye. In our code, that means: "Low profile, I'm calling Mister Splitfoot to the rescue." In the darkness, under the unusual clarity of the candles, the pedestal started to balance from right to left and to turn, like a kite held on a tight string, a bandalore and a fat top all at once. Apparently without any special effects. Unbelievers decidedly do not want to understand that modern spiritualism brings to light energies still unknown, as Leah so well explains it. Neither Kate nor I are going to tell them what is really happening behind the scenes, nor what happened *really* in Hydesville. We were still children then; children are surprised that the world can go on without them. At night we often tiptoed to our bedroom door to check whether a black abyss had not suddenly replaced the staircase. Nowadays, somewhat less naïve, we know that the abyss is inside us, in people's heads, and that only spirits exist. It doesn't bother me at all to cheat a little when none of them are answering.

We stayed almost three months in New York. Anyone who doesn't know this city is a hick. Everyone exists there with the mad agitation of a beheaded centipede. Everything there is immense and opens to the river or the sea, everything there resonates like on a dizzying dance floor where everyone in the entire world, including horses, wears Irish tap shoes. Leah got married there, to the great chagrin of Mr. Strechen, our manager. Kate, that kind of pale lunar creature all men want to protect, became the muse of a media baron who doesn't believe either in talking tables or any other materializations. Is he expecting instantaneous prophecies of the weather from her? It's crazy, the journalists' and bankers' interest in spiritualism! Let's just say that without my little sister's sleepwalking, we probably never would have been put on a big train to Broadway!

Kate and I have a developed a direct method of automatic writing. No need any longer for the rectangular tablet on wheels, equipped with a pencil that you animate with the tips of your fingers. Once the spirit is manifested, it's enough to separate the arm that is writing from the rest of the body with a little curtain and let the hand equipped with a graphite stick move all alone across a blank sheet of paper. Here, I just tried it myself out of the blue:

> *A centipede in the staircase*
> *Climbs steps four at a time*
> *His shoes are down on the ground floor*
> *His shoes are up ahead on my landing*
> *A staircase in the elevator*
> *Complains to my sister about only having one foot*
> *I walk on the ceiling in slippers*
> *With a flyswatter and a shoehorn*

When to burn my diary? It's getting to be time, before unfriendly hands seize it. What a shame it would be for me if Leah were to come across it! But she has too much to do with that Underhill, and soon we'll hardly see her anymore. She's a New Yorker now, the spouse of an artist of high finance and holding court, while Kate for her part invokes the spirit of the little peddler from Hydesville and I languish alone in Rochester. Do Prince Charmings have to be rich bourgeois in this damn country? What became of my dear Lee in Rapstown, my beloved with the skin of an angel?

Now that scoundrel Frank Strechen, the unemployed manager, is falling back on me, for lack of any other leads. He is offering me the going rate for a solo demonstration in Philadelphia. I'm off for Philly! City of Quakers and brotherly love. Provided that I do not lose my means along the way!

> *If you have the time to listen to me*
> *Blow your nose with your toes*
> *And pull the spinach out of your ears*

XI.

The Sleeping and the Dead

Lady Macbeth and some specters took the stage of the East-man Theatre. Charlene Obo played the role with an unsettling energy, throwing her audience, all dressed up for the premiere night, into a state of stupor close to terror.

"Why do you make such faces?" she declaimed. *"When all's done, You look but on a stool!"*

In a side loge of this Italianate auditorium, leaning on the balcony railing, Lucian Nephtali sat paralyzed. Charlene outdid her character in a lugubrious chiaroscuro where the shadowy recesses were contending with the purple of a perpetual twilight.

The sad Macbeth himself seemed to be trembling more at the hallucinatory determination of his wife than of the consequences of their crime:

> Ay, and since then too, murders have been performed
> Too terrible for the ear: the times have been,
> That, when the brains were out, the man would die,

And there an end but now they rise again,
With twenty mortal murders on their crowns.

Soon, in the midst of walk-on actors, the usurper reacted with a bewildered terror at the sight of the specter of his victim, which he alone could distinguish:

> Approach thou like the rugged Russian bear,
> The arm'd rhinoceros, or th'Hyrcan tiger;
> Take any shape but that, and my firm nerves
> Shall never tremble. Or be alive again,
> And dare me to the desert with thy sword;
> If trembling I inhabit then, protest me
> The baby of a girl. Hence, horrible shadow!
> Unreal mockery, hence!

A cold sweat stung Lucian's neck. Alone in his loge, hands trembling on the guardrail, he had the impression that all the faces below, haloed in a vermillion light, were turning ostensibly toward him. Sponging his temples dry, he had to admit he was still feeling the effects of his time at the Golden Dream that afternoon, magnified tenfold by the playwright's thunderous parables. Sometimes it happens that a mild discomfort takes on such an intensity that one would willingly leap into a pyre to escape from it. The nearest real person at this moment, the only one who would be able to help him, was separated farther from him than the ghost of the King of Scotland! For almost another hour, Charlene belonged only to the stage, as did for that matter the audience transfixed by her performance.

But the hellish couple "still young in action" was going to retire in order to quench themselves in the soothing waters of sleep. Haunting the illusory moors, the three witches, made up to perfection like transvestites for All Hallows' Eve, came to the front of the stage to consult Hecate, mistress of evil spirits, under the faraway rumbling of a storm.

Lucian didn't let himself watch the interlude, so much did he fear a new setback of a completely falsified reality. The play continued on with these supporting roles. By concentrating on the exterior details as if immersed in the dark gold of opium, he perceived, like a little isolated flame, the face of Kate Fox among the many masks, and was irrationally frightened of some kind of singular collusion between her and Lady Macbeth, who came back on stage in the fifth act in a trance, without even having to mimic the act of sleepwalking.

> Out, damn spot! out, I say!—One: two: why,
> then, 'tis time to do't. Hell is murky! Fie, my
> lord, fie! a soldier, and afeard? What need we
> fear who knows it, when none can call our power
> to account?—Yet who would have thought the old
> man to have had so much blood in him?

A murmur crossed the auditorium when, after some hypnotic confessions, Lady Macbeth cried out as expected: "To bed, to bed! there's knocking at the gate," for it became clear that the actress had found herself alone under a magnetic influence. Her role finished, she stood crazed in front of the side curtains backstage, while her partners went on with the scene. Clad in the same combination of colors as the decor, a stagehand came to lead her offstage. Charlene appeared to fall down flat, stage left.

In the hands of the makeup artist removing her greasepaint, little by little she regained consciousness in front of a mirror just after the curtain had gone down. The reflection of Lucian Nephtali appeared, smiling tensely.

"What happened?" she asked in a faint voice.

"It's best to spare you," he said only.

"I don't remember being applauded . . ."

"The applause happened without you, but it was for you that the public cheered."

"Are we going to Buffalo Street?"

"The car is waiting for me and Kate is already on board. But you, *to bed, to bed, to bed!* Go home to sleep. Your nerves are on edge."

"Not at all! *Come, come, come, give me your hand . . .*"

The next day, Lucian woke badly with the certitude of having killed his friend Nat Astor. His foggy reasoning led him to believe that this murder was not such a big thing, considering the immortality of souls. Was it really so terrible to push a mortal into eternity? Kate and Charlene had reached no conclusions in front of his friend's grave: some dematerialized intruder wanted too much to intervene; not counting the destitutes of long ago and the fugitive slaves from the common grave. One legend claims that every cemetery has as its guardian the phantom of the first person buried there. That night, during the ceremony, a Negro dressed in charcoal sacks suddenly appeared a few steps away from Nat Astor's gravestone. His face lit by oil lamps, he alleged that he was the caretaker of the place, which made the gravedigger paid to guide them laugh maliciously.

"That would surprise me greatly," he shot back. "Negroes have their own section!" But the shadow returned with a laugh of his own.

"Long ago," he declared, "in the time of the British Empire, the throat of a Redskin or a baptized slave was slit in secret to ward off evil spirits on the eve of the inauguration of a new white cemetery. This is how I came to be the first person buried here."

Seated on the couch where he must have ended up last night, Lucian took some time before getting his bearings. The bluish light announcing the sunrise bathed this interior in the unreality of dream. Mounted on the wall above a full-length mirror tilted toward the ceiling, a recent photograph of Charlene in a frightful rhinestone frame left him perplexed, until he recognized the pattern of the carpet, the ebony and mahogany furniture around him. Quietly he put on his shoes and went off to find a spirit or a body, once again surprised by the accumulation of mirrors and painted portraits, drawings or photographs, all of them endlessly reflecting from one wall or partition to another.

He found the actress in her bedroom, lying across the bed, a satin negligee bunched above her naked body. The emotion he felt had nothing to do with the sensual. Seated at the foot of the bed, he contemplated her beautiful breasts, spread apart, and the circumscribed forest of mystery between the groin and the border of her pubis. To him a woman's sex looked like a cross of burning eyelids with a bloody heart. Could he put his lips there without fear, like on the mouth of a dying man? Gently, he pulled the fabric down over this perfect body and sat next to the sleeping woman. It's the face that saves a body from monstrosity.

Everything becomes spirit in its prism. There is no longer woman or man. A face is the imprint of an angel's glance. With her eyes closed, this one resembles the one in his dream—a mask drowned in the ocean's depths . . .

"Is that you, Lucian?" murmured those lips between two worlds.

"You were sleeping half-naked."

"*You should have taken me as dead.* I love being made love to in my sleep . . ."

"I just woke from a dreadful nightmare. A gravedigger was leading you and me to Nat's grave. Kate Fox was accompanying us. It was night. Under the gravedigger's dull lamp, you couldn't stop laughing, a mad if quiet laugh. Kate was in a state of extreme distress. She asked Nat's spirit to manifest itself but a shadow stood up before us and claimed to be the guardian of souls . . ."

"Is that so terrible? It's just grief. Nat's spirit is still linked to yours."

"I'm the one who killed him."

Charlene sat up, letting her bare breasts oscillate in a beam of sunlight.

"I was with you on the terrace when he shot himself in the park."

"I was also in the park."

"Lucian, Lucian, we were coming home, all three of us intoxicated from the Golden Dream. I recall that Harry Maur was furious when he let us into his house. That bear hates honey. He made us drink some of his whiskey to remind us of ordinary drunkenness."

"I remember all that too, Charlene. But in the state that you were in, that all of you were in, you could very well have imagined me at your side on the terrace while I was arguing with Nat in the park. In my nightmare, Kate exclaimed: 'No, no! I cannot hear this,' while staring at me with horrified eyes."

"Calm down, Lucian. If all our dreams described exact reality, what place would there remain for spirits? They are who come to visit us in sleep, they communicate with us through great symbols and small insinuations. Not all of them are benevolent. Human dream is the domain of spirits more or less stuck in their memory, and disembodied criminals prowl around there alongside God's angels. Besides, you can't have forgotten that we drove Kate back home last night?"

"That was our plan when leaving the theater."

"In the car, she appeared to have been deeply affected by the spectacle of the witches, those three fatal sisters, and the carnage of Dunsinane. She said a strange thing that seemed to have permanently marked you: 'All of those around us who die, die by our own fault.' You threw a startled look at her as if she'd guessed your thought. This I saw quite well, thanks to the passing headlights of a sedan traveling at breakneck speed."

Emerging from the shadows, a ginger-colored angora cat jumped onto the bed. Out of its slightly opened mouth came the droning of a hive. Intact, a large blowfly escaped from it, which the cat re-caught and bit, wounding it. The stunned insect circled loudly on the bed between Charlene's legs.

"Rid me of this horror," she said.

Not knowing if she was addressing him or her cat, Lucian picked the fly up between two fingers and without even thinking ate it.

XII.
The Life of Phantoms

The big house on Central Avenue had lost its copper plaque with the *Fox & Fish Spiritualist Institute* insignia as well as some of its furniture, which was distributed to relatives. The two younger Fox sisters were living there temporarily—though Margaret was currently on tour in Philadelphia along with Leah's ex-manager. Kate sat grieving over this abrupt dislocation of the restless and complicit little family world she had known. Disciples and supporters had quietly returned to their churches, or had joined propaganda societies; some of them had set out on their own, increasing the army of mediums that crossed America and Europe by the hundreds to appear before crowds of converts, believers, and supporters who these days numbered in the millions. Now a pythoness adored in Washington, Wanda Jedna carried on her same divine plan in the battle for universal emancipation. For the living as well as spirits, there could be no segregation. Many of Leah's companions had taken their leave, encouraged by recent theories positing that the gift of mediumship was available to every soul. If with a little study every Puritan could become minister of a cult or another sect of the reformed church, it was even easier to take part in the spiritualist doctrine since no certified congregation could limit the practice. And the spontaneous conversions were by now far too many to count. Spiritualist networks scattered throughout organized private séances, mediumistic seminars, and group camps—like Onset Bay Grove or Lake Pleasant in Massachusetts, the Wonewoc Spiritualist Camp in Wisconsin, and even Lily Dale not far from Rochester—where fervent crowds often coming from very far away congregated, in the manner of those great Puritan meetings that came out of the Revolutionary War.

There was hardly anyone left but the Catholics to ostracize the new faith. The archbishop of Quebec or Paris hurled anathemas at the necromancer wave that was fast outpacing the baptisteries. The Congregation of the Roman and Universal Inquisition condemned for its part the use of magnetism and other methods of divination. Talking tables were commerce with the devil. It was the devil himself responding to their trances and invocations.

Kate doesn't open the anonymous death threats addressed to the three sisters any more than the uncountable letters from learned societies, mystic factions, or of single individuals anxious to confess, a number of whom were melancholics, maniacs, or other fanatics stricken with insanity. From all over the world came these requests for long-distance divination with scraps of fabric, strands of hair, or photographs to help—and the hope of receiving news from their dear departed by return mail.

While waiting for a sign from her sisters, Kate sorted piles of paper and hovered half-asleep over her notebooks. She hardly received anyone anymore, except the occasional relative, leaving Maggie in charge of paying the bills and Janet in charge of housekeeping. Maggie seemed delighted about her stay in Philadelphia, according to the single letter that had reached her, after more than a month: her handwriting was beautiful, that of a passionate being, leaning into the wind of inspiration and oddly riddled with details about the public demonstrations, galas in progressivist circles, and other notable encounters, like the worried joy of a child surrounded by all the colored paper ripped from her presents. There was the question of two or three mentions of a certain Elisha Kane, a doctor by profession and explorer, with whom she'd had exchanges as fierce as they were friendly. Thus she declared: "Mr. Kane is an unbearable rationalist. He claims that there is nothing true in our practices." And a few lines later, "This dear Mr. Kane showed himself to be a perfect gentlemen in ushering a clique of unbelieving Puritans away from me."

This very night, Kate had reread several times the single letter from Maggie, a bitter smile at her lips, thinking of the shadows that were about to extend under the high ceilings and how she wouldn't have the courage to confront the maid hiding in the kitchen by ordering her to light all the lamps. A weariness had taken hold of her like it had done in Hydesville. She wandered through the house for hours with an intense feeling of dispossession. Soon to turn eighteen, she felt old, completely forsaken from the inside. Between the death of her young brother and then of her mother, blocks of nothingness had crossed through her; now the dead pursued her mercilessly, little white souls, demons, octopi in tears over a repeated drama, detached hands grasping daggers sharp with grief. She didn't want to hear the lamenting widows of the world confronting the grave anymore. In a matter of a few years, this naughty game of little girls had shaken the foundations of Puritan society; but was it her fault that most grown ups didn't really exist, that they were puppets frightened by their own living image? How could a child more alive than fire and water be transformed one day into this scarecrow of God? Patchworks of cadaverous things, all adults had a little of bit of Frankenstein in them.

Kate was wearing her only fancy dress, brilliant with embroidered flowers. Barefoot, she went through each of the rooms with a slight shudder of terror. What she was feeling had no name in English, and she doubted it had a word even in Enochian, the supposed language of angels. A sort of rippling undulation was coming from objects and particular spaces: it seemed to her that the times lived by others here and there manifested themselves to her in a thousand mute innuendos. What advantage was there having this paroxysmal vulnerability? A kind of sponge more innervated than the cornea, ready to fill until soaked by the least impression, that's how it felt to her in the worst moments. Quite despite herself, a dull pain at each moment, nothing escaped her senses, not the twitch of an eye, not the belated private sigh of an admission. From an out of place chair or a particular shift of dust motes in a luminous ray, she induced intentions or unsuspected events. Which didn't prevent her from being dismayed at her own lack of culture and ignorance about the things of life, like love and sexuality. Seeing other people love and desire each other taught her nothing about herself. She stopped with curiosity in front of the big mirror in Leah's otherwise empty bedroom. Was she pretty or seductive, would someone one day want to unbutton her dress and undergarments? She started to laugh, twirling, and ran to an adjoining door. Her brother David and her cousins had pillaged her mother's bedroom after her funeral, but a negligible remainder was spread on the chimney mantel and in the corners, enough to ignite flares of emotion in the young girl's face. These little items had belonged to the old woman as much as the spots on her hands and her wrinkles when she smiled. Knitting needles in a skein of wool, a pair of well-worn slippers, and a bandage for her varicose veins all brought the indivisible effect of her presence to Kate. She staggered while sobbing.

"Little Mother, where are you?" she implored in a tiny voice.

Something trembled around her. Was it the Rochester night, with its red and black tentacles? Alert, she stood petrified, arms drawn up close to her chest, pupils dilated. The pair of slippers had moved, she saw it without seeing it, the right one moved in front of the other, taking turns very slowly with the left one and so on in a simple movement of walking. The long needles flew up with the yarn and started to stitch above the slippers like the mandibles of a beetle or crab. This lasted an indefinite time before the light of the full moon supplanted the night's darkness. Then came the sonorous knocks, like a box being nailed shut. Suddenly dizzy, Kate could no longer feel her legs. In a cottony listlessness, she fell to her knees and patted the floor with both hands. Janet called to her from below in a shrill voice. Coming back to herself, the young woman fled the room and stumbled into the staircase at the end of the hallway.

As if collapsed upon herself, looking like a dropped puppet, she was stared at blankly by the maid. Finally Janet rushed to gently gather her up.

"A gentleman is here to see you, Miss!"

"At this hour?"

"He has come before, back in your mother's day."

Kate thanked the servant, intrigued by the sort of religious cornet that she had fastened to her head. In the entryway, Alexander Cruik made no excuse for his late intrusion.

"I dreamed about you," he blurted out while removing his hat. "My dreams are thoughts that come to me from God. *'Departing dream, and shadowy form of midnight vision,'* that's from Thoreau. Do you have a few minutes you could grant me?"

Preceded by Janet who was holding a candlestick, Kate invited the preacher into the downstairs living room. She asked for a fire, some light, and drinks, troubled to see this austere figure emerging from out of the night. With his silver hair standing in a crown on the top of his head, his eagle's profile, the blue edge of his otherwise colorless gaze and the lanky presence of a meadow runner, the missionary had a little bit of the presence of an Iroquois Indian ghost of the Great Lakes disguised in the strict suit of a Puritan. His voice, made hollow by preaching, had an unusual sweetness.

"Don't worry, I'm just stopping by. I just wanted to be sure . . ."

He cast a quick glance at a photographic print of the three sisters framed on the wall, the youngest standing between her seated older sisters, who, despite their difference in age, seemed nearly to be twins—identical duenna hairstyles and that stoic expression of waiting for the blinding blow from the photographer, that Cyclops hiding under the drape of a Spanish prelate.

"Loneliness is not good for you, my little Kate, you are cloistered in a ring of ghosts here. You must get out, spend time among the living . . ."

"Janet's enough for me."

"That sad caryatid? I strongly doubt it. You need exchange, fraternal awakening. Exclusive commerce with the afterlife can only lead to depression and madness . . ."

"Margaret will come back."

"Your sister has thirsted for independence ever since Leah moved to New York. I learned that she is getting along with some success in Pennsylvania. But she is not built for the role, I'm afraid."

Alexander Cruik did not press the subject. He deciphered with apprehension how the delicate features on this young girl's face were locked inside memory, the heart's fortress. Without her really knowing it, her sisters had only variously pursued the supernatural impulse that lived inside Kate for their own worldly ends. She suffered from a nervous condition that aligned her with other dimensions; her nerves reached out long as antennae, vibrating too intensely as energies concentrated themselves there like on Dr. Franklin's metallic rods. But instead of flowing back into the earth, the electric fluid accumulated inside her. Could one protect oneself from lightning by holding a lightning rod in both hands? The evangelist would have loved to snatch this delicious child from the funereal silence of this house and take her with him, far away to the great plains where the Great Spirit breathes freely. *Hey-a-ahey! Hey-a-ahey!*

"I have an exciting message for you," he said finally in a soft voice. "That's why I allowed myself to trouble you. I've just returned from a meeting in New York for the protection and defense of the American Indians killed on their reservations in many states of the Union. During this visit, I had the occasion to be invited by Mrs. Underhill, your sister, and her husband, who is an influential man. Leah organizes private séances that are highly prized by polite society. Thus it was that I was able to speak with Horace Greeley of the *New-York Tribune*. You know that this great man represented our state in Congress for many years. He spoke to me for a long time about you, Kate . . ."

"I know him, of course, he was very generous when Mr. Phineas Taylor Barnum, the circus entrepreneur, had invited all three of us."

"Well, he would like to invite you personally this time. Mr. Greeley thinks it would be criminal to abandon you to the merchants of the temple like Mr. Barnum, and to leave fallow your psychic gifts. Much of your instruction still awaits, Kate . . ."

"I've read Fenimore Cooper and Longfellow, you know."

"Longfellow? We all love him. I don't think anything is better than *Songs of Hiawatha*, listen to this:

> *And the desolate Hiawatha*
> *Away amid the forest,*
> *Miles away among the mountains,*
> *Heard that sudden cry of anguish,*
> *Heard the voice of Minnehaha*
> *Calling to him in the darkness,*
> *"Hiawatha! Hiawatha!"*

Kate looked with surprise at her visitor and, as if the words were being dictated to her, continued the poem in a weary tone:

> *Then they buried Minnehaha*
> *In the snow a grave they made her*
> *In the forest deep and darksome*

"I myself have spent time with the Ojibwa Indians of whom the author speaks so well . . ." Alexander exclaimed, distracted by this evocation before continuing, *mezza voce*: "However tonight is not about the Ojibwas but about your future, my dear Kate! Mr.

Greeley believes in you, he thinks that you deserve better than cabinet consultations. He appears determined to take charge of your affairs and support you financially and morally in your studies. Isn't that wonderful?"

"I don't know, why didn't he address me directly?"

"A man like him is very busy with his duties. To be frank, he asked me to sound you out. If you accept the idea, you will be hearing from him very soon . . ."

XIII.
The Conquest of Ice

Nothing resembles the life of a hero. The most intrepid man still has the heart of a child. Margaret regrets having burned her journal because of the final pages where she had recorded, or rather affixed, like rare or common flowers in a herbarium, the first moments of their love, back when intimacy was still limited to letters and some sighs exchanged lip to lip. She had met doctor Elisha Kent Kane at an evening gala in Philadelphia. It was a celebration for the victory of Democratic abolitionist William Bigler in the governmental elections, but she cared little about the event and the heated debates that erupted here and there about the indignity of agricultural states of the south and Republican potentates. Here at this party, where she was finally left alone with the spirits, she had just abandoned the lively hustle, between the orchestra and the dance floor, when she abruptly found herself facing him. Was that before her mother had died? She no longer remembers much. The stranger's gray eyes immediately invaded her mind and soul. He had a large curly beard that mingled at the temples with waves of long hair, the head of a prophet framing an intelligent mind and of a severe beauty. "We know each other, Miss Fox," he had said to her just after the long look they'd exchanged. Her anonymity was suddenly broken, but he did not bother her about her public life. Undoubtedly they danced, and discreetly entwined, thoughtfully felt the possibility of happiness.

She saw him two or three more times in Philadelphia. Doctor Kane, so reserved and careful of judgment, was also an adventurous scholar, a hero of the Mexican War, a tireless traveler, and an explorer returned from Africa and from a relief expedition in the Arctic area. But his ambitions remained unfulfilled. Talents, knowledge, diplomas, and successes supported by a nice family fortune had not yet conjoined with that brilliant beam of fame that would have finally given him proof of his native election and salvation. A preceptor of his own destiny, Doctor Kane secretly lacked confidence in himself. From anywhere in the world, he could hardly escape its clutches; Margaret, who had suffered plenty of servitude, had ample time to see it in this magistrate's son, affecting the independence of a rationalist mind. Audacious and refined, Elisha loved poetry and the arts as much as the crossing of a Himalaya or a sea of ice; distant sirens called him and, having just survived a shipwreck or scurvy, he would already be dreaming of the next departure with an incomprehensible longing. Back under the Stars and Stripes, the weight of Puritan conformity— the Victorian version of which he'd had a taste of in London— had caught hold of him at the same time as ailments from the Tropics and the persistent mortifications of an education based on the necessity of consideration.

For a long time the only proximity Margaret had known was an epistolary intimacy with this ambassador of the wind. In his letters Elisha showed a sentimentality both heightened and recriminatory. Brimming with requirements for the present and the future, he of course disapproved of her spiritualist activities and urged her to break with that entourage of charlatans, convinced that Leah had exploited her two young sisters for greedy ends. Having had the opportunity to meet Mrs. Underhill up close in New York, his verdict remained unchanged.

Deeply moved at being able to be an object of passion without her spiritualist trappings, Margaret quietly allowed herself to be persuaded. Presented to his patrician Pennsylvanian family, to the parents and allies of the rich heir, she kept her role of promised one with all the required discretion. She could not hold his hand or touch his shoulder in public, though he begged her to be all his in her letters, to scent them with her perfume or to include a lock of her hair. Resolute, after going to the point of threatening her manager with prosecution, Elisha eventually forbade her psychic exhibitions. Reduced to a trifle by the man she loved, Margaret was tempted to strike back. When he was giving lectures in Boston or Washington at the invitation of scientific societies, she tried in vain to win back equivocal powers. But the credulous excitement around her was missing. In morgues or cemeteries, on certain nights of intolerable solitude, she went to invoke the silence of the dead that, in the lightheadedness of the unspeakable, sometimes strangely resonates from the depths of the grave or the void. No one ever answered, however, no spirit, no expeditionary from the kingdom of shadows, and she no longer had the heart to crack her knuckles to deceive that fact. Margaret could have recited her letter of surrender word by word: "I explored the unknown as far as the human will is capable. I went to death in order to obtain from it any manifestation, even symbolic. Nothing ever happened, nothing. I was in cemeteries in the middle of the night. I sat down alone on a tombstone, hoping that the sleeping spirits would rise up to me. I tried to obtain a sign. No, no, the dead will not come back, and no one knows how to escape hell with impunity. Spirits cannot come back. God didn't want it."

Flattered that she would accept leaving an unhealthy glory behind for him, but doubting that it was her deliberate choice, Doctor Kane showed her his gratitude in a missive full of leniency, addressed from Boston where he was giving a series of lectures: "I understand well the necessities that were yours, poor child, don't I in the end have quite similar obligations? Facing the crowds come to hear my wild stories of the Far North, I sometimes feel just like you. My brain and your body are sources of attraction and I admit that there's not that much of a difference . . ."

Thwarted in its prerogatives, the religious establishments of every denomination—from Methodists to Anglicans—then tried hard, in the name of the Christ Resurrected, to win back the sheep under the influence of imposters, while the academies of science on their end were sanctioning those apostates of Cartesianism and the same experimental method that the already elderly chemist Michel-Eugène Chevreul was working to formalize. He and Michael Faraday, spearheading a general outcry, harshly criticized the spiritual doctrine's new claims to objectivity. Doctor Kane, who was pulling out all the stops to disenchant his beloved once and for all, likewise summoned Catholic dogma and its theater of punishment. Shamelessly, in a bitter play, he made her a list of the mortal sins to which she'd been exposed. More than the arguments of accurate science, the Catholic fulminations decided her renouncement. With a devil that Elisha didn't believe in, he managed to disabuse Margaret; didn't he have the right to use all means imaginable? The spirits that not long ago she actively believed she was divining, along with the quite convenient deceptions linking the invisible to physical occurrences were thus nothing more than the work of the Prince of Darkness . . . For she had no doubt about the irrational. All the instruction that her volatile fiancé was imposing—at the home of his Aunt Susannah, who'd been assigned the task of chaperoning her—only deepened her belief in mysteries and her fear of endings.

In order to please her lover on the page, Margaret solemnly read *The Wide, Wide World* of the very Victorian Elizabeth Wetherell. The *Narrative of the Life of Frederick Douglass* seemed equally incredible to her. Was it really possible that, even if black, an infant could be torn from its family, that innocent women of color could be hung upside down and whipped to the point of bleeding, and that a miserable little black boy had to swap bits of bread in order to learn how to read from the little white boys almost as poor, but at least in school? Taken with the invocatory game of reading—this sweet interview with phantoms—she also discovered, though not without trouble, a translation of Friedrich de La Motte-Foucqué's *Ondine*, which recounted the story of a water sprite who, in order to acquire a soul, marries the knight Huldebrand.

At least she was taking a rest from the general din of the dead, and for her it was a blessing to be excited in her living body, even at the expense of a meager intellect. Tables stopped turning for her and the bones of armoires stopped creaking. She hardly had news of Kate anymore, also in the hands of educators. Considering the multitude of scholars converted to spiritualism, the instruction couldn't be a panacea against the bedlam of spirits, but undoubtedly it was enough to enlighten simple souls. Leah alone persisted with her symposia as well as salons, firmly established with the authority of being founder of this new doctrine, despite the competition now coming from Europe under the auspices of the French pedagogue Hippolyte Léon Denizard Rivail—a.k.a. Allen Kardec—who evangelized his religion of salvation through metempsychosis wherever it had some resonance, particularly in Brazil and the Philippines. Encouraged by her fiancé, who was indignant about the press's intrusion into one's private life, Margaret no longer read the publications of the mediumship societies where her name had so often appeared these last several years. "Don't trouble yourself with the world," he wrote her. "Never answer the questions of journalists. How horrible a life is autopsied while still alive!" As she'd done with her private diary, yesterday she fueled the stove with three notebooks filled with articles carefully cut out and pasted.

Finally satisfied with her renunciations and at how she'd applied herself to learning, Doctor Elisha Kane promised to marry her upon his return home. By the way in which he phrased it, Margaret could read between the lines the conditions implied in this promise: that she would remain steadfast in her conduct and that his impending expedition would go without pitfalls. For this had to be one of the most dangerous and risky operations ever undertaken. It was nothing less than chartering a specially streamlined vessel to break the barrier of the polar Arctic in order to find the trail of Sir John Franklin's lost expedition. Chief Medical Officer during the initial foray financed by the rich philanthropist Henry Grinnell, Kane had decided to lead under his own command this second mission leaving from New York. His services in the United States Marines or the Africa Squadron, like his missions in China and Europe, hadn't cured him of a sense of adventure. The vocation of explorer only meant something with the discovery of new spaces. He worshipped the Scotsman David Livingstone, doctor and missionary who departed on the quest of locating the sources of the Nile and who would not rest until he'd made that latitude legendary on the map of the world. Or his defunct compatriot John Franklin, who, on his three journeys to the boreal arc, would end up mapping most of the northern coast of Canada, continuing up the Mackenzie River to the Beaufort Sea, and finally, aboard two ships fitted with steam engines and reinforced to last years, ventured in search of the northwest passage, wandering in the Greenland ice floes and disappearing with his crew in 1847. But for the most part, wasn't it more exciting to discover, ice pick in hand, an unknown mountain than to lose oneself in conjectures on the smoky hallucinations of the afterlife?

Elisha Kane's farewells on the eve of his departure on an express train to the port of New York filled Margaret with apprehension, but she had the perspicacity not to let on about these forebodings, knowing that he would only see them as a hardly promising symptom of irrationalism. Aboard the expeditionary ship, along the inhabited shores, Elisha did not fail however to write long letters posted at each stop to his sweet and disciplined promised one.

Grinnell's second expedition would fail to further explain the endpoint of John Franklin's arctic line, but because of it, the whole North coast could be mapped up to a latitude of 82°2'3. At the risk of being trapped by walls of ice that, barely broken up, would close back up right behind their ship, and suffering from scurvy and malnutrition, Kane and his crew heroically crossed Smith Sound to the ice floes of the then-unnamed Cape Constitution. Nearly a year without news after the rare missives that had come from the Atlantic shores of Canada, Margaret rebelled against her superstitious nature, vowing to forget the spirit-chasing devil if Elisha came back safe and sound. Saved *in extremis* from the grip of ice by a British bomb vessel with a steel rostrum, the explorer indeed reappeared with an almost-intact crew.

He returned home safe to Philadelphia, burning with tragic and sumptuous recollections that he started to transcribe with a sort of dazzled haste, but his health declined quickly after their wedding. Although tolerated by her in-laws after this test of interminable waiting, Margaret, who had only her husband's financial support to count on, had to defend tooth and nail her assets as woman and spouse. Without any regard for the love she had bore for him, they sought every means to take over her duty to care for her sick husband under the pretext that she lacked the experience and quality of judgment assumed proper by the cream of society. Margaret drank deep draughts of the waves of fever that intermittently struck her companion. Vestal virgin over his breath, she watched for each sign of weakening and at night stood awake beside his burning flesh with the feeling of drowning.

As soon as he was better, before the inevitable relapse, Kane gave himself over with no qualms to the obligations of a finally achieved celebrity, even accepting honors and distinctions with a sort of exasperated appetite, all the while meditating on new odysseys. He didn't think twice about crossing the Atlantic to give an account of his expedition to Sir John Franklin's widow. Back from London, taken again by illness, he yielded to the entreaties of his doctor who promised him restored health in the Caribbean. The trip undertaken this time on a three-masted frigate of the United States Navy, Margaret was surrounded for three days straight by a terrible sea of steel that swung its giant scythe as high as the masts.

In Havana, at the loading dock, Elisha looked almost joyful under the glare of the sun, which the royal palm trees barely shaded. But the spectacle of a long column of chained slaves led to the harbor by armed militia quickly broke his enthusiasm. The young couple had time to enjoy the privilege of island life and knew some beautiful days. But the too-intense light seemed to reduce him little by little. The local doctors recommended a more temperate climate for Kane; however, the return trip would have to wait for a remission. Instead, death's access had been increased.

Out of sorts, mouth dry, Elisha turned to his wife one night to recite one of the poems he'd written for her with edifying ends:

> *Weary! weary is the life*
> *By cold deceit oppressed*

Margaret heard nothing but a groan and, waking instantly, found him dead by her side.

XIV.

And Now We Roam in Soureign Woods

It was while going down Norton Street headed toward the lake and river that William Pill, at a slow trot on his Quarter Horse, recognized the youngest of the Fox sisters in the back of a carriage loaded with three beautiful leather trunks with gold hardware. He immediately turned around to accompany the car. Accustomed to troublemakers, the young woman mimicked indifference.

"You don't remember me, Miss Kate? Yet it seems to me that I was of some help to you during a night of rioting in Hydesville . . ."

She stared frankly at the rider, surprised to see that beautiful, cheerful, all-pockmarked face.

"I'll never forget how you saved us from hanging, you and Miss Pearl . . ."

"Are you leaving Rochester?" he asked, nodding toward the luggage.

"I'm taking the train to New York in half an hour."

"Well, good luck!" he said. "Maybe we'll cross paths there someday? They say there's fortune over there to be plucked like clover on a battlefield."

Turning back around, Pill thought that there was surely room enough in New York for one more swindler. Soon he heard the great wooden bridge resound as the locomotive squealed. The mention of Pearl—he couldn't lie to himself—had affected him rather strongly. That woman carried in her every blessing and every perdition. Once again he had tried to forget her after their surprising reunion, which had certainly been a surprise only to him.

Galloping this time toward Lake Shore Boulevard, he remembered in two parallel streams of reverie the vagaries of his career as conjurer and of the incomprehensible success of his new livelihood. At poker or roulette, Lady Luck was linked as much to bluffing as the little fetishistic rituals and would almost certainly elude him once he put faith in her star; but in front of a public gaping at ghosts, every turn was good for filling his wallet. Once the illusion had reached its height, he would be overwhelmed by unexpected phenomena, some kind of uncontrollable fantasy, as if hoaxing the most unsuspecting hearts and consciences sometimes provoked, quite surreptitiously, the repercussions of something supernatural. It was fashionable to assert the nonexistence of chance, that thing concealing a necessity that would answer to higher laws. With their genius for competition, the mediums coming from Europe also claimed that there was no hell, suffering cannot be unpardonable, and that our lives were all subject to reincarnation. So that the present life would come after innumerable others, always revolving, and all of this in order to atone for this exhausting relay of crimes and transgressions that have dragged on since the expulsion from Eden and will go on into the future, ending with incalculable and successive human husks falling one after the other into the dust, perfectly immaculate in the light of God. It amused him, these hobbyhorses of false pastors. He adapted them to his purpose by promising better lives tailor-made: so and so, who toils at boiling wool, will be the son of the governor in the next life, and the old leprous woman pouring with sweat after walking from the hospice will be reborn princess of Grenada or Norway. But metempsychosis didn't help much with the everyday.

On the shores of Lake Ontario, at this cool morning hour, he set out on his Quarter Horse so quick to pick up speed, holding the reins with one hand and his hat with the other, happy to see her dancing mane the color of beer and blonde tobacco. A cigarillo added its smoke to the low-hanging fog. He told himself that the episode with the blind man and his female guide, dating back now already several months, would have remained suspended in the realm of the absurd, its insane images digging their spurs in his side. For a long time, incomprehensible, it remained inscribed in him, like a living tattoo on the skin of his dreams . . .

One evening last winter, under the unoriginal name of Mac Orpheus, he had agreed to go to this curious solicitor's home for a private séance at a reasonable price, on the west bank, downstream from the Great Falls. The same young, short-haired blonde woman greeted him at the door of a big sad house in the Rochester suburb. The darkness inside was carved hollow by the light of an occasional candle. Apart from some bituminous paintings on the walls, heavy drapes and rosewood screens, the room where they received him was furnished only with a round table and three chairs. He presented himself with a peddler's bag containing his basic equipment, his planchette rolling board, an alphabet, some scarves, magnets, a tarot deck, two boxes filled with painted glass plates, a lantern with swiveling magnifying glasses and his precious fumigator scented with pontifical incense. Only after he was settled behind the table did he notice that he was in the presence of the old man, seated several meters away in a dark corner, a leather briefcase on his knees. He was also able to perceive that the young woman now acting as governess was wearing a very flattering though out-of-fashion dress. Dimly lit since greeting him at the doorway, her beauty finally flowered in the candle's flame. He was stunned once again by a panicked feeling of déjà-vu. At that moment the blind man handed him a photographic plate, face-up. "It's about this person," he murmured in a slightly quavering voice. It was a calotype, that method of chemically capturing light invented by Talbot two decades earlier, which showed the portrait of a gracious Puritan woman of not long ago, a white shadow in her faded eyes. The blind man was pressed all the way back in his seat. Behind him his alleged housekeeper, backed by the heavy curtains at the window, motionlessly observed the scene with an absent expression on her face, as if she herself were posing for some cameraman hostile to the least blink. As usual, Pill started out with his huckster hermeneutic of proven clichés before testing out his "rigorously scientific operating technique." The first raps that he produced from the table, his hands in the air, neither the blind man nor the young woman appeared to have heard. But the lugubrious atmosphere filled with incense fumes was favorable for apparitions. From his improvised medium's cabinet, he began to project by means of his lantern and his fumigator a materialization in good and due form between the panel of a screen and the angle of a wall. The woman's silhouette that took shape, moving, on the broth of white smoke, made no impression, as he had expected it to, on his only female spectator, and consequently she remained silent for the blind man. Frustrated by this lack of cooperation, he was resolutely determined, without any more unnecessary effects, to render audible any kind of manifestation coming from anywhere whatsoever. And so he pretended to focus like a paid oracle on the calotype, after inquiring from the old man what he really wanted to know. He quickly lost control of the situation at the moment of the alphabetic transcription of knocks. "Violet! Violet!" the blind man cried out. "I beg you to answer me this time! Was it an accident, was it an accidental drowning?" This pathetic exhortation ended with a groan. Taken ill, the old man suddenly doubled over and toppled head first onto the leather suitcase. The other woman left her prostration, and rushing over, very pale, she began to drag the panting body away from the table and smoke.

"Open the window!" she ordered him. The curtains raised, the full moon inundated the room with metallic clarity. He had helped her lay the old man down on a couch, then unfasten his collar and belt. Several times the hands of the young woman brushed against his. "It's his heart," she stated with some hoarseness, wrapping her fingers around the old man's wrist after having crossed his hands as befits the blind. At this moment, stung with a violent attraction for this woman while being assailed by a vague whiff of decomposition, Pill had still understood nothing of the mixed disorder of his mind and senses.

The wind had picked up on Lake Ontario. William Pill walked along the waterfront where a motley group of porters and sailors bustled between the warehouses and steamships that were docked at the quay. Able to transport at least a thousand barrels, some of the steamships were carrying giant wheels or railroad ties. A little further on, under full sail, a departing frigate reminded him of his eventful journey across the Atlantic and the Plymouth

Brethren evangelist, his shipwreck companion who died of cholera on Grosse-Île. The only thing that remained of his adventure was a moldy and dog-eared Bible. It hadn't been wars or mildew that had caused his departure for America, before the millions of other starving Irish, but a rather pugnacious boy's dream to put the Ocean between him and his miserable home back then, family included.

Pill headed back toward Sodus Bay, impatient to get back to his cabin on Briscoe Cove where he was not far from leading, on days off, the natural existence prescribed by that good Thoreau, between a canoe for fishing and the leafy forest. "I am in the frightful necessity of being what I am," that was his motto and his fate. He could have certainly lived there permanently, dressed in skins, a leather belt around his waist, like Elisha the Tishbite. After all, the soul of a swindler could be just as straight as a stalk in water that optical illusion portrays as bent. It was enough to assume if not completely count on one's redemption. Faith could very well do without the truth.

Sitting on a fence rail, she was waiting for him in front of the stable. Her blonde hair fell in ringlets across her shoulders. Had he ever known, on all the routes he'd traced in the world, a woman more resplendent with vitality, more built to set aside the black scum of mourning and nostalgia? When she had led him away from the blind man, in another room, he still didn't know her identity and what contract linked her to this bewitched old man. How could he have guessed, even pierced by a dizzying feeling of familiarity, that the pastor, stricken with amaurosis and selective amnesia after a stroke and his only daughter were reenacting the tragedy of *Oedipus at Colonus* in this Rochester suburb? But the reverend Gascoigne, haunted by his crimes as a holy man, passed away serenely in the arms of this Antigone, without recognizing his Pearl other than by a lightning intuition at the instant of his death.

William Pill dismounted his horse wild with joy and, not stopping to tie the Quarter Horse, ran to lift the young woman into his arms.

"Ah, I've missed you like the devil, did you know?"

"The devil has nothing to do with it!" laughed Pearl.

"Neither does the good Lord! Nor any other master of this world or another!"

XU.

With the Permission of Frederick Douglass
and Ralph Waldo Emerson

Crowds were gathering at the John Street Methodist Church newly rebuilt atop the relics of Wesley Chapel. In the climate of excited nervousness reigning in New York, the overall mix, caused by the disorder of those entering the church and the massive presence of Negroes from Harlem and the Bronx under the vaulted ceilings vibrating with echoes, gave the event an air of revolutionary frenzy. Invited to this forum at the initiative of the American Anti-Slavery Society, Frederick Douglass reconsidered his destiny as a fugitive slave from a tender, as we call it, age, in the plantations of Maryland, when children were prohibited from learning to read, when the slave breakers punished ruthlessly over the least infraction. With a thundering voice he recounted his escape by train and steamer to the enlightened city of New York, thanks to the solidarity of a black sailor from Baltimore and some Quakers from Philadelphia.

Frightened by the unstable crowd at the entrance of the church, Kate listened to him while standing in a sea of shoulders. She had lost Miss Helen, her Irish chaperone, right at the entrance, and all the while her searching eyes marveled at the phenomenon of adhesion caused by this outspoken, aging Negro. She'd happened to cross paths with him in Rochester, where this man they'd nicknamed the Lion of Anacostia had founded the *North Star*, an abolitionist newspaper. Now she was hearing for the first time this confrontation, by turns affectionate, inflexible and passionate, of an inspired speech with its audience. Even the spirits at such a moment had been subjugated, deprived of any recourse in the face of this power of persuasion. Rightly demanding freedom for each of its citizens in America, but also for women and all the oppressed in the world, Douglass claimed to one day make his dream coincide with reality, without violence, solely by the power of faith. After evoking the Dred Scott decision and Bloody Kansas, he strongly disapproved of the call for armed insurrection by the white radical activist John Brown, all while paying tribute to his inflexible ally.

His equalizing homily ended with an ovation when he formulated once more his credo: "Right is of no sex—Truth is of no color—God is the father of us all, and we are all brethren!"

Jostled toward the exit by the crowd, Kate felt a previously unknown sensation of possibility. This pacifist leader couldn't be taken in by the agitation spreading across the country, revolts and strikes even in New York. Mr. Greeley, her benefactor, had explained it to her at great length: the Southern States were challenging the authority of the federal government; they were consequently threatening to break accords with the Union, more because of the economic ascendancy of the industrial North than for a simple matter of human rights, whereas the Union vaunted the Constitution as a means to rein in this league of rich land-owners, pro-slavery farmers, and illiterate pioneers endangering civil peace. There was a life possible in broad daylight, however, even in the peril of action, and this man who'd survived the worst yokes had come to demonstrate that to her without bragging or mystification. Above all, she felt the freshness of a wind on her cheeks and her neck, like the beating of sails on the bow of a ship. Life was not limited to being confined with the spirits of the dead, in the dark confusion of all those tables, those screens, those walls that she had to constantly probe and question to please the experienced. One could, for several hours or even longer, forget the hereafter, so close and so rustling with omens, for a here and now that was perilous but vast as hope.

At the end of John Street, deep in her thoughts and soon surprised to find herself lost, without even enough to pay for a cab, she watched the blue floats on the East River where the steamers' smokestacks were sending up plumes. Despite the brisk wind, she would go back to Sutton Place then by foot, where they were waiting for her for who knows what visitor at the home of the director of the *New-York Tribune*, even if it meant muddying her shoes and the skirts of her dress. Ever since being spared the public séances that often turned into a circus and the challenging consultations in the cabinet with rich neurasthenics, it seemed like she opened herself to a thousand exterior details that yesterday were ominous symbols, like the palpitation of the North Star in the blue of the sky, this cloud in the shape of a schooner figurehead, the play of leaves and birds in a maple tree. A large brunette woman pressing the paws of a fox stole against her mouth passed along the row houses. If it only took Kate a glance

to understand what drama she was living, she could free herself
from it by humming briskly:

> *O carry me back to my home far away*
> *All quiet along the Potomac tonight*
> *To my one true love, she's as fair as the day*
> *All quiet along the Potomac tonight*

No sooner had she started off on foot toward Sutton Place
than her name rang out from the opposite direction. The opulent
Miss Helen was rushing as quickly as she could, arms in the air.

"Where on earth have you been? Ah, but let's go home quickly
and change clothes. This is really not the time to be received . . ."

An hour later, still flanked by Miss Helen, who went discreetly
to hide in the office, Kate was greeted in the second vestibule by
Horace Greeley in a stiff collar and frock-coat. If the progress of
his baldness, offset by enormous sideburns and a full beard of an
immaculate whiteness, revealed the huge forehead a little more
each year, his good smile kept a youthfulness intact. Kate let him
embrace her and take her hands. Since the decline and recent
death of Mr. Fox, who'd fallen into drunkenness after years apart
from his family, Mr. Greeley had become the paragon to her of
the fatherly figure, which he found somewhat amusing.

"Come in my dear, tonight we have some important guests . . ."

There were already thirteen or fifteen people of sprightly humor,
women in evening gowns, one of them dressed as a tiger tamer,
men of venerable appearance, and some younger men, swirling a
glass in their hand. Solemn as a judge, the butler was filling flutes
with authentic Champagne.

"My dears," Greeley announced while turning toward this little world, "I would like to point out to the distracted or unaware the charming apparition of Miss Kate Fox, whom it would be inappropriate to present . . ."

"And her sisters?" blurted out a dandy in ruffles still holding his cane. "I thought they were Siamese . . ."

"So you don't know Leah Underhill, then?" exclaimed the wife of a Boston publisher. "Ever since her return from London, she only accepts the spirits of lords at her tipping table . . ."

As other conversations intersected, indifferent to their neighbor, the harsh words and fine taunts were hardly of consequence. The topic went from the English question to vice and religion, to the revival of ancient glories, to the truth of miracles.

Kate turned away, a smile on her lips, and pretended to examine the paintings, landscapes, illuminated portraits of the Catskill Mountains, and still-lives imported by Dutch settlers. On the fireplace mantel, in a brass frame, a daguerreotype protected in smoky glass drew her attention. One could make out the infinitely melancholy face of a young woman covered in white lace. The press baron saw Kate's cocked head and, suddenly nervous, forsook his guests.

"It's Jennie, my favorite daughter," he said, approaching the frame. "She died of consumption like three of her younger sisters. I was hoping she would be safe once she reached the age of sixteen, but she died the day after her birthday."

"She's not dead!" Kate exclaimed without thinking, in a voice that was just a breath.

The old man's glasses fogged up. He caught his breath and, pivoting slowly on his heels, playfully addressed the person approaching, his hands crossed behind his back, leaning forward like a skater on the parquet floor.

"Ah, there you are! 'The poet is the sayer, the namer, and represents beauty.' Wasn't it you who wrote that? Well then you cannot help but be understood by this child of light . . ."

The director of the *New-York Tribune* headed off toward other civilities, leaving Ralph Waldo Emerson to consider with an amused eye the woman who came over to be presented in a whirlwind and before whom he didn't know what to say. It was indeed one of the Fox sisters, those mad, gentle girls capable of apprehending in its own individuality the genius of a dead butterfly! The ashen face of his son, snatched from the world twenty years earlier by scarlet fever, superimposed itself onto that of the young girl. Memory, that's the eyes' daily bread!

Kate for her part was timid and unsteady on her feet under the attentive eyes of the man of letters, whom she had read, pencil in hand, under the advice of her mentor. "Every soul is a heavenly Venus for every other soul"—he'd thought of them, those hardly intelligible and so deeply moving words? Did he really imagine that there was a single and unique Oversoul in all the universe from which each creature received a reflection or a wound? He looked like a great hieratic bird with the beaked nose of a hornbill. Beyond a nice smile of abnegation, his silver eyes stared at her so profoundly to the point that the anodyne woman's self-awareness helplessly dissolved.

While the shouts of voices and laughter multiplied around them, a lady interrupted this silent *vis-à-vis*.

"Mr. Emerson, you who are our Goethe, what credit do you accord to these stories about mediums?"

Kate didn't have time to hear the response. She watched the couple move away into the hubbub. Other famous figures, or those who enjoyed coming across as so, accosted her for a friendly conversation, a compliment, or a dig—but she appreciated not being the center of attention, just a low-level curiosity like that elegant man with an ivory cane or of this adventuress known for improvising her way, depending on the circumstance, as a medium, actress, or businesswoman and who was pressed close against a rich entrepreneur of the railroad and maritime industry nicknamed the Commodore. This woman presented herself frankly to Kate.

"I am Victoria Woodhull, my name will perhaps mean nothing to you. But I find it overwhelming to approach you. We are many in America who owe you an eternal gratitude. It's your example that we all follow on the path of spiritualism . . . Isn't that right, Cornelius . . . ?" she added.

"Look who's coming in!" the entrepreneur cried out without listening, his arm around her waist.

A clamor arose in the rooms. The guests clapped their hands, moving toward the newcomer. Kate, motionless by the fireplace, recognized without real surprise the wavy mane of the Lion of Anacostia. Where else would an activist on tour like Frederick Douglass finish his day's tribune than at the home of the most influential reformist in New York? A lively exchange was heard where words like liberty, rights, and equality rang out.

Then, imagining herself forgotten, thinking of rejoining Miss Helen back in the office, another individual appeared as if engendered from a dream and addressed her in a flat voice.

"Kate, do you remember me?"

The young woman paled, brought back to some unplaceable time. But she pulled herself together, certain she did not know this stooped man with dull eyes and sickly skin, who seemed to have mustered a Herculean effort to approach her.

"No," he said, "you do not remember me. I am Charles Livermore, New York financier. You have before you a desperate man. I need your help. You are my final hope . . ."

Cheers rang out around Frederick Douglass. The brilliant speech of the former slave drowned out the whispered confidences of the banker.

"Once you let the black man get upon his person the brass letter, U.S., let him get an eagle on his button, and a musket on his shoulder and bullets in his pocket, there is no power on earth that can deny he has earned the right to citizenship . . ."

Kate promised whatever was wanted by the banker and escaped to the stairs, taken with the impression of imminent danger beyond anything she could dread in this world. "It's nothing, it's nothing," she repeated to herself, subtly terrorized by the idea that something bad could have happened to Margaret. Entering the kitchen, she discovered with disbelief Miss Helen, seated on a bench, legs splayed, drinking a strong whiskey in front of the enormous stoves.

"Oh, I'm so happy!" Kate cried out from far enough away to allow her chaperone time to regain composure.

"And by what good fortune?" stammered Miss Helen, gathering up her skirts.

"I spoke with Emerson, imagine that!"

While the good woman showed her ignorance with a dignified silence, Kate went on to recite with pressing eloquence:

Far or forgot to me is near;
Shadow and sunlight are the same;
The vanished gods to me appear;
And one to me are shame and fame.

Part Three

NEW YORK

Tread softly because you tread on my dreams.
—William Butler Yeats

I.

Recent Disagreements

As a consequence of the election of Abraham Lincoln, who promised the abolition of slavery left in abeyance since the 1820 Missouri Compromise, South Carolina's secession precipitated a national divide in a matter of weeks. In New York as in Rochester, one watched with a sort of stupefied amazement the escalation of events that could only mean a general uprising was on the horizon.

No one had yet experienced the battle of Bull Run, in July 1861—three months after the overall benign confrontation at Fort Sumter at the origin of hostilities—but it was definitely war. Convinced of the superiority of the Loyalists and even more of the efficacy of industry at the Union's service, the brand new Republican President flanked by two young telegraphists launching his orders, firmly incited a staff of armed forces hardly familiar with such grand military maneuvers.

It all began with disappointment. In position after an exhausting night march, it was in front of the political and financial elite of Washington, come to watch on lawn chairs the announced defeat of the rebels, that the Yankee troops led by General Irwin

McDowell surrounded, not without panache, the area of Bull Run. But the skirmish at Blackburn's Ford improvised by senior officer James Longstreet quickly turned into a fiasco, with a hundred killed and more wounded. After some uncertain exchanges with swords drawn, the Confederate Generals Beauregard and Johnston, veterans of the Mexican War, supported by the Virginia brigade of Colonel Thomas J. Jackson, under the imperious command of Generalissimo Robert E. Lee, rushed in to defeat the enemy camps, tearing off the foot of an eighty-year old widow who couldn't leave her bed in the process. All of this happened over the course of a few hours around a hill and a stone bridge. Following this panicked start that had had the worst outcome, McDowell's undermined forces retreated to the outskirts of the capital, on the other side of the Potomac, leaving a crowd of prisoners behind. At the Executive Mansion in Washington, which had just missed falling into enemy hands in this first real battle, it was clear that the war was just beginning and would require important sacrifices in material and in men. The subject of riots in New York, a presidential decree soon launched the mobilization of half a million citizens. Hardly a year later, there were victims in the tens of thousands on both sides of the fluctuating line of the front.

The missionary Alexander Cruik, who had volunteered as a chaplain in spite of being banished by his congregation for his measured defense of spiritualism, experienced hell every day on the front lines and in the country hospitals, where young men's limbs were being amputated, having been shattered by bullets coming from grooved musket barrels, the recent invention of a French gunsmith. In the middle of pitched battles, even at the risk of being taken as a target, the evangelist wandered like a harvester of souls in the bloody fields where the dying moaned, wandering from a Southerner with a blown-open stomach to a dismembered Unionist. Obsessed by the abomination of mass murder without offense or insult, he saw the disadvantages and defeats of his side facing the Confederates, who were inferior in number but fiercely defending their territory under the banner of aristocratic officers. When Lincoln had resumed the offensive by proclaiming the emancipation of slaves long before the hour of victory, thereby increasing the war effort tenfold through the mass conscription of Blacks and the intensive use of rail and water transport of troops, the horror of the battlefield also found itself multiplied. Armed only with his faith, carrying only his word or his silence, Alexander Cruik could no longer tell what was at stake in all this carnage. How could he find any difference between a massacre displaying Yankee prowess and a mass grave in honor of a generalissimo? In the snow or the mud, uniforms were too torn and stained to recognize which side they belonged to. Therefore, between two dying adolescents, was it necessary to tend to one first before the other? Were their souls brothers or enemies at the moment their armor of passions and identities dropped away?

During the move from one position to another, with the cavalry and artillery wagons preceding the advancing infantry battalions, the wounded at the back letting out cries and moans, Alexander Cruik believed he was watching the dead walking in dense rows and kept hearing the wild screams from the attacks. They all called for their mothers, those who fell. Children were playing at killing each other and believed they were only playing. At Chancellorsville, after four days of shelling and bayonets, the army of the Potomac suffered such setbacks that Cruik saw a band of defeated Yankees lynch one of their own because he was black and therefore the cause of the war. General Robert Edward Lee, in triumph, then pushed his cavalry of apocalypse up to Pennsylvania. Uninformed by the military advisors, the disoriented infantrymen grasped little of these advances and setbacks, other than from the hoarseness of the bugles after the fighting.

Cruik, who had witnessed the consolidation of the North under the leadership of General Grant, no longer reacted as he watched the Confederate troops, now on the offensive, plow the front line with artillery between two hills south of Gettysburg. Considering the sky-blue uniforms of those on the lookout, he couldn't help but speculate on the survival or imminent death of such and such recruit nearby who, for the moment, was squinting his eyes at the enigma of the horizon, one of them gently touching his ear and the other smiling at some dreamed-of face—all of them on the edge of the abyss, so full of slender eternities.

But there was a shudder, and sighs spread out at the sight of those enigmatic flickers quickly surrounding Little Round Top, countless, on the front line of enemy guns. Rather than giving command to use the artillery, head of the Maine regiment Colonel Chamberlain and his counterparts from New York State ordered their troops to charge. Hidden behind the 48- and 64-pound howitzers, which had been shipped to them by rail and which the bomb blasters surveyed with a rogue tenderness, Alexander had the feeling he was participating by his trembling in every limb at the immense devastation being committed, from this distance similar to a game of colored figurines. A great clamor swept by winds from the west swirled through the hills, where muskets and repeating rifles crackled while artillery sporadically thundered with a kind of phlegm. Already, stretcher-bearers on duty and fellow soldiers brought back the first of the torn-up to the tents. From his point of view overlooking the hills, Alexander discovered beyond this monstrous duel of bayonets, a multitude of other engagements as far as the eye could see, where cavalry and footmen were intertwined in dust raised from the force of their impacts. Called in by a nurse, her arms red with blood, he entered the ward of the field hospital, the odor of chloroform and entrails seizing his throat. At the bedside of a mortally wounded Negro calling for Christ's help, he began to entreat the unknown powers to come to his aid. Astonished on the brink of his dying, the man had the time to tell him, vomiting his guts, that he wanted only for his name, Ben Crosby, to be written on a piece of paper and pinned to his shirt. Seeing him do that, a wounded man in a bed nearby, who was about to be amputated, asked the same favor in a low voice, adding the name of his village. "Gangrene will set in," he said, "and I will only get the common grave." A young woman in a smock who was assisting the surgeon at work on another pallet had turned toward him a worried face, of a feverish beauty. He smiled at her desperately and rushed out of the tent.

Guns and howitzers now thundered forth over a crackling of muskets and one could see here and there, without a plausible link to these sustained shots, fallen groups of soldiers or spurts of earth and stone carrying numerous puppets blown to pieces. The fighting shook the most beautiful slopes under the impeccable azure. A lark shrilled, inaudible. Alexander Cruik remembered the hidden miracles of sight and speech. He raised his head toward the bird perched on its summit and cried out, his eyes filled with tears: "Don't prophesy! One mustn't prophesy such things!" Although half destroyed, the Union battalions were at this moment retreating in good alignment to their outposts while the dislocated enemy columns ebbed in disorder beyond their positions, leaving room for a few scattered soldiers who, severely shocked by the intensity of the charge, were still firing in isolation, unable to come to their senses. A non-commissioned officer with flaming hair, face pockmarked, his uniform stained with blood, appeared suddenly before him like a handsome devil, bayonet high, staring perplexedly at him in passing. Those in his company followed him with heads down so as not to count the missing comrades.

With the steps of a sleepwalker, despite the calls from the returning sergeant, Alexander rushed toward the deserted battlefield that the relief workers, waiting for the signal of a truce, had not yet entered. As he stepped into the open field, imploring God's mercy, his dark silhouette stretching over a pile of corpses, a Southerner wounded in the legs and head, thinking he saw a vulture circling above him, had the strength to lift his musket and shoot before rendering up his own soul. Hit in the chest, Alexander Cruik fell to his knees, hands on the ground, face to face with his murderer. He thought to himself that this dead man resembled him like a brother. Sobbing for the first time since he was a small child, he kissed that bloody face full on the mouth.

The sergeant had observed the scene from the shelter of a cannon breach. After a moment of disbelief, he stepped over the fascines and tangled remains, crouched down, and came quickly to join him.

"It's not worth it anymore," said the chaplain.

"I recognize you," William Pill cried out. "You are the evangelist of the Redskins, the friend of the Fox sisters!"

The officer raised Cruik's head up off the ground to moisten his lips with his alcohol flask. "It's going to be all right," he said, "I'll take you back . . ."

"Useless, you'd just be bringing back a corpse. I remember you too," the chaplain added, leaning on one elbow. "But come closer. I have loved only one woman in my life. We could have done such great things, she and I . . . Listen: I'm wearing an amulet of no monetary value around my neck. Promise me to give it to Kate Fox. It came to me on the day my mother was killed by the Cherokees, right before my eyes. We had been heading west like so many others. The Indians discovered me at the bottom of the carriage, but they didn't hurt me. Before abandoning me to my kind they tied this amulet around my neck, I don't know why. It has never left me . . ."

William Pill brought the cadaver back anyway. And it was in front of a witness, recording the last will of the chaplain Alexander Cruik, that he pocketed the iron chain and amulet.

In the meadows and hills battered with the holes of shells, where disemboweled horses rotted in the sun, tens of thousands of soldiers from both sides lay who hadn't had the time to write their names and addresses on a scrap of paper. Mass graves were dug throughout. Faced with such carnage, the governor of Pennsylvania subsidized a sanitation committee for the site as well as the construction of a cemetery. However, the battle of Gettysburg gave the advantage to the Unionists and Sergeant William Pill, taking his chances at each new engagement, won his lieutenant's stripes there. The front line delimiting the warring territories moved like a snake in its cage for months, from one region or state to the other: no victory brought about a truce and the two camps were by now tallying their martyrs in the hundreds of thousands. In April of 1865, President Lincoln who, thanks to the war effort, had raised the Union to the status of industrial power, was finally and triumphantly able to enter Richmond, the capital of the Confederates that General Grant, his chief of staff, had just conquered.

With one finger on his left hand blown off by a Minié ball, his chest slashed by a bayonet, and having miraculously survived a fire provoked by a famous general enthusiastic about scorched earth, William Pill left his uniform without regret. Not an hour of his life since his recruitment in the first months of the conflict had passed without his thinking of Pearl Gascoigne. Despite his ordeals, the Union's victory mattered less to him than the possibility of seeing Pearl again. He had watched his companions die fighting, and himself had killed without fail, carried by a single thought: of one day seeing again the woman he loved more than God or America. Pearl, however, had left him, she'd betrayed him for a chimera, a figment of the imagination, the worst of insanities: to be a free woman, to write books, to be accomplished.

Barely off the train, Pill reclaimed his American Quarter Horse from a breeder in Monroe County to whom he'd entrusted it three years earlier. The animal had also aged, but still turned on itself like clockwork, and it was at a gallop that the demobilized lieutenant headed back to Rochester, determined to forget the recent troubles and grumbling, unable to get out of his mind an air that the black recruits loved to hum in hoarse voices before the fight:

> *Oh, Babylon's falling, falling, falling*
> *Babylon's falling to rise no more*
> *Oh, Babylon's falling, falling, falling*
> *Babylon's falling to rise no more*

II.

Livermore's Good Influence

Nothing more appears after one pulls out her first white hair—
age must wait for the second. Kate put on her golden fox coat
and crossed the sparkling, dewy park along a flowering path
that intersected the road. Walking from the gamekeeper's house,
which had been converted into a small office and salon next to
the Livermore mansion, there was hardly time to breathe in all
the beds of roses and lilies that were the pride of the grounds-
keeper—an almost-black Jamaican with a cockney accent who
Charles Livermore kept in service in memory of his wife. Was
there any object or custom that wasn't being kept in memory of
Estelle? The financier had settled into his memory, and mourning for him could only be an acute form of attention paid to the
absent woman. From then on, his banking career on Wall Street
had in no way been troubled, business only being an abstract way
to occupy his time, an opportunity for circumstantial oblivion
that not even sleep could provide better.

Kate had accepted the widower's proposal in the middle of the
Civil War, one year after Estelle's death. The years of studies lavished on her by Horace Greeley couldn't add up any longer. The

more one learns, the heavier the tray of ignorance becomes. The exclusive engagement proposed by Livermore had been nothing more for her than an opportunity to untie herself from a singular alienation—for what music theory or philosophy could restore the medium eye-to-eye with the other world?—without which she was under the same constraint to follow the example of Margaret who, disinherited by her in-laws, had resumed touring city to city in the grip of an unscrupulous manager, or else of Leah Under-hill, who for her part only practiced spiritualism for the additional fame and fortune, in hostage to a sterile pride.

In this unspoiled corner of Manhattan Island, close to the development work of a giant park and acclimatized gardens with wildlife reserves, Kate forgot the fever of New York City, where all the world's wars seemed ready to break out at any time in miniature. Her employer and a trust of businessmen led by Mr. Greeley were even strongly opposing the hare-brained idea of Fernando Wood, the mayor of the city who, under the guise of economic dealings with the Southern States, was plainly recommending that New York be the next to secede.

Unaware of the disorders of politics and finance, Kate spent the war in her little island of green, preoccupied only with what was expected of her. As she did each morning, despite the coldness of the air, she left the mansion first thing, curious about the dying colors of the Portland roses, the scarlet Rembrandts, or the dwarf double-blooms with the ridiculous name of Pompon Perpétuel. The autumn roses were certainly the most exquisite. Mr. Livermore left her free to roam at this hour—during the week a carriage would have already delivered the banker to Wall Street—but it was her pleasure to go visit the manor house, a large colonial building on two floors with an exterior staircase and peristyles, in order to have lunch or tea and cookies in the office, in the company of the cook, an old Caribbean vendor of roast meats, and sometimes with the Jamaican gardener who came swigging a jug of fresh water. The other employees of the house, a German chamber maid with six arms, a Calabrian porter, and Mrs. McCords, a housekeeper with multiple functions, kept their distance from her, one of them out of superstition, the others from jealousy or mistrust. By far the oldest servant of the mansion, the cook told what she knew whenever she felt like it, by instinct and even bluntly, without taking the time for clarifications, considering the least question indiscreet. Kate gladly listened to her while contemplating the tea leaves at the bottom of her cup or the flames licking the throat of a huge cast-iron stove with its two ovens and three cooktops. From distracted scraps of conversation or obsessed soliloquies, she had gleaned much more from the cook than from the small tearful confidences of the widower.

Estelle had been a young woman of the Southern aristocracy, daughter of a Tennessee plantation owner, a man with opinioned ideas who employed a good thousand slaves flanked by a militia that was under his thumb. She had fled her town and family after being forced to attend the public hanging of a runaway slave that she had seen fit to help. Cursing any affiliation with them, Estelle reached New York by railway where Mrs. McCords, a relegated parent, received her without too much grumbling. Through the involvement of the latter, an educated woman who, in addition to her good company, served as his private secretary, the financier was one day put in the presence of Estelle. He was immediately smitten to the point of reforming all his old ideas for her and investing considerable sums in the anti-slavery struggle. It was a few months before the default election of Jefferson Finis Davis as president of the Confederacy. The battle of Fort Sumter hadn't yet taken place, but with Lincoln surrounded in Washington, the outrage did not weaken after the hanging of John Brown, the radical abolitionist hero who led his own army, ten men strong, again the federal arsenal of Harpers Ferry in Virginia.

In the context of dislocation from clan and family ties that augured dark days, the marriage of Estelle and the financier undoubtedly participated in the social upheaval underway. But neither the ostracized young wife nor Charles Livermore lived those hours on the planet any differently than Adam and Eve. Although he was her senior by more than twenty years, Estelle still found herself loving him with an ever-increasing amazement. Nobody in the world could have shown her such a tender, soothing, and sensual attention. In the face of this ever-present sun, the many treasures of seduction that he lavished on her in the name of attraction had, in contrast, the pallor of a moon. Always available despite the ups and downs of the profession of international trader, Livermore loved Estelle like an absolute, without intelligible comparison. Everything that was not her had almost no value, his own life included. The exacerbated passion of love took on an almost quasi-cannibalistic aspect in him—covering her with kisses, he had to restrain himself from nearly devouring his wife. The businessman gave the impression of being present everywhere around her; the better to adore her, he would certainly have abandoned his fortune in exchange for being able to be ubiquitous. At the mansion, there was alarm at his metamorphosis into a tribe of gallant ogres. Joyful but languid, Estelle lost her strength. The more she abandoned herself to the devouring love of her husband, the less she offered resistance to the seasonal illnesses and other maladies. She took to bed one icy and snowy day. The doctors diagnosed a galloping consumption. She died without lament after having called the staff of the mansion to her bedside to declare solemnly that no human being would ever be loved like her.

Livermore had a kind of igloo built on a hill in the immense park, and until snowmelt kept vigil night and day over the dead woman wrapped in an ermine cloak. He had a grave dug in the same spot in the park, and built on top of it a tall chapel of white marble, an altar window on either side, an alabaster angel, and a statue of John Calvin. In his outfit typical of the Renaissance era, Calvin had Livermore's exact traits, at least his profile looking at the other figure. Kate, who'd been led here on her second day by the Jamaican with the cockney accent, assimilated all at once the angel that was Estelle. This image of beauty offered by the rock's durable phosphorescence left her confused, in an enigmatic silence. Nothing came to her anymore from the world nearby. No one had the thought to inform her of the assassination of President Lincoln, let alone the recent crimes in Estelle's hometown of an organization of former Confederate soldiers with a name like a Mongolian tribe. Kate felt the atmosphere of places with a pathological acuity; decidedly nothing of her interlocutors' mental states escaped her. She could endure the martyrdom of Saint Sebastian in front of the tree flayed by lightning or of Saint Stephen finding some frog stoned by a scamp. Kate refrained from this sensitivity in isolation; she turned by predilection to places free of any influence and to beings manifesting a healthy indolence, like the cook or the gardener, who was dumb but not deaf. Attentive to her desires, and perhaps to her thoughts, he helped the young woman be less of a foreigner in this place devoted to the worship of a dead woman.

Charles Livermore, for his part, divided himself into two mental planes, his body coming and going. The Wall Street financier, handicapped in no way in his abstract operations, would fall back into a great melancholy upon returning to the mansion, ready for any of the mantic arts to touch the illusion of a relic. Lost in a Kabbalah of signs, his meeting with Kate Fox, one year after losing Estelle, had seemed to him a good omen. This young woman had given him the look from the beyond. He sought out mediums in vain in New York, Boston, or Rochester: all betrayed a prosaicism and even a vulgarity of the soul incompatible with his needs. The charlatans among them, easily visible, boasted the gifts both of mediumship and hypnotism, a Janus with a twisted neck. The authentic psychics, he'd figured out over time, were only passive intercessors, simple transmission belts; many were recruited from the washers of corpses or uneducated cowboys, assuredly the ones most apt at annihilating consciousness and will in themselves. It was, however, impossible for him to conceive of a communication with the world beyond via an unbalanced person, or some crook or ecstatic moron. Aside from her reputation, Kate had immediately attracted him by her quality of presence, a childlike simplicity and a graceful charm so close to the core of his memory of Estelle. Livermore had a pretty keen awareness of her nervous condition, but her melancholy was a refuge for him and it mattered little to him that insane asylums these days were teeming more with spiritualists than syphilitics.

For years, two or three nights a week, in the room where Estelle had passed away, séances were perpetuated, all doors and windows closed. In a trance state, before a little pedestal table clearly in view of her host, Kate was free to proceed with any kind of invocation, to write with her bare hand or through a rolling planchette. On the forty-third séance, between the four-poster bed and an armoire mirror that reflected the motionless flame of a single candle, Livermore perceived a halo to which he could not give a name. The phenomenon amplified in the sessions that followed, without any sound. When the first knocks were heard, he no longer doubted the success of the experiment, but in his thirst for certainty, he imposed all sorts of precautions and controls on Kate Fox, binding her wrists and even holding her bare feet in his palms. When the knocks didn't stop, wild with the darkest happiness, Charles Livermore wanted to add evidence to his certainty and on a few nights invited over unimpeachable witnesses, authorities such as Professor Mapes of the National Academy or the jurisconsult Edmonds, who had eventually gone along with the late Robert Hare of the University of Pennsylvania, fighting on the side of the Fox sisters after having long constituted an inquisitorial tribunal persecuting the new heresy. By different operating strategies, Professor Mapes was able to anticipate or thwart all the usual ruses of illusionists and other falsifiers. Kate Fox was one of the very rare mediums with physical effects never caught in the act of deception. The energies set in motion in her presence could never be assigned to any artifice, unless the whole thing was faked. Satisfied and confident after all the tests and audits—hands isolated in an aquarium, zinc separator plates, levers arranged on a spiral scale with a mobile indicator to measure the forces in action—Livermore asked Kate to intercede with the spirit of Benjamin Franklin, whom he had worshipped from a young age. That one of the founding fathers of the United States agreed to appear in Estelle's company had been a transcendent confirmation for him, more credible than all the physical evidence, of the substantial incarnation of his late wife. Estelle never ceased to write with the lead pencil held in Kate's left hand, and what she recounted, her style and written form, brought back so well the happy life of yesteryear, with warmth and in the smallest details, that Livermore soon found himself overcome beyond any consolation. That he was transitorily in love with Kate, through whom the voice and appearance of Estelle kept manifesting, in no way contradicted his passion for the marble angel. The materializations followed one another with ever more influence, and the weak Kate, permanently besieged by a monstrous energy, disintegrated little by little like a straw mannequin between two burning lenses.

On her three hundred eighty-eighth apparition, Estelle announced that it would be her final one, that the hour of deliverance had come for her. Kate must have fainted at the end of the session. She woke up in a nightshirt, in her room on the pavilion, at the dawn of the new day, and realized that she had been entirely undressed.

Charles Livermore, become once again the respectable man she had known in town, left to her the choice between a life of leisure and study next to him, or freedom. Knowing that her mental and physical health were hanging only by a thread, Kate bade him farewell before visiting one last time the angel of the chapel. As a sign of gratitude, in order that the cause of spiritualism might progress, the Wall Street banker offered to her, whom he considered his savior, a stay in England and the means to pursue her investigations for some time. In a long letter vibrant with praises and saturated with exhortations, he recommended in advance Kate Fox to his correspondent Benjamin Coleman, freemason and fervent follower of what was now referred to overseas under the name of spiritism, imposed by the very scrupulous Allan Kardec, coauthor with the spirits themselves of the *Book of Spirits*.

Sitting in his upstairs office with large bay windows overlooking the entrance to the park, the banker reread his letter with the mild recoiling one always feels in front of the written expression of a well-kept secret:

"Miss Fox is incontestably the most marvelous medium alive. I received so much more from her during these grim years of grief than I can say, in my own house, to the point of feeling indebted to her. It's now to you, my faithful companion, that I entrust her. Above all that you will take good care of her while she is away from her family. At thirty-five years of age, Kate still has the heart and spontaneity of a child; she feels the particular atmospheres of each individual so strongly that she can become excessively nervous and apparently capricious. Take measure quickly of her natural genius and learn well how to tame her, it's on her esteem and trust in you that her extraordinary receptivity to other dimensions will depend . . ."

At the moment of sealing the letter, Livermore saw down below, leaving the chapel, Kate's silhouette headed into the tall trees of the park, and felt, without wanting to explain it to himself, a sharp twinge of sorrow.

III.

The Green Fairy and the Murderer

S low waves of snow fell obliquely onto Floss Avenue. Margaret was immobilized among other passersby in front of the windows of the J & M Nicols department store, where frightening mannequins with human figures dressed in manufactured clothes had just been installed, immediately evoking the materializations of the so-called medium William Mac Orpheus, barker at Barnum's Great Circus Museum and Menagerie, which had pitched its tents for a few days in Rochester. Such a novelty brought forth the gloomy memory of a beautiful dead woman embalmed with an injection of vitriol and nitric acid, whom Margaret had had to work to make speak.

Collar gripped tight against the cold, she made her way close to the buildings' façades to avoid the splashes of mud from the carts and carriages. Her return to Rochester, in deep winter, had the effect of a private cataclysm on her. She had lived a fairy tale in this city in her youth; here she and Katie had known a kind of glory under the yoke of their older sister. Fortune, even managed by a third party, made everything back then obvious and right. Wasn't it Mister Splitfoot who had encouraged them to bring the good word to town? The spirits loved fashionable furniture, high wood-paneled ceilings and heavy drapes. In their former home on Central Avenue, Margaret had long believed in these stories of communication with the afterlife. Besides, the tables really were tipping, there was no doubt about it. And when she forgot her failures and resentment, certain phenomena still occasionally occurred. But a part of her had been consumed in the dreary fire of the years. Her living forces devoured all along by a public of vampires, she turned sometimes, more and more often, to various contrivances, expertly calculated ruses. The conjuror's tricks of this Mac Orpheus that she could have seen at the Barnum circus were without mystery for her now. Moreover, spiritualism was no longer what it had been since the mass arrival of spirits with the flow of new Catholic immigrants. Margaret understood nothing of all these spiritual hierarchies nor of the purgative effects of reincarnation on the soul in transit to the divine light. From what she could tell, except for the women suffering seizures and a few authentic necromancers in a pact with obscure powers, everyone was faking and mystifying in that domain.

But she had to live somehow, and despite everything she still kept a little of the Fox sisters' prestige in the shadow of Leah Underhill, now become high priestess of a religion of five or six million converts. Her own immortal soul she continued to sell off for a few dollars' representation. Margaret shrugged before a blind beggar crouched under an awning who, dark glasses on his forehead, was counting his money. She turned onto a dark narrow street where, like feathers from a plucked chicken, thick flakes flew in every direction. The shop sign of the Good Apostle creaked in the wind, adorned with a stalactite beard. She pushed open the yellow-paned door and was comforted by the stove's warmth. Thankfully, one could have the green fairy in the wet states. Nose in her glass, the absinthe of dubious quality and the cheapest in the house, a woman no longer has a reputation; it made no difference to drop her guard alongside the sailors and the millers. She poured only a thin stream of water on her slotted spoon and the sugar never entirely melted. At her third or fourth absinthe, its color like that of zinc sulfate, she felt better, finally able to examine the world. There behind the counter was John, the cafe owner, distiller, and brewer behind the scenes, among his bottles, glasses, and barrels, holding forth with a hymn-singer and the driver of the next stagecoach to New York, ahead by a few drinks.

"Laws," he was saying, "there are too many of them, each governor wants his own, we've lost all common sense! I allow that we hang criminals, but look: in Boston, one law forbids playing banjo on the sidewalk, in Idaho, it is formally illegal to fish astride a giraffe, and in Tennessee, one doesn't have the right to lasso a fish . . ."

"I know all about it," said the singer of canticles. "Where I come from, in North Carolina, it's illegal to sing off-key."

A middle-aged man opened the door, as if pushed in by the snow, and shaking himself off, came up to the counter. He immediately ordered the best absinthe in the house. His sheepskin coat dripped as he beat a rigid, black, wide-brimmed hat with his palm. Margaret thought she recognized a visitor of the late Spiritualist Institute, or maybe a former guest of Leah's salon—back in the time when she was the very dignified Mrs. Fish-Fox! Who ever heard of such a creature. The olive-skinned man had heavy eyelids, smooth graying hair, and features as delicate as they were bruised, showing the exhausted relaxation of an asthenic reveler.

He lightly set his hat on the counter, then lifted his eyes toward the sparse population of the nightclub. Intoxicated, her head poorly attached, Margaret held her scrutinizing gaze. She had learned never to lower her eyes, which allows one, *presto digiti*, to divert the public's attention when juggling acts.

Intrigued, Lucian Nephtali picked up his hat and walked over to the slouched absinthe drinker, her neck leaning against the rippling marine background of a large mirror.

"We know each other," he said without taking the time to introduce himself, "aren't you Leah?"

At the moment of pronouncing those words, approaching this creature without makeup, his error appeared flagrant, but how would he justify his interruption?

"Excuse me," he said, "from far away you look a little like . . ."

"A person twenty years older than myself who is none other than my sister," she replied in a breath before raising her hand and launching out in a voice pitched too high: "Bring me another one, John, for the love of God!"

"Two!" Lucian corrected while sitting down. "And of the better kind!"

Margaret looked at the intruder with amusement. She reconstituted in fragments the person, his social position, the people he associated with. It was always a point won to show, casually, the amplitude of her memory despite her psychological degradation.

"And what has become of Charlene and that dear Harry Maur?" she said after a brief moment of silence.

"Charlene lost her mind, you didn't know? It's odd, she was playing the role of Mrs. Mountchessington at the Ford Theatre in Washington, the night of Lincoln's assassination. She knew the murderer well. Maybe you remember, she had played *Macbeth* with that lunatic John Wilkes Booth. That was anything but *My American Cousin*. Once his crime was committed, Booth jumped onto the stage, shouting, 'So die the tyrants!,' it was like a Shakespearean intrusion on this bourgeois farce. 'Birds of a feather gather no moss . . .' But all of that has nothing to do with it. Charlene was transferred to Athens, Ohio, shortly thereafter to a luxurious asylum that had just opened its doors. Whereas Harry . . ."

The cafe owner came to exchange glasses, a worried eye on his client. "I hope you'll help the lady get back home," he muttered into the ear of the more respectable drinker.

Blasé, Margaret smiled and lit a cigarette.

"To you, we're all just a bunch of jokers, eh?" she stammered in a caustic tone. "You never believed in all of that, you! Magnetic fluids, communication with the beyond, knocking spirits . . ."

Taken aback for an instant, Lucian conscientiously wet his sugar. It was quite true, he never believed in any of it, even if he couldn't have admitted to himself that his friend no longer existed. From the grave of his being, Nat had reemerged as his own buried soul.

He leaned over in confidence toward Margaret. "Spirits inside an end table? That's perfectly ridiculous. But once I was able to sense in your sister Kate certain remarkable properties of her psyche that I wouldn't know how to analyze otherwise. A kind of hypnotic dividing in two or an extra-lucid torpor, maybe, a natural empathy, a power of impregnation of things and beings she herself doesn't know . . ."

"Kate's a real medium, that's all."

Drawing back in embarrassment, Lucian noticed her crow's feet, the fine wrinkles at the corners of her lips, and especially the way this woman had of biting her lower lip and batting her eyelashes. With a good dye job, the dignified Leah, who was living the good life in New York, could hardly look any older.

"Why were you in need of my younger sister?" Margaret pursued in the shelter of a screen of smoke.

The question was inescapable, at least from himself, the absinthe not permitting lying any more than opium, and he had just come from an underground smoking den that had opened on the port since the closing of the Golden Dream. Although unbelieving down to his marrow, he had long consulted in moments of golden limbo numerous soothsayers living or dead, Simon of Judea, Paracelsus, Robert Fludd, or the Marquis de Puységur, and he himself was on the threshold of disappearance, bombarded by all the morbid influences grief unleashed. But he had survived, still unbelieving, thanks to little Kate. Hadn't she known, on one unforgettable night, to link the tenuous threads of the soul's depths between him and Nat Astor, saving him thereby through the great mystery of the damnation of love?

"Why?" he said finally. "Probably to understand my crime. Your sister enlightened me on the matter. She blew on the fog of my spirit and there I saw a bloody footprint. Subsequently, I turned myself in for the murder of my friend—the Rochester coroner had been expecting it for years. There was a sensational trial. I just missed being sentenced to death, you know. But Harry Maur, cited from the beginning as a witness for the prosecution, testified at the end of the trial that he had been present when the tragedy occurred and that it was in fact a suicide . . ."

Margaret was hardly listening. Blurred images were superimposing themselves, undulating across this face from the past.

"But it was no suicide!" Lucian nearly shouted, stepping back. "No, no," he went on in a calmer voice, "there are only murders more or less thoughtless . . ."

Margaret shrugged. Would she too have killed her husband without thinking? She saw again the tender and serious Elisha increasingly weakened upon returning from his expedition, and suddenly felt again the sharp pain of lack, that blade lashing the entrails, then she remembered her banishment after the funeral. Without a fortune, driven from her belongings by his family, she found herself back where she started, more alone than ever, chasing after an already strained fame to once again earn her living week by week, under the name of Margaret Fox-Kane. But mediums by that time abounded. America, naïve about leagues, congregations, and multiple sects, had been handed over entirely to new charlatans with hosannas, with no recognition for the two pioneering sisters, while Mister Splitfoot was surely snickering under the snapping banner of Old Glory!

Her mind lost by the alcohol's vapors, Margaret hadn't really followed the substitution of human scenery, Nephtali ceding his place without a word to another figure in her life.

"You're drunk again," said this one indignantly. "Have you forgotten that we have a séance with two dollar entry tonight?"

"It's coming back to Rochester," she admitted while re-lighting her cigarette. "It's shaken me up . . ."

"Like what was shaking you up to the point of falling down eight days ago in Philadelphia!"

Frank Strechen pulled Margaret out of the tavern before she had finished her glass. The still dense snow was being matted into a black mud. He hailed a cab and gave the driver the address of their hotel. On their way, Margaret heard from another planet the bitter reproaches of her manager. She thought about an erased world from which arose clusters of memories quickly covered by this pallid avalanche. The big house on Central Avenue, all shaky on her left, seemed tiny and dull to her under the storm's redactions. At that moment, she remembered a promise and cried out to the coachman, leaving Frank Strechen speechless:

"Buffalo Street, right away! To the old cemetery!"

No one could have forbidden her this visit to her dear old Mother. In the last letter before she left, Kate had written her: "If ever you happen to pass by Rochester . . ."

It reminded her of a song for drinking and crying that she sang with gusto:

> *If ever you pass by the old homestead*
> *Pray step right inside for to see if I'm dead!*
> *And drink to our love if you find I am gone*
> *But love me again if you find me at home*

IV.

The Necromancers of the Old World

The *Oceanic*'s twelve boilers fired one after another, vibrating the ship's rigging and steel plates while the liner's enormous funnel repeatedly exhausted its broth into a motionless sky, subsuming for a moment the two rear masts and nearly motionless sails unfurled by a rakish team of sailors. Leaning on the railing of the promenade deck, the first class passengers watched the maneuvers without understanding anything. Was there a lack of wind or too many crosscurrents? On the stern and bow of the lower decks, the third class crowd, less dense on the way back, made themselves comfortable as if on holiday. Chartered last year by the White Star Line and flying the British flag, the *Oceanic* had left New York and was en route to London without much fanfare, with its contingent of *nouveaux riches* heading home for the new year, disenchanted emigrants, and graying rejects of the British Isles or the old continent.

During the two weeks the crossing lasted, Kate, usually on deck, wrapped in her fur, let herself be invaded by the versatile breathing of the sky and the sea, sometimes more tenuous than the exhale of a dying person and then suddenly of an abyssal violence. She had never felt more delivered of herself, almost disembodied, stripped of that weight that a dream drags along in the guise of the human. Back in her cabin in rough weather, she couldn't take her eyes off the sea. Poor dragons of foam and spray danced before her. This contrast of grays resembled her life: all the loneliness in the world behind a flashing porthole. Kate imagined an endless voyage to find serenity. After ten days of imprisonment behind the guard rails of bridges and the gangways, the restaurant, or her luxurious cabin, she told herself that nothing would prevent her, one night with a full moon, from letting herself slide overboard. Similar to the miraculous wind vibrating in the light, wandering souls that perished at sea were not burdened with those crippled obsessions around old cauldrons. Even the worst among them would cross one day the Cape of Good Hope on his ghost ship. And then what idiot medium would have the idea of invoking spirits on board a ship—everything there creaked and moved only in accordance to Neptune's wishes! On the tenth day, finally delivered of a fearless sadness and completely astonished by the geyser of a whale or a ballet of porpoises, Kate knew that she wouldn't lose equilibrium. One rolling morning, rushing to catch a flying fish that, while she was alone in her seat, landed thrashing on the deck, she had the vivid sensation of releasing a dove of ice back into the waves.

Approaching the Old World, washed of funereal influences by the ocean, she wanted to believe that everything would work itself out far from those fanatical Puritans, who from lack of roots had crowded around capricious spirits. On this side of the Atlantic, according to what she'd read, ghosts had the manners of propriety and a sense of family. "I am thy father's spirit / Doomed for a certain term to walk the night," wasn't that in *Hamlet*?

At the sight of the English coast, an unnamed fright gripped her again. What would they require of her now? And what kind of face to put on before her hosts? Like the end of a dreamed bridge, she crossed the landing stage like a sleepwalker. On land, destitute crowds, staggering women, hordes of raggedy children were bustling feebly at undefined tasks or prowling around the pontoons and docks like hairless dogs in the shadow of sailors and longshoremen. For one distraught second, Kate realized that a matte-complexioned porter was following her, her trunk hoisted upon a trolley. Then, with a determined air, a coachman in purple livery with copper buttons approached her.

An English eight-springed carriage was waiting for her on a quay shining with rain. Inside, after two nights of not sleeping, she gave herself over to the swelling sensation to close her eyes, head nodding, to the sound of the little trot ringing on the road, the carriage making a turn in her dream with the exact sonority of Old Billy's hooves.

Benjamin Coleman's staff had received her without ado in this Chelsea manor. It had the look of a dwarf fortress with its Gothic turrets and narrow windows, its paved courtyard between gargoyled façades and carved projections over an enormous gate armor-plated with fittings. Kate found herself without any transition in another universe, where the uncertain light and fresh air conflicted with the marmoreal mists from which arose antique architectural profiles. Everything there was different, charged simultaneously with mystery, almost of enmity, and with a very distant familiarity. This insidious sensation of having traveled back in time came over her on certain meanderings, when the cries of children behind the high walls of an institution, the brick-red face of a harmonium player on the corner of a street black with soot, the bird's eye view of a park where a large folded paper bird was thrown, or simply this immutable iron-colored rain— they reminded her of something that she hadn't lived, at least not yet, and that filled her with a mysterious nostalgia. If she'd had a doctrinaire head, like all those fresh zealots steeped in the antediluvian allegories of India or Tibet, Kate could easily have been convinced of spiritualist conjectures about the transmigration of souls, but she could not or would not understand the muddled speech of her peers. Past lives for her were tangible every minute. As for the enlightened progression of souls, Mister Splitfoot had never said a word about it. However, that gave her enough free time to bear with good grace the sagacious interrogations of Mr. Coleman's friends.

London fascinated her even more than New York by what its dark and adventurous reputation concealed: it was there, in those monotonous streets, along the Thames when the Tower Bridge raises as the offshore rigs enter the harbor, among the serious crowds of Oxford Street, under the arcades of the Royal Opera House or in the gardens of Hampton Court, that so many of her heroes suffered the drama of their destiny. She hardly made a distinction between such literary characters and their authors. And so Shakespeare, Anthony Trollope, or Dickens, whose recent death she'd just learned of, haunted the same places alongside Ben Jonson's alchemist or Daniel Defoe's plague victims. Discovering *Vanity Fair* in the Livermore library, shortly before her departure, she identified with the young Amelia only because her good friend Becky seemed irresistible despite suspicious origins, and it's actually her rather than Thackeray that she caught herself looking for in the streets of London. Alone on board a horse-drawn carriage or flanked by a silent chaperone, she loved to lose herself in this immensity that in her eyes was more populated than the whole of America, albeit with fewer colors, except for the turbaned Hindus with cobra stares. In the unreality of an unfamiliar environment bringing up false memories in her, Kate saw everything strangely slowed-down, as if emerging from out of a dark cloth woven in different times. Each time she crossed over a bridge, those drowned below made a sign to her. On a hill in Hyde Park, surprised by the snow one late afternoon when the gas lamps were lit in the city, she thought she saw through the swirling one of the washers of the shroud, one of those materialized spirits—infanticide mother burned alive or decapitated streetwalker—that are called *Midnight Washerwomen*, and returned in a hurry to Chelsea, overwhelmed by the fear that some misfortune had happened on the other side of the world.

They were expecting her that evening in the salon of her host. She had just enough time to change her dress and powder her pale cheeks. Three large chandeliers illuminated the space, varnished parquet floors, ceilings painted by Rubens or his school, colonnades that opened on both sides to stairs or a series of interconnecting doors along galleries. Squeezed into a black coat like all the gentlemen present, Benjamin Coleman showed a joyful impatience on seeing the American woman in the grips of a couple of ladies of the world particularly interested in physiognomy.

"Allow me to borrow her," he said, leading Kate off by the elbow. Once they were clear of them, he leaned close to her ear: "Beware of Perdita and Fantasima, they are disciples of Ellis Brotherwood. They practice the magical orgasm . . ."

With Kate's hand in his, Mr. Coleman climbed the two steps of the small stage crowded by a grand piano. He pulled his guest to him.

"My dear friends," he uttered in a majestic tone, "I am immensely proud tonight to present to you the one you are all waiting for . . ."

A number of somber people were there, some with beards and monocles and some in sumptuous jewel-encrusted dresses one would marry a prince in. That's what Kate thought, intimidated by the sudden keen interest she'd become the object of. Her back against the black mirror of the piano, she regretted at that moment not being a concert performer who could escape through Bach or Beethoven. However, her host saved her from embarrassment by asking the audience not to test such a medium as ultra-sensitive as Miss Kate Fox.

"Need I remind you that we followers of spiritualism owe almost everything to this beautiful person who comes to us from New York and who, now over twenty years ago, though she is still a little girl, was the first to enter into communication with the other world, if one makes the exception of course of the Cumaean Sibyl or of Jesus conversing with Elijah and Moses . . . Our cause however has acquired the most eminent scholars like the astronomer Camille Flammarion, who declared loud and strong at the funeral of Allen Kardec: 'Spiritism is a science, not a religion,' or our friend the chemist William Crookes, member of the Royal

Academy. Tonight I borrow these words of the discoverer of thallium: 'Confirmed spiritualists owe this lady an immense debt for the joyous news that she was to a great extent the herald chosen by Providence . . .'"

Receiving an ovation, Kate felt a blush rise to her cheeks, but luckily neither a detailed response nor séance was asked of her. Mr. Harisson and Miss Rosamond Dale Owen, two editors of *Spiritualist* journal, came over to congratulate her around the buffet.

"Have you ever been attacked by evil spirits?" Miss Owen couldn't help but ask.

"Would you agree," Mr. Harisson interrupted her, "that Spiritualism is announcing itself to us as the third revelation of God?"

At that moment a young man of an unhealthy thinness, a diamond in his tie, bowed to the company from the top of the platform.

"The previously unpublished sonata you are about to hear was dictated to me by Mozart's spirit to Allan Kardec. And it's the communicator spirit of my deceased master, it's his biomagnetic energy whose interpretation you will hear through me . . ."

While the skeleton of a man lifted his coat tails to sit on the piano bench, Kate felt the burn of a glance; a little drunk from three glasses of champagne one after the other, she considered a quite ordinary physiognomy that, with simplicity and relaxation, appeared before her in the guise of a cheerful forty-year-old.

"Rest assured," said the man in jest, "I am not a spirit."

A little wobbly, Kate felt immediately at ease, a little like when one spots a good place to hold on to while on a merry-go-round. She would have liked to wrap her arms around the neck of this wooden horse, whose first name was George and who camouflaged his left eye with a tinted monocle. The stranger replied with a hilarious jubilation at her tipsy curiosity. Had he had too much to drink, too?

"In fact, I am the lawyer of our three-striped clownfish, for what concerns his purely material affairs."

"Is Mr. Coleman on trial?"

"An influential man such as your host sometimes has to be defended. But it has to do only with capital and investments. Between us, I don't think that spirits, if they exist, have much need for lawyers . . ."

For a whole year, sponsored by Benjamin Coleman, whose eager efforts to treat her like a parent and ally did not escape her, Kate was exhibited to the fascination of the London gentry, to the benign curiosity of neophytes up from the suburbs, or to the species of fervent rivalry of international followers. Spiritualist circles, congregations, and learned societies invited her to well-attended séances, with or without conferences of experts, all over England and the capitals of Northern Europe. Kate learned at these meetings much more than what she thought she knew. For instance, the spiritual world preexisted us with its hierarchies of angelic substances not unlike the Catholics'. That souls evolve from the mineral into the human. That spirits, all wandering and more or less dematerialized, are heading toward the indivisible way of perfection and are broken down into the impure, the spirits that knock, spirits who falsely claim authority, neutral spirits, etcetera, on the low scale still dependent on passions and matter; and on the high scale illuminated by divine intuition: the benevolent spirits, learned, wise, and superior spirits, like Jesus, Gautama Buddha, or Zoroaster, just before the beatific erasure into divinity.

The formidable challenges of an omniscient seer such as the Scottish Daniel Dunglas Home, of a certain Madame Blavatsky upon her return from Cairo, or of the illustrious Florence Cook who materialized a full-length ghost walking for the first time in her darkroom (that of the not least venerated Katie King, who had died two centuries earlier), were only building in a spectacular way upon a multitude of experimenters of the shadow who, recently, were pronouncing with the projections of ectoplasms and other remarkable phenomena the hypothesis of the *perispirit*, an intermediary element between spirit and matter, a sort of fluid continuation or electromagnetic division of the astral body in two, with evidence gathered of fingerprints in paraffin molds, the levitation of furniture or operators, the contribution of objects from the other world or even the glimmers on photographic plates, the new infatuation of darkrooms.

Kate however had still benefitted from the prestige of origins and was for many a symbol and an augur. Thus the Empire's wars and revolutions did not prevent Queen Victoria, eternally mourning the prince consort, from secretly welcoming the little American so that she might comfort her with a thought of the afterlife between two government meetings.

There were other parties at Chelsea. Kate met new faces. The naturalist Alfred Russel Wallace explained to her the effect of rivers on the distribution of inbred animal species and offered her a magnetite from the Malaysian Islands. An old French writer accustomed to exile invited her to Guernesey where he voluntarily resided since the death of his grandson and wife. A blind countess made her the gift of a silver plaque of the divinatory virtues that represented her from the time when she could see, eyes wide open. Several young girls of the aristocracy fell in love with her out of whimsy, mimicry, or contagion.

One night in November, 1871, the lawyer George Jencken resurfaced, invited by circumstance. Suddenly free of his tinted monocle, with one eye gray and the other green, Kate understood while staring at him the agitation that had inhabited her ceaselessly for months. Encouraged by the good omen of her pallor, George, without the knowledge of her protector, dreamily asked her hand in marriage.

U.

A Normal Life

Real life, after so many years of summoning the dead and occult forces, was linked in Kate's mind with the exclusive love of a man. Just married, she had withdrawn from the social comedy with an unknown emotion, entirely devoted to the service of the lawyer George Jencken, whose name she had donned the way one dons the veil. Freed overnight from the regard of others, that servitude which ultimately turned into torture, she abandoned herself to her new status as anonymous wife with an affinity for detachment close to the confused notion she had of happiness. Incapable of complete serenity because of those difficult skeletons, those detached hands, all those ectoplasmic tentacles that almost naturally inhabited her dreams, she worked to regenerate herself on a canvas of omission whose loose weft gradually wove in the ancestral motions that she had seen carried out in Rapstown or in Hydesville, and that moved her so much to recollect, how her good mother attended to the household chores while humming, suspecting nothing still of the machinations of her abominable little girls. Putting away the towels and bright sheets on the shelves of an old armoire, for example, without counting the suspicious creakings, washing the crystal glasses under running water without listening closely to the rattles or acute vibrations, lighting the phosphorous lamp or candlesticks very simply in order to knit a sweater. And to read the poems of Keats offered by her husband:

O tender spouse of the golden god Hyperion

Or those of Dante Gabriel Rossetti bought at Alexander's Bookshop, in her neighborhood of Notting Hill:

> *The blessed damozel lean'd out*
> *From the gold bar of Heaven;*
> *Her eyes were deeper than the depth*
> *Of waters still'd at even;*
> *She had three lilies in her hand,*
> *And the stars in her hair were seven.*

That the author, mad with grief, had buried in the coffin of his beautiful and young wife the manuscript of his verses only to exhume and publish them eight years later was something Kate didn't want to have inflicted on her. George, discovering this editorial novelty in her hands, had reported the anecdote to her while caressing her breasts. After so many evanescent hysterics, libidinous puritans, heavy-handed patriarchs, it pleased her to be desired without hindrance or intercession, like any other woman that one would kiss and undress. The body of a man, its ligaments and strength, occupied her fingertips and her entire body enough to think of nothing else than imminent pleasure—at the small of the back, between the plexus and perineum, from the neck down to the toes—which attenuated her happiness while increasing her love tenfold. Kate couldn't keep herself from finding an exhilarating taste of death in physical possession, which she brought herself out of each time with a little ritual of childish coaxing that astonished the lawyer after the excess of embraces.

To no longer avoid the world of the living, Mrs. Jencken protected herself from the morbid declivities of her mind by showing her enthusiasm at the worst moments. Joy was for her a symptom of anxiety. She also appreciated more than anything the drizzly and bland languor of autumn days, the vacant nights before a crackling fire and the unsinkable boredom of Sundays: wasn't she alive in sweet contrast? She loved the oscillation of the large trees in the wind, in the London parks, the clouds above the river, when she would descend on foot to the old Battersea toll bridge, bought back by the Metropolitan Board of Works and again threatened with demolition, and even the strange desolate streets of Whitechapel where thousands of children orphaned by cholera wandered, growing up on the street to become ragpickers, collectors, thieves soon to be hanged—or if lucky, to become apprentices in the factory.

Busy during the day with his study of the City, on the Queen's Bench Division or in conference with one or other of his clients, George was long unaware of her sleepwalking fugues. Until the night Kate came home late, looking wild, her gloves torn and stained with blood. He figured out that she had been assaulted by a bunch of East End kids where she'd gone to stroll without protection, a defector from the good side of town, and had broken her nails while heartily defending herself. He lavished her with soothing words and nursed her scratches, discovering that she had been frequenting for months perhaps the canvas shelters of the

Christian Revival Society, where the most needy of the countless underprivileged were helped under the leadership of the preacher William Booth. Out of a natural generosity, but suddenly concerned about the mental health of his spouse, as much as he had always hidden from her his own ailments, the lawyer became closer to her and made sure that his driver and right-hand man followed her diligently from the moment that she declined being driven somewhere.

But a happy event—as those usually indifferent to the event love to say—soon changed the mental state of the Jencken couple. Kate gave birth to twins so exceedingly identical, even down to the details known only by mothers, that she herself must have permanently confused them two or three times, leaving to good fortune the choice of identities until their father decided to attach to their ankles thin gold chains engraved with their names. That one would be called Arcady and the other John Elias—or the reverse—before this initiative, was hardly going to change their reciprocal existence a hair. Which one was the eldest by a few minutes, Kate couldn't have said, which eventually disturbed her with generative vertigo. She lived through her pregnancy like a bird hovering so high, so far above the dark marshes. Flesh fertilized opened the mind to the joys of childhood as well as to the white locks of age, with the influx of stars and the dazzling abysses of ice. For her, giving birth was bringing her own self into the world; Kate was born from her own stomach or the bowels of the universe with two twins as a sign of the zodiac. This moment contained all moments, the streaming of generations, the infinite metamorphoses, and the heart of the shadow of death palpitating across the billions of lives with ephemeral stigmatas.

One recovers quickly from birth when taken by frenzy to save the mystery of life by pouring it out in careful sips. In motherhood, Kate distanced herself from the terror of procreation. Her two boys grew strong and got big, still always interchangeable, playing on every occasion with their twinning, Arcady answering to the call for John Elias, the other fooling his parents in false stories, the both of them exchanging their clothes when the adults wanted to tell them apart, up until the day when one of the two, stricken by a purulent meningitis and placed into isolation, was brought out after two weeks of treatment with memory disorders persistent enough for the twins to abandon their favorite game, having become impossible to play by the force of circumstances.

Between the education of her children and a redoubled attention to her husband, Kate no longer felt the need to flee into the London streets or into her cataleptic dreams. The nostalgia for American cities, so different from the big London checkerboard where sooty neighborhoods alternated with parks in undefined suburbs, seized her sometimes unexpectedly. There, everything was possible overnight, glory and madness, unhappiness and fortune. The memory of Horace Greeley, her indulgent patron, who died the year of her marriage after running unsuccessfully in the presidential elections, still throbbed in her, but like a good star about to fizzle out. She missed above all the beautiful days of Rochester and pined for Margaret. She even missed Leah. There comes a day when siblings replace the buried memory of the elders, since in them alone are found now the inflections of voice and the attitudes populating one's intimate background.

From time to time Margaret wrote her long rowdy missives where she cursed everyone on Earth, starting with Leah who gave herself the right to reprimand Margaret publicly in the name of the spiritualist cause, under the pretext that she was giving herself over to alcohol and, in a series of degradations, to the disloyal charlatans of French and German spiritualists touring Main Street America and the entire East Coast. It was apparent from her letters, without her daring to admit it, that her manager and probably lover Franck Strechen was exploiting her with the cynicism of a pimp or circus-freak showman. Kate sadly felt very glad while reading of no longer having to deal with that spiritual brotherhood, in some respects as fratricidal as it was incestuous, and of having preserved her twins and her husband from the miasmas of the other world, for she no longer had any doubt that frequenting the dead too often meant giving oneself over to them body and soul. George who, in marrying her, had lost Mr. Coleman as his client, was half-ruined but not unhappy to distance his beloved wife from the crowds, more and more numerous, applauding her in their grief from the wars, catastrophes and epidemics that traditional faiths were no longer able to console. Such dangerous heresy was in his opinion more contagious than gangrene.

It was a fact that neither Mr. Coleman nor Charles Livermore, warned belatedly of her defection, were interested any longer in her since her marriage: a woman of family goes better with stoves than spirits. The only company Kate had were George, her children, and her family-in-law. Uncle Herbert visited them once a week, always jovial, so happy to play the great uncle that the twins, delighted at this diversion, celebrated him like one of the Magi. Gifts accumulated in their room, all different: little islands of toys would have sufficed to betray Arcady and John Elias if the illness had not long shut down their mimetic emulation. Although he was a radical atheist, admirer of the Paris Commune and great reader of Karl Marx, starting with his *Contribution to the Critique of Political Economy,* Uncle Herbert kept the former pythoness of the pedestal table in relative mistrust. He had learned never to judge individuals on their alienation and treated his sister-in-law with the same distant charity that Plague doctors must have had in the time of the miasma theories. Once a month a less amiable grandmother came up, a jealous widow who monopolized the attention of her son and grandsons at Kate's expense, suspicious in her eyes of casting a spell. Wasn't she one of the three Fox sisters, like the three Gorgons with snakes for hair, like the Fates or the monstrous Grey Nuns of legend who had among the three of them a single eye and one lone tooth, taking turns watching and devouring?

Kate was never happier than in the fisherman's house they rented sometimes in the summer, at Gower, between the beaches and cliffs of Wales, when the lawyer could accompany the children. It was upon returning from a week on the peninsula that his health problems, up until then inconsequential, took a dramatic turn. After having gone valiantly to his office in the city with the help of his coachman, several days later, swearing that it was only a little fatigue, George took to his bed and died one summer night in 1881, in the sole company of his wife, to whom he had never stopped promising that it was really nothing serious, that he would go on loving her for many more years and even more once he felt better.

Alone in the house, the children entrusted that night to their grandmother, Kate shook the body of her husband while begging him to respond, screaming at him that it wasn't funny, that he had never ever abandoned her, then wept her fill on his already cold hands, kissed his lips and eyes, and suddenly petrified by the evidence, searched her empty mind to remember a prayer from her childhood. After a silence that lasted nearly an hour, she stammered the creed of John Wesley she'd so often read, chiseled on the pediment of the Methodist church in Hydesville:

Do all the good you can
By all the means you can
In all the ways you can
In all the places you can
At all the times you can
To all the people you can
As long as ever you can

VI.

The Two Widows of Notting Hill

At nine years old, nothing about the schemes of adults escapes you. This is what Arcady and John Elias told each other without saying a word on the return home from the cemetery. They conversed and thought by exchanged glances. Needless to bother with words, unless for putting on airs. Silence isn't just for the deaf.

Uncle Herbert, grandmother, all sorts of aunts and old cousins had invaded the apartment after the funeral as if to hide a secret or to take the place of their father. And then those people went home, leaving the house full of shadows. Kate would come to tuck them into their twin beds and, very solemn, tell them stories of blessing and paradise, but she would cry a long chain of iron tears. And it was they, the children, who night after night had to console her. Explain to her that he was there, close by, that George was watching them with his different colored eyes, one blue eye in this world, the green eye in the other.

Weeks later, a thundering night in autumn, Kate started to smile prettily, like Mary of the Images. She promised them a surprise: Margaret, their aunt, was going to cross the Ocean to come meet them. One more relative or one less, this piece of news was fleeting, but Katie's smile kept up its promise. Arcady and John Elias, for months now, had listened to her lessons of healing while she herself had been using both hands to hold open her own wounds. One night very late, she led them into the room where their father had been laid in his coffin. There was a table with three chairs, just across from the bed illumined by a bedside candelabra. "Who is there?" asked Kate, after having them sit down, their little hands flat on the table. It was winter, an enormous gust shook the roofs and chimneys in a torrent of noise. Sometimes a gust charged with rain seemed to cross the exterior wall. Then the alphabet started to answer Kate's voice with numbers and the table knocked the floor from one foot or another: one, two, three, four, five . . . Was it five? The numbers had to be translated back into letters and words in order, then she read:

A-R-C-A-D-Y-J-O-H-N-E-L-I-A-S-I-L-O-V-E-Y-O-U.

Was that all? They already suspected that their father loved them. Although this game without any playing cards was fun, with the candles, the agitated table and those mysterious noises, their eyelids were heavier than the earth on a grave. Kate had to carry them one after the other up to bed. Another time, the table rose, oscillating like a little hot-air balloon. Arcady could not believe that his father, once so reasonable, was returning from the grave for such mischievous turns. John Elias was of the same opinion and, without either one of them expressing such a thing, declared all of a sudden:

"Mister Splitfoot, will you soon finish with your antics!"

Kate, horrified, stood straight up, letting the table topple. "Who told you about him?" she stammered.

The twins, side by side, looked at their mother with the unusual attention one gives to a loved one confessing to a defect or hidden perversion.

"You did, Mommy!" said Arcady, "when you sleepwalk at night through the rooms . . ."

"My boys, my boys!" she cried, incapable of finding the salutary words, clutching their heads to her chest.

It was by telephone, from the central post office, that Kate made contact with her sister who, just arrived at the port of London, was calling from the offices of the maritime shipping company at the agreed upon day and time. Yes, there was no change, they were expecting her at the indicated address, she was still living with her children in their Notting Hill apartment. Kate wasn't surprised by the hoarse and listless voice on the other end of the line, thinking of the hardships of that voyage.

But when her sister presented herself at her door, two grumbling porters beleaguered with trunks behind her, she could not conceal a startled jump at the sight of her ravaged face.

"I've gone to pot, no?" Margaret said gently to help out. "Soon I'll be ready for the scrapheap! But you, you haven't changed so much. They say that one's face reflects one's heart . . ."

Once the luggage was deposited and the coat hung, seated face to face, the steam from a teapot undulating between them, the dialogue was renewed as if it had never stopped, and the discord between a very real aging and the transience of this decade of not seeing each other was reduced to the point of disappearing entirely: hadn't she always carried Margaret inside her, branded like a cross of fate on her bare skin? Already, she was asking what there was to drink, some wine, some beer, some whiskey, to get her back on her feet after a crossing drowned in spray.

"By the way, where are my nephews?" she asked in surprise, somewhat confused by this lack of propriety.

"With their Uncle Herbert for the birthday of a little cousin."

"I'm excited to meet them!" she said, helping herself to a bottle that George had been the last person to open. "And you, you've pulled yourself together some? Here we are, sisters in bad luck . . ."

"You're drinking too much," Kate whispered.

"It helps me get over the old times . . . Will you take me to visit the Metropolitan? I'd also love to discover the old streets, palaces, churches. Ah! what a fortune we could make here, the two of us, in the largest city in the world . . ."

"I'm done with all that."

"I understand, protect yourself, even faking with all one's might, it still brings out dangerous forces . . ."

"What!" Kate exclaimed. "You were pretending?"

"Everyone fakes it, what are you thinking, you can't always be inspired, and then there are nights when the spirits shun you, so what do you do, in front of an audience wanting knocks, levitation, and the whole shebang, you bluff, you know it well, even a stew sometimes boils over, though sometimes it falls on a gas burner. I don't know a single one of them, of those so-called mediums, who hasn't been caught one time or another with pockets full of tricks . . ."

Chin resting on her fists, Kate gazed at her older sister in a state of deep confusion, less because of her revelations, which entertained as much as scandalized her, than because of the mutations showing in her whole person. Her voice, her language, her face had suffered ten years of strange insults. Shivering, Kate wondered what her life must have been like since the death of Elisha Kane.

"You're looking at me like a stranger," declared Margaret. "I'm the same, don't you worry. I've just known some distress and adversity, like a lot of women back home. And Leah didn't help me . . . Would you happen to have anything else to drink?"

They didn't leave each other all night, remembering the fortune of the old days, the lost celebrations, and all the light ghosts of memory, handsome Lee in Rapstown, the children of Hydesville, Pequot, Lily Brown, and Harriet, the girl from the ranch where a slave was hung, and Pearl, their teacher.

"I crossed paths with her in Rochester," said Margaret. "She became an influential woman, an activist in women's rights. She writes novels . . ."

"And her father, the reverend?"

"Dead and in hell, I hope. He deserves the hell of papists!"

The next day, when the twins were back, Margaret hugged and kissed them to the point of terrifying them, wept about all the children she wouldn't have, while laughing the whole time at herself and singing like an old pioneer:

> *O boys, we're goin' far to-night*
> *Yeo-ho, yeo-ho, yeo-ho!*

No doubt from the logic of opposites, she turned astonishingly quiet in the weeks that followed, absent by day and plunged at night into the study of religious works. Since she had stopped drinking and becoming angry at every mention of Leah, supreme usurper of the kingdom of ghosts, Kate thought that the distance had calmed her back down. Maggie was resting in London from the extravagance of energies, spiritual insurrections, and conflicts of all kinds that were overflowing from the American cauldron.

Distraught, with no other desire than some support from beyond, she actually ran to churches and temples. Despite her dyed hair and the powder on her face, age had adulterated the comforting reflection that glances in the mirror used to return. Emptied of any *sentiment de soi*—that hot evanescent roundness that is perpetuated in a waking dream, a sort of inner sanctuary where one waits endlessly for who knows what—she wandered under a changing mask, by turns tragic or as indifferent as the London sky, from a nestled chapel in a dungeon at the church of St. Marylebone so similar to the churches in New York, to the St. Paul Cathedral, then to St. Clement Danes next to Covent Garden. This deserted splendor, under the shadow arches, between two directions of crowds during the divine offices, soothed her without having to determine the nature of the sect at work, be it Anglican, Methodist, or Presbyterian. The misery that circled the city, beyond the buildings and kept parks—in Whitechapel, in the East End, the area surrounding St. George, where weary prostitutes paraded among packs of grimy children, drunkards, and crippled seekers, in Limehouse or Lisson Grove, with its wide streams of human distress between the railways and channel gaps—seemed to her like an unknown, more ancestral species across the Atlantic, flourishing on its own cankers or as if moored to its own shipwreck.

From wandering to wandering, it was in the heart of London, at the end of Whitehall, in the City of Westminster, that she found her haven. The splendors of the abbey astonished her without emotion. Neither the tombs of a king and his queen behind the altar, nor the heraldic banners of the Knights over the stalls caught more than a moment of her attention. But she came to a stop before a statue of the Virgin, under a big dome fanned with sculpted shields, in the center of the stone circle of apostles and saints.

For several days she returned to Lady Chapel, weary perhaps from a vain wonder, trudging to the old prison yards where the cathedral must have been built, next to the preserved oratory of the former Catholic church adjoining a building probably used as a presbytery. Margaret entered the sanctuary feeling a mixture of oppression and deliverance. The burning bush of candles and the blue smoke from the censers at the foot of an effigy of the Immaculate Conception along with the shadow cast by a large crucifix of the dead Christ, sides pierced, conjured for her in some ways the arrangement of a medium's cabinet. She remained so long in front of the Virgin, haggard, with an imploring look, that a priest sitting in prayer in the shadows of a recess began to worry about her. The apparition came over and leaned down to her, thin in her black dress with red piping and buttons.

"You need help, we have all been in sorrow; are you Catholic?"

Those words of this clergyman, encountered by chance in the remains of a church, shattered Margaret who, after a long interview and a complete confession, feverishly accepted conversion. The influence of the priest over her was immediate and without reservation. She learned later, at the moment of the sacraments of baptism along with the company of other converts, that he was the Archbishop of Westminster, the Cardinal Henry Manning, one of the most influential Catholic theologians, fully committed to John Wesley's idea of social justice. Manning himself had converted after a heretic past and, on one finger along with the episcopal ring, wore the ring of his young wife who had died shortly after their marriage. A secret necromancer in his own dreams, the inconsolable prelate perceptively understood the emotional challenges of the new doctrine. Margaret was for him an easy prey as well as a trophy: already won by the Virgin Mary, she was persuaded as by her husband before her of the highly terrifying register of damnation. Didn't everything in spiritualism fall into demonic practices? Captivated by the spells of the Catholic liturgy, but duly unbewitched, she felt better in the months that followed, in a convalescence with no pharmacopoeia other than holy water and the bread of angels.

Kate no longer recognized her sister. They had never discussed between themselves the perpetual virginity of Mary or the worship of the Eucharist. Even less in the participation of the unknowable being of the Trinity. The variety of vices and sins, with interior delight or conscious and voluntary transgression, had hardly been their concern up to now. Margaret returned home solemnly each night without swearing or trying to slake her thirst. Temperate and frugal, she considered all things from the point of view of grace. By nature generous, Kate provided for her happiness by offering her all the little things necessary for her asceticism. Since George's death, she used her modest portion of the inheritance without ever counting; but no income led slowly to collapse. The lawyer's old lessors and billers eventually objected to the widow's debts.

When it came time to turn in the keys to the house, proof of their misfortune, Margaret sold her jewelry and some dresses to help with the costs of moving. With the twins, her sister, and two carts of furniture, Mrs. Fox-Jencken went to settle in the East End. School being mandatory only up to the age of ten, a recent age limit due to recruitment in the factories or the coal mines, she devoted herself to providing the secondary education of her sons, mixing disciplines, teaching the erroneous and the apodictic in the same way, the infestation of evil spirits and some notions of algebra. Fortunately, under the impulse of Maggie who, divided between ecstasy and sagacity, had little by little gone back to drinking, the twins were able to attend courses free of charge in a Catholic institution. At no point in their poverty, deprivation, and eventual destitution, did Kate consider the idea of going to complain to her in-laws, who associated meanness with propriety, or to reclaim her fame on a music hall stage, numerous in London, as a historical medium of quality.

When Maggie, worn out by homesickness and the uncertainty of her own vocation, took the boat back to New York, Kate found herself so distraught that she obediently began swallowing all the remains of the bottles left by her sister. This she did between visits to the immense park of Kensal Cemetery, bordering Notting Hill, where the Jencken family mausoleum, shaped like an ancient temple, stood among mourners and the statues of archangels. Facing her husband's tomb, Kate noticed one day an old solitary tombstone, strewn with daisies, the family name indecipherable, but whose epitaph was still clear:

I'd rather hear something to make me laugh

The exclamation from the grave rang mockingly in her. Thinking of her twins, she quickly fled the cemetery and returned with a decided step to her neighborhood on the East End, between the gate and the river.

VII.

Mens agitat molem

New York was smoking like a thousand locomotives under the falling snow. Mills and factories, numerous construction sites where pyramids of brick and scrap iron were being erected—with, as its emblem at the mouth of the Hudson, the immense framework of the future Statue of Liberty on its granite fortification—and likewise the mouths of the metro and the sewer, the conical or terraced roofs, and ferry boats crisscrossing the river and the strait, were all sending up fat clouds of vapor and gray-black plumes. These traveled in a rolling boil denser than a mountain fog toward the plaster casts of the sky, from which the solstice snow seemed to crumble and fall in discontinuous waves.

It was three o'clock in the afternoon on a day that had not quite fully risen and was already starting to wane when, both arms leaning against the back of a chair facing the windows—on the corner of South Street Seaport and with a view of the new Brooklyn Bridge, the dock harbors and fluvial escape toward Governors Island—Leah Underhill wondered humorlessly if her health troubles and annoyances would grant her a reprieve from the end of year festivities. At her age, one could still overcome the small warning signs of passing time, the creaky wheels of age were still oiled well, provided that one was not constantly worrying about various troubles. "They lose it that do buy it with much care," she'd heard the other night at the Standard Theatre, at the premiere of *The Merchant of Venice*. And she estimated she'd inherited the bulk, and in tons, of worries, during a life devoted to the Spiritualist cause with its varied fortunes and a constant adversity from the side of barkers, hypnotists, jugglers, snake oil salesmen, and other disloyal competitors marching off in packed rows to distort the message of spirits. They were organized throughout the United States, without ever even thinking of inviting her, these conferences of mediums under big tops, in churches, and community halls. George P. Colby, somewhere in Florida, proclaimed himself prophet of Spiritualism *urbi et orbi*. The Anglican priest William Stainton Moses, another champion of deep trance, claimed to transcribe in shamanic dictation the living conditions in the afterlife. Emma Hardinge Britten claimed to understand in detail the works and miracles the disembodied used to answer us. And what about that half-wit Eusapia Paladino, going out with her sleeves all twisted from her *perispirit*, or of that stuck-up thing Frickie Wonder, who knew so well how to use her breasts and hips to captivate the old geezers of the universities while spouting the worst philosophy for girls, or still yet, to top all this bluffing off, that joker William Mac Orpheus, now one of the star attractions in the new Barnum three-ring circus! The inventory of all this deception and prevarication would have required an almanac. Baffling enough to make her lose her Latin! Leah felt much too old and betrayed to sort the wheat from the chaff. And it mattered little to her whether she was in good or bad faith, since she alone knew how to assemble the flags and drums. Modern

Spiritualism was her exclusive invention, no one could contest it, and certainly not these poor rookies who had benefitted from the enterprise as apathetic and capricious associates. Like John the Baptist, she had given the impetus to a new religion with no messiah or legislator, expanded now all over the world, with crowds of proselytes more or less devoted. Thanks to her, all the dead were like Lazarus, ready to answer as present. There was no longer that plague wall between the world of the living and that of spirits. She had even contributed to the liberation of women, those slaves, white or black, by offering them a spiritual forum impregnable to most men, so stupidly full of themselves with their brute force.

But her pain was mitigated by the spectacle of the snow. Without a doubt it was the virtue of angels, this cottony and indistinct slowness that leisurely dresses the soul. But Leah still had one more demon in her head. In addition to a share of the Underhill fortune, her investments in the railroad had earned her enough to languish for several lifetimes in New York—if it occurred to God to reward her troubles—without having to give conferences on the Doctrine any more. She was abandoning without regret the emptiness of precepts and systems to the teachers of the other world. From spiritualism to spiritism, there was just one syllable missing, cheerfully replaced by the "third revelation of God."

Leah told herself that she would have suffered it all, the lynch mob, the skeptics, the scientists incapable of admitting that there is no miracle without faith, the imposters by the dozen, and even spiritism, to top it all off, which had made off with her discovery, just as the converted persecutor Paul of Tarsus's words were taken by a revenant named Jesus. Too old to take the offensive, she had only to look toward her retirement so long as the enemies kept their distance. But they'd been grinning at her front door ever since her sisters' return. Without resources, always between drunkenness and madness, Margaret had displayed herself grotesquely in music halls for a few dollars, pushed by a crooked manager who had the sole ambition of denigrating her. At seventy-five years old, Leah Underhill was the only one upholding the legacy of Hydesville. And the pitiful Kate, landed back in New York this autumn with her twin warlocks, exposing a spectacle of deliquescence for all to see . . . Leah had given the order to her lawyer, a good man efficient and naturally respectful of propriety, to take legal action to stop these scandals. If he could detain the one for her pattern of repeated scandal before the public, and begin the procedure to remove the children from the other for proven negligence and moral abuse, then Leah would be back on track.

With a migraine and an aching back, Leah moved away from the windows and went to her room. Her two lapdogs, Horace and Wildy, jumped onto her bed once she was lying down. They wagged their tails in search of a caress, tongues hanging out. Touched, the old woman dug her bony fingers into all that white wool. "My little loves," she said, eyelids heavy. "You'd never make any trouble for your mommy, no . . ."

Sleep would have resembled a soothing death without these pains and parasitic dreams. Over time, Leah had honestly come to believe in visiting spirits. And never more so than in the floating cities of dream. A business woman suffers more than other women from the idleness of solitude, and there was nothing her lapdogs could do to help that. Waves of images from her youth in Rapstown came back to her in fits and starts, lashing her memory. Amid a lowly breed of people destined for the dirt and the barn, she had rebelled, desperate to one day be like the ladies who came down from the city to do charity work, whether by spending sleepless nights studying books loaned by a sympathetic pastor or giving lessons to the young educated girls to have access to their drawing rooms. Her first ambition, barely pubescent, was learning to play the piano. The rich farmers proudly furnished their ranches with that enchanted sideboard. And the pastor was pleased to have at his disposition a wise young woman to put back to liturgical use a small portable organ donated by the congregation.

Asleep in an instant, her consciousness asymmetric as her heartbeat, the eldest of the Fox sisters suddenly had the feeling of a great pillaging of the well-ordered cabinets of memory. The images of her life were merging, absurdly and without correlation, reducing a great ocean of light to a desire to urinate or twisting one into the other, like a marshmallow pastry, the faces of the dead and those of the living. She herself was burning, a witch from another century, on a stake where each flame represented a day of her life. "You're bringing out dangerous forces," an old man wearing a compass and sextant breathed in her face, while tearing out the flesh of her neck in fistfuls that, thrown in the air, were flying with the cries of a nightjar. How to escape the morgue of dreams? Heads and limbs, parts of cadavers rising up from an autopsy table encircled her in a burlesque sarabande of suicides, drowned persons, and assassins. Dressed in animal skins, her Welsh ancestors were now flocking to steal her things right out from under the old spinster. Do millennia have the same value as a single instant in the other world? A scarlet parrot, sprung from one of her ears, chased the ghosts away with blows of its beak and then the fiendish bird perched on her shoulder, deafening her endlessly with *"Mens agitat molem."* Even dead, she thought she could hear herself thinking, she would have had to give birth before she could begin to comprehend such a phenomenon.

But these vapors vanished. Revived from the grave, mind in tatters, Leah Underhill let out a low groan that frightened her little dogs. She raised herself up to sitting, a little more certain of being safe after each tick of a pendulum clock hanging on the wall. Soon on her feet, she stumbled over to the bay window, hands on her hips. The snow was redrawing the ribs and shoulders of the Brooklyn Bridge. One could barely make out the hills on the other side of the strait, and the islands at the mouth had receded into darkness. Woken up badly, she rubbed her scalp at length as if delousing herself of her dream, then grabbed a silver bell sitting on a pedestal table.

Impatient, ringing it several times, she admitted that it was useless to doze off in the middle of the day, irritated by a hissing sound in her left ear and even more by her inevitable lateness now to the Spiritualist Circle in Union Square where under her presidency they were receiving the pacifist Colonel Henry Steel Olcott and Mr. William Quan Judge, both founding members of the Theosophical Society. Although their driving force, a Mrs. Helena Blavatsky, also made claims about her mediumship, the two of them hunted in different forests, so to speak. And good for them! It was clear that the spiritualist cause, rather than letting itself be overtaken, should display a healthy ecumenism.

Finally appeased, Leah saw her Virginian maid coming toward her contrite, curlers on her old head.

"I could have died a hundred times over," she let out in a falsely serene tone.

"But Madam, you had given me the afternoon off . . ."

"Even if it were three days, or an entire month! You must still be there when I ring!"

In front of the red dye-job and googly eyes of her maid, she suddenly remembered the scarlet parrot in her nightmare and froze, suspicious.

"*Mens agitat molem!*" she exclaimed. "*Mens agitat molem?* What on earth could that mean . . ."

UIII.
Three Letters for a Betrayal

Apart from the blizzard baptized the "Great White Hurricane," which paralyzed the northern United States and Canada for several days in mid-March under an enormous sheet of ice, fifty-inch snowfalls, hundreds of victims, and tons of iced-over bridges and railways, the journalists of the *New-York Tribune* had nothing exciting to sink their teeth into. That was according to old Oil-stone—his editorial staff's friendly nickname for him since he'd gone completely bald—who was stuffing himself with cold cuts at Katz's Delicatessen, a new bistro on the Lower East Side, when he thought he spotted a familiar chin wavering behind the head of a beer tycoon. In his line of work, one ended up being able to recognize any sort of celebrity under the disguises of time. The use of photography in the press had accustomed his eye to trans-formations: one had to be able to recall the portrait of a beautiful woman who went off her rocker. This puffy old broad, bags under her eyes, a mop of hair like crow's wings: it was definitely one of the Fox sisters. He had interviewed them during the time of the Barnum Museum. Aside from Mother Underhill, female pope of those devoted to the old school of knocking tables now

280

become a sort of New York institution, the Fox sisters and how many legs they had between them had been forgotten. Novelty, that was the sole watchword in New York. One had to be on the train, a fashion dandy, up-to-date. Old Oilstone, who did not lack for a nose and knew by heart the extent of the public's intrigue, didn't have to think too hard to figure out how to take advantage of this revenant. It was an ordinary expedient of the journalist in calm times to make use of a fallen glory, who was sipping her own bile, in order to fill the newspaper plate under the disgusted but complacent eye of the column editor. Scandal always pays, failing a prodigy. One can always turn to the past, provided it's to stir things up.

The old journalist kindly offered Margaret another drink, which for an instant made her think he had taken her for a prostitute.

"Wouldn't you be Kate Fox, or rather her sister?" he whispered with a feigned enthusiasm.

Being nearly recognized would have almost flattered her, if the mirror facing her hadn't been reflecting the mask of a shipwreck. She accepted without protest to answer some questions, letting all the bitterness of her last years rise back up to her lips. Taken into the game in her inebriation, she spared no detail for old Oilstone, who broke his pencil on his notepad several times.

"Modern spiritualism, as they call it, well I'll tell you a bit of history from its very foundation. At first, when the whole business began, Katie and me, we were just kids and our damned older sister, already an old woman, played us. As for our mother, she was a fool, a fanatic, if I may say so myself. But our mother had an honest heart and believed in these things. Leah, though, that's a different story. She prostituted us in exhibitions without any scruples. And all the proceeds, they went straight into her pocket . . ."

These comments appeared a few days later, rewritten into good English, on the front page of the *New-York Tribune*, and Margaret, who hadn't taken this chance encounter seriously, discovered them in a different bar on the Lower East Side, paging through the house copy fastened to a newspaper stick. Immediately paralyzed, she finally shrugged and read the date above the headlines with a renewed superstition: hadn't she been converted on September 24th? Still clinging to her Catholic faith, Margaret saw in the number of the year a great symbol: 1888. Nothing less than the divine Unity flanked by the three infinities of the Trinity!

She wasn't unhappy about the racket this off-the-cuff interview was going to provoke in the spiritist and spiritualist circles: the world would remember her. She could easily imagine Leah's fury. But the long letter she received by general delivery a few days later quite cleverly showed nothing of it. Her sister sermonized her for five pages, in the name of the cause, presenting her with her complaints, the unspeakable discredit she was guilty of, the shame that her conduct was inflicting on the family, and in conclusion guaranteed her a lawsuit at the next prank. The stationery was beautifully printed with the name of Mrs. Leah Fox-Underhill, and the handwriting in blue ink was neat and proper. Margaret crunched it into balls that she threw into the fire.

From a furnished room on the Lower East Side or in Greenwich Village, her only luggage a trunk where she kept her stage outfit and a few accessories, Margaret fell back into a sullen anonymity. Her whim had hardly dented the reputation of Leah, who grandly used her right to respond by inviting the best writers of the spiritualist cult to defend her honor. Cleverly inverted, stigma is only a stepping stone.

Left to herself more than ever, Margaret dreamt of returning to Monroe County, where she remembered a few people she'd known who were probably still alive, some of whom might be willing to help her. A remote town like Rochester is willingly flattered to have what London or New York are tired of.

Margaret considered more and more seriously getting a one-way ticket at Grand Central Station when, again by general delivery, two letters delivered on the same day changed her mind. One of them overwhelmed her with sadness and anger, the other handed her the means necessary for that divine justice named revenge. The first came from Kate, who in her despair didn't leave an address. Leah had now gotten her way. On the basis of her accusations, Katie had been arrested for vagrancy on a public street while looking for a place to live, she and her sons loaded down with luggage. Custody of her children was withdrawn in the wake, under the allegation of abuse. Despite all of her appeals and petitions to the court, before the judges, to the governor, the court decision was upheld. Placed in the Saint Vincent de Paul orphanage, the twins claimed their mother as much as she claimed them. After the judgment confided the custody of Arcady and John Elias to her British in-laws, Uncle Herbert hardly tarried in having them delivered on a liner of the General Transatlantic Company. That was all the contents of her letter. Kate added, a little wave falling over the shipwreck of her signature: "Maggie, defend me! Help me! I cannot survive without my angels." The other letter she opened with trembling hands and read through her tears:

Dear Margaret Fox-Kane,

I had the opportunity to learn with surprise and satisfaction of your disillusioned declarations a while back in the New-York Tribune. *You are perfectly right to set the record straight. Leah Fox-Underhill scandalously injured you, you and your little sister. I thought that you might push the envelope further in a profitable way. Essentially, why not make a public demonstration of it to New York itself. The idea occurred to me that we could earn a lot of money by renting the biggest hall in town, that of the Academy of Music. With a good slogan like "The Return of the Fox Sisters" or "Margaret Fox Denounces the Sham," it's two thousand dollars guaranteed. I would charge for my services of course, with the usual terms, for the organization, promotion, and success of the event.*

Remember, dear Margaret, what a devoted agent I was for you for a long time, etc.

Frank Strechen

The card of a Brooklyn hotel with the telephone number underlined in the same ink accompanied the letter. She got back in contact with the manager that same day and, determined to ruin the reputation of Leah Underhill, agreed with him without going into all the details on the protocol of the event. Strechen wanted a show, something vengeful and bloody.

In the weeks leading up to it, Margaret had long had a single thought: to find Katie. Margaret returned in vain to the sumptuous mansions of old contacts, financiers, and amateur traders in the unknown, but only their vestibules remained accessible to her. In desperation, and banned entrance to Leah's building on Cotton Street, she had humbled herself to beg Leah in the premises of the Spiritualist Circle of Union Square. They unceremoniously kicked her out after her sister had demanded the solemn confession of her crimes toward the cause. "I'll die first!" Margaret had responded. The followers present had carried her out like a sack under Leah's glacial eye. For entire hours that day, brooding over her hatred in the chalky June light, Margaret had wandered in search of Kate between the ponds and hills of Central Park. At the end of one path, under the inclement glare of the sun, a preacher of the end of the world was perched on a bench, holding forth to himself alone:

"Behold, I stand at the door and knock; if anyone hears my voice and opens the door, I will come in like a friend to his friend's house."

That was just it, she thought, "if anyone hears my voice," but no one would answer her anymore in Heaven just like on Earth.

At the approach of the month of August, impressive storms sliced with torrential rains didn't diminish the tropical heat wave by even a single degree. The New York newspapers soon announced with various caustic or bemused commentaries, and along with an unattractive photograph, the exceptional performance of Margaret Fox in the grand auditorium of the Academy of Music. Never letting go of the daggers of her anger, Margaret could feel a wave of panic rising in her. Being recognized once or twice in public terrified her like the pronouncement of a curse. Among the bustle of the streets, in one neighborhood or another, she'd stop to catch her breath at the first shop sign for absinthe or any kind of alcohol to revive the part of her that was dying, and was able to pay thanks to the advance of two hundred dollars burning a hole in her pocket. But it was necessary for her to feed this covert fire day and night without losing control, until the moment of surrendering herself to the invisible, several brutal hours where, poked by myriad waxy demons, the hell promised to the intemperate would welcome her in for an atrocious prelude from which she would escape twenty times over in her sleep, dreaming that she was running after a sleepwalker more elusive than a flickering flame. Finally, eyes wide open, crying voicelessly into a stony silence, she thought she was calling for help. But there was nobody in the world to answer her.

Then, wide-awake, she recognized a little voice:

O the good times are all dead and gone
Singin' hi-diddle-i-diddle
Still I love you dear, my whole life long
Singin' hi-diddle-i-diddle

IX.

Poltergeist at the Academy of Music

A crowd is just a kind of maelstrom of opinion, a whirlwind, an open mouth of hungry souls. Wherever this Leviathan of circumstances arises—cyclonic dragon, serpent of storms—all trace of altruism or of simple humanity disappears and the most one can hope for is a speedy return from primitive chaos, the animal brain, before all cataclysm.

In the grand auditorium of the New York City Academy of Music, the stampede released into the stairways and halls worried the staff of this institution more accustomed to the airy gait of music lovers. Behind the scenes, trying to get a count of heads coiffed or not, Franck Strechen was rubbing his hands together. This was a turnout to dream of, an audience of great opportunity, even if it augured no future, given the poor state of his contractual associate. At least she was abstaining for the moment and letting herself be made up, ready it seemed to demonstrate being a medium with physical effects according to the rules: they could expect some classic conversations with the table, experiences of directed writing from afar, and of Ouija according to the upside-down-glass technique, as well as some levitation exercises using a single support, partial materialization by densification of the astral body and, perhaps, contributions from the afterlife, a bouquet of flowers or an old Bible, given all the stage equipment Margaret Fox-Kane had taken the time to spread out before the doors opened. Closets, diversions, miraculous escapes: they were all the rage! He was worried only about the effects of the trance on her weak constitution, for he had never doubted the excessive nervous energy Margaret channeled, as much for conjuring tricks as for the embodiment of spirits.

Still camped behind the stage curtain, Franck Strechen began to closely scrutinize the first rows: everyone was there! The spiritualist crème de la crème of New York. He recognized, among other luminaries more or less documented, the unpredictable William Mac Orpheus, Thomson Jay Hudson behind his martial handlebar mustache, clairvoyant mediums from the hinterlands, mediums of Christ more dangerous than the Medusa, a quantity of orderlies from spiritualist organizations, and the most faithful of the faithful, Andrew Jackson Davis in the flesh. The yellow, white, or black faces mingled noisily throughout the auditorium. A candid mass of uncontrollable instincts, the curious people— unusual amateurs, spellbound by principle, enthusiastic laymen— were to be feared more in the case of defeat.

A spectacle had been expected, no doubt, but the announcement, a tad bit sensational, added some spice to the event:

Modern Spiritualism
exposed for the first time
by one of the Fox Sisters

The tremor behind the curtain didn't escape the notice of a spectator from the two-dollar seats who had slipped in between two blind cohorts. So tiny, unrecognizable, Kate Fox-Jencken hid unnecessarily beneath a floppy hat with folded edges and black veils despite the stifling heat. Hours earlier, checking the hallways, offices, emergency exits, she had tried unsuccessfully to reach her sister to beg her not to put herself into peril. The bottled-up negative energies that they had released without the crowd's knowledge had accumulated to their own loss. Kate was convinced of this ever since her despoilment by the law; after a rebellious and struggling time, she remained concealed in the shadows. It was necessary that she protect herself from a universal conspiracy. Diverted by Leah, the obsessive little fears of Hydesville had taken on a crazy amplitude, disturbing all the dead in cemeteries, channeling millions of slaves to their devotion. Soon the spirits would overwhelm the living. What might happen then surpassed all understanding . . .

Wearing a dark dress with a headband in her hair, Margaret greeted the room after the presenter's disclaimer: it was necessary to observe a religious silence conducive to demonstrations. Very pale in her medium's cabinet reconstituted for the stage, she initially produced the expected effects: various noises and knocks, the movement of objects, the spontaneous combustion of a sheet scrawled with the directed writing in a closed and locked cabinet. One moment she even seemed to take up spiritual telegraphy, her eyebrows frowning as she invoked Benjamin Franklin and Abraham Lincoln. Then, standing up to face the audience gratified to applaud her, she announced there would be an exceptional second component to her presentation.

To everyone's amazement, she then said very calmly: "Spiritualism is from one end to the other a deception. It is the biggest fraud of our century. Kate Fox and I embarked on this adventure while still little girls, much too young and innocent to understand what we were truly dealing with, the two of us propelled on this path of deception by unscrupulous adults . . ."

"That's shameful! She's crazy!" someone exclaimed from the front rows.

Before the rumblings and indignant exclamations had time to discourage her, Margaret, back at her cabinet, undertook a demonstration of each of her turns. Calmly, she began to deconstruct for all to see all the phenomena of conjuring and apparitions. Then she revealed her method of knocking by exposing a sounding board installed under her feet and a quantity of compartments under the table top. Barefoot, she cracked her toes together to produce the desired sounds. She proceeded with a clinical determination, as if reconstituting a crime scene. Her slowed-down gestures and the extraordinary expressiveness of her face substituted for paranormal manifestations with a power that seemed even greater. A deathly silence fell over the stunned audience. There was nothing more to see. The theater of the Fox sisters was forever destroyed. "It's madness, a well-planned suicide," was whispered from one part or another. Strangely, the crowd left the Academy of Music in the biggest calm, as if at the end of some funeral ceremony.

Outside, on the twilit square where the blue lights of the gas lamps danced, people dispersed with lowered heads, not looking at each other, some toward public transportation, whereas others, impatient despite the mildness of the air, waited in the endless line for their horse-drawn carriages. An old man still alert, with large shoulders, showing a slight limp in the weakness of a hip, appeared to be looking around for somebody and, suddenly raising an arm to a retreating figure, walked as quickly as he could in its direction. Kate found herself caught in a narrow and badly lit street when the individual reached her.

"How you run, wait up!" he said. "Don't be afraid, I recognized you in the stairway of the Academy of Music, wait!"

As the silent shadow went on her way, William Pill, alias Mac Orpheus, placed himself firmly in front of her, blocking her from every direction, and gazed at her, overwhelmed to find again through the wrinkles of the years the face of a Hydesville girl.

"We knew each other well," he said, "don't you remember?"

"Yes, yes," Kate murmured, "but let me go."

"Why did your sister do that? Do you know?"

"I don't know anything about it, it's her problem, now let me leave . . ."

He stepped aside without leaving her, limping alongside her. Kate gave the impression of hardly being aware of his presence. Looking like a raw-boned elf under her veils, she seemed to move outside all reality, in some parallel world where things were perfectly identical, although of a different substance.

They passed vagabonds, puzzled women smoking along shop windows, drunkards in the grip of their demons. Out of breath, misty-eyed, William Pill wondered over the strangeness of this little woman who, despite their lack of acquaintance, was the source of his good fortune. Thanks to her, he had become rich enough to be honest, from his point of view, and had met his angel, the fickle love of his life, a damn bluestocking fled today to Rochester with a trunk of books.

"Were you ever loved, Kate?" he couldn't help but stammer, seized by that uncontrollable emotion of old men.

As she remained silent, he gently took her arm and, while walking, leaned toward her ear.

"Of course you were loved, and even passionately. During the Civil War, in the battle at Chancellorsville, a man who you'd often spent time with gave me, at the moment of his death, his only treasure to give to you. It's an Indian necklace, I've carried it with me for twenty years, hoping to be able to hand it over to you one day . . ."

"A man?" Kate said.

"Alexander Cruik, the preacher," Pill answered, unclasping the necklace from his neck. "This amulet will bring you fortune, it contains the umbilical cord of a Sioux chief killed in combat . . ."

The necklace held tight in one hand, Kate looked at the slightly vacillating shadow of this secondary actor in her life who'd appeared out of nowhere and who, after walking her to the hotel where she claimed to live, returned to the great residence of oblivion into which disappeared everyone we have met on this Earth. Taking up her way toward the Hudson away from any of the numerous walkers in the summer night who might have tried to bother her, she opened her hand to look at the amulet, which a street child would immediately have run to snatch with the vivacity of a bird. Facing the shifting constellations of the river, while a ferryboat descended to its mouth, all pennants lit, she undid her veils and cape to taste the sea breeze.

Two sailors went up along the dock without seeing her. Falling down drunk, they bellowed loudly an incomprehensible tune:

> *Adieu foula', adieu mad'as*
> *Adieu guenda, adieu collier-chou*
> *Dou-dou à moi, y va pa'ti'*
> *Hélas, hélas, c'est pou' toujou'*

X.

With Congratulations from Mister Splitfoot

S ome years later, all the water in the sky had passed over the memory of men, and the death of Leah Fox-Underhill one winter night in 1890, who was significantly less influential after the family betrayal, was less widely talked about than the excruciating death of William Kemmler, the first person sentenced to execution in an electric chair thanks to the work of Thomas Edison, or the arrest and assassination of the Sioux chief Sitting Bull, followed by the massacres at Wounded Knee and Pine Ridge, which spared neither women nor children, or the vote of new segregationist laws in Mississippi and the southern states, or even the inauguration of the New York World Building, the tallest building in Manhattan. Spiritism, the uncompromising religion that, without recourse to hell or purgatory, assured the salvation of everyone through positive transmigration and the upward path of spirits toward the celestial light, had supplanted Modern Spiritualism and its avatars worldwide. Which in no way caused braggarts, fanatics, or speculators to give up, or any kind of the socially confused, those multitudes without imagination who had never known how to behave confronted by the unknown.

Masses of immigrants continued to rush in from Europe and Asia. To the Irish Catholics were added those from Poland and Italy. The Germans fleeing cholera or *Weltpolitik*, the Taoist Chinese or the Buddhists from Fujian and Guangdong, the Jews from the Russian empire escaping pogroms, all landed continuously by the thousands on Ellis Island and its pontoons on the East River. Each of them wandered like convalescents in exile, distraught under the same sky, with their nostalgia returning as a foolish hope. In this anthill of fermentation, the margin was a fine line between the asocial needy and the workers, reckless or trafficking bourgeois, dignitaries and mafia, excited devotees and foolish free spirits. But all were working blindly, in various ways, under justice or outside the law, for the grand melting pot in the making.

Away from that human cosmos, living from begging or mysterious gifts, sleeping here and there, in shelters, rooms where a cot cost a dollar or two a night, or under the stars between the high walls of buildings, Kate Fox managed to keep her appearance neat and shoes clean, letting her hair be done by charitable prostitutes, keeping her clothes spotless thanks to the helping hand of the laundry room of an evangelical home. She'd only seen Margaret again once since the catastrophic revelations at the Academy of Music. Both of them, overcome with remorse when learning of Leah's illness, had attempted to seek her pardon. The moment after, downing whiskey upon whiskey in a port-side tavern and forcing Kate to drink along with her, Margaret got carried away, cursing again their madam of a sister who had to give up the ghost without a word of reconciliation. The two younger sisters separated shortly after that, frozen in the lucidity of intoxication, and the weeks and seasons had flown by like the clouds in a great wind, with a sort of disenchanted haste.

Vagabond, Kate was at home in her meandering. She could no longer see herself as wandering, going from one palace of leaves illuminated by a bright round moon, to the distracted temple of a bar from which she left drunker than *five giants sunk in the soil*. In her bewilderment, everything finally made sense, forever, forever, forever! How beautiful reality was, finer than a cigarette paper between the fingers and charred lungs of God. She perceived the voices of Creation, barely audible, and the geometric figures of an infinite precision that were endlessly in the middle of her skull. She laughed all alone sometimes, passed by the faces mixed in crowds between Fifth Avenue and the Harlem River. Who hears the Spirit? You or me?

> *O sister in the bath, the water is so cold*
> *That your tears burn me*

An eternal Negro came to take her in his arms, one night when she'd fallen, a footprint in the shape of a heart on his forehead. Don't cry Madame, God doesn't forget you, don't cry, life is not down here. She stood up, very small, like in the days of Pequot. There remained for her the path between the Palace of Leaves and the Temple of the Bar. Alcohol is like eternity. Lost secret, I'm coming to you, hair already white. One night, in a dollar-a-night hostel, a princely man came to inhabit her dream. Oh Katie, little sorceress, it's almost time to end this play-acting.

"But who are you, I don't recall."

"The ghost of a man who didn't love women and who loved you, star of the final hour."

"It's you, Lucian, you're dead, you too?"

"Dead? Living? Who can affirm that he isn't sleeping?"

"I remember. You told me: don't be afraid."

"I told you, when you were sleeping, forever, forever, forever, I will be next to you. What importance is today or tomorrow, and all the kings covered in sweat?"

"I don't understand."

"It's necessary for us not to stray from the path of flowers."

"I don't understand."

Kate loved the pigeons rising all of a sudden, like a saber dance. In Central Park, for entire days, she watched other people's twins, all the children were twins. She told herself there was no sound louder than memory. Her children were playing next to her, grown up, now bigger than her, they were there in spirit. Why should one weigh the soul and matter? *No, no magic.* She would have liked for Margaret to be with her, not angry, in the violent insomnia of specters. She knew well, Maggie, that all their lies hid a bigger truth, immense, knees bent on the misty hillside, in a dying autumn in Hydesville . . .

> *Am I your sad king*
> *Your lover on the last night*

When the Salvation Army sanitation services, quite busy in winter, found her on a bench, a blanket of snow barely scrawled on her chest, she was smiling in archangelic crystals, perfectly alive, and endlessly murmuring words that the ambulance volunteers couldn't or didn't want to understand. Was it, "don't come to console me," was it, "the fallen life is homeless," was it, "we are all wandering spirits"? In the rickety cart, at the exact moment of being all finished with flesh and these memories, Kate bristled, her eyes immensely open.

"Oh!" she said, frightened. "You are very funny, Mister Split-foot, perched in my lap like that."

"I don't weigh that much, Katie darling!"

"Oh!, oh! Mister Splitfoot, how I'll miss you!"

"Don't worry about anything, Katie, spirit's blood, I'm waiting for you under the light scarves."

In the Bellevue Hospital emergency room, a doctor on call casually noted the death of the incoming patient and crossed himself just in case.

"What should we do with her?" he asked the service nurses.

"No paperwork, she's homeless, probably an immigrant escaping scurvy or typhus who caught cholera instead."

To ward off the risk of an epidemic, the corpse was not sent to the anatomical theater. It was delivered to the gravediggers, who for compensation hardly got anything more than the gold or silver teeth and, on rare occasions, a little furtive affection. They made a pile of other remains at the bottom of a trench and covered them all with quicklime. Was it at Woodlawn Cemetery? Though hardly consoling, the common grave does accomplish the ideal community. And the morning dew passes for human memory. One marvels at the hardened mortals who swear that their minutes have the weight of turnips and squash blooming in their garden!

A few months later, in a funereal intoxication, Margaret Fox dreamt so strongly of her little sister that it killed her, her body rotten with lethal ulcerations. Lacking resources or identity, she too had a common burial.

Thus ended—as precisely as the concentrated work of mediums in these pages would allow it—the uplifting and pathetic adventure of the Fox Sisters.

No one will ever meditate or dance on their remains. Who ever takes the time to bow over a mass grave?

Epilogue

Good-bye my Fancy!
Farewell dear mate, dear love!
I'm going away, I know not where,
Or to what fortune, or whether I may ever see you again,
So Good-bye my Fancy.

Now for my last—let me look back a moment . . .
                                        —Walt Whitman

Behind the wheel of a Panhard-Levassor with a two-cylinder engine, whose original owner had passed away, Pearl Gascoigne quickly developed the taste for speed. The whole way from Rochester to Hydesville, they had only passed one other automobile, an Auburn looking like a luxurious carriage, and a few fiacres and peasant carts. The road, in the process of being asphalted, crossed or ran alongside the railway tracks several times, but they saw no locomotive.

"Don't forget that you're driving with a thirty-six horsepower engine!" William Pill was frightened. "Would you like me to drive?"

"No!" Pearl replied. "It's too exhilarating . . ."

"Well, slow down then. You're going at least twenty-five miles per hour on the uphill slopes!"

They reached their destination in the early afternoon, under a cold sun white as snow. It was a sharp day in April, bright, with an Eastern wind carrying a marine taste. Several kinds of fruit trees were already in bloom after the early start of the season.

The outskirts of Hydesville seemed unrecognizable to them. They had expanded the roads, drained ponds, erected electric power lines, and built a water tower, stone houses, and a rather beautiful building that must have been a school.

The automobile having reached the center of town, Pearl missed a gear-shift and nearly ran over a procession of geese, with other animal witnesses—goats, pigs, dogs—scattering out of the way at the first sounds of backfire. Two horses hitched to a drugstore railing flinched and whinnied. Children wild with joy ran by the dozens and circled around once Pill managed to apply the brake. Housewives curious about the uproar leaned out of windows. Several of the regulars came out from the saloon with laughing faces, legs spread as if standing on a ship's deck.

Pearl took off her leather cap and goggles under the amazed eyes of the farmers, who had certainly never seen an elderly woman so pretty and determined in her kidskin boots, with thick, milk-colored hair, and a delicately drawn face and eyes of an almost alarming clarity. The solid old man who accompanied her, barely stooped in his suit, looking like a rich farmer or circus director, aroused vague suspicions among the elders without being able to translate them into memories. A grandfather leaning on his cane, which was quite useful upon leaving the bar, stepped in front of the car, with a look that seemed to say, "Now *that* is an automobile!" Then he raised his stubbly chin toward this interesting bourgeois couple.

"It seems to me, sir," he began while rubbing his hand over his forehead, "I have the impression . . . Well, it wouldn't surprise me if, sometime, that we'd met before . . ."

"Of course!" the other answered while lighting a cigarillo. "But it was well before the Great Depression, the strikes, the invention of the automobile, the Civil War . . ."

"In those days, I was a man of the law, just in this lost hole of a place . . ."

"And I, the professional player, passing through here rather often . . ."

"*The Faker!*" belched the man, leaning into his cane. "So it's you, William Pill!"

"Alive and well, Marshall McLeann!"

The latter, barely recovered, gave a polished wink to Pearl, who, wet-eyed, was studying every detail of each wooden façade.

"Is that your wife?" he whispered.

Pill let out a laugh and, after a slightly annoyed gesture of denial, thumbs in his pockets, took on an air of importance.

"Enough of widows and orphans! Let's be serious: what's going on these days aside from the bullet dance between the bumpkins and the ranchers?"

"Bah, my goodness, fields are still fields and whiskey's the same color! There's a little bit of tourism now, because of the Fox sisters' farmhouse being under construction over there. Getting some big ideas in his head from folks in town, the mayor dreams of making some kind of monument . . ."

Seized with emotion, Pearl drew away in small steps toward the church. Partly rebuilt and repainted, but identical, with its fretted awnings, its slate steeple above the roofs, it reminded her of nothing happy. The reverend had long terrorized his world every Sunday with his granite faith and the rigors of a morality worked over by remorse. She only glanced at the adjoining house, to the narrow window of her bedroom, at the empty room on the ground floor where she used to teach her class. Eyes closed for a moment, she turned quickly back to find the main road, followed closely by two mischievous little girls and a small dog with a black muzzle.

William Pill was waiting for her, seated behind the wheel of the Panhard. Through the smoke of his cigarillo, he smiled at all these years that had passed by more quickly than a single day of his childhood. Now established in the good city of Rochester, he had put away at the bottom of an armoire the trappings of Mac Orpheus and lived off his private income, as sanely as possible. Pearl had never wanted him at her place among her things, too busy making war with the country's institutions or writings stories to make you fall asleep standing up. So refined, dismayed over a broken glass, she also found him more cumbersome than a carnivorous bison. But he had only settled in Rochester with the idea of sharing a few happy hours with her—incandescent memories, a good dinner, long walks along the shore of Lake Ontario—with no declared motives other than to be at her service, from time to time, like for this stunning pilgrimage to Hydesville. There's nothing picturesque to see here, really, in this damn countryside, where he'd on more than one occasion barely missed being hanged or lynched!

Pearl, in a sweeping movement of shoulders and hips, had settled at his side without arguing this time for the right to drive the racing car.

"Take me you know where," she said.

At the moment of releasing the brake, he noticed that it only took a few seconds for the perfume of an elegant woman, albeit in sportswear, to reclaim her empire. And with Pearl it was more than a perfume, it was a kind of balsamic grace that emanated from her entire being, a sort of evanescent favor granted, he didn't know by what miracle, by his fondness for her . . .

"What are you thinking, William?"

"Nothing, stories of grandmothers."

The fields marched by, lined by beech and ash trees, leaning into the light around the hills of the Iroquois that dominated the horizon. Two kilometers away from there, on Long Road, Pearl marveled at the hitches blocking the path that led down to the pond. One could make out a group of people around the clapboard buildings.

"They're doing some kind of work," said Pill, pulling over to the median to park.

"It brought back awful memories, for a moment, all these people . . ."

They walked down to the farm without saying a word. Apart from this curious influx, nothing had changed in a good half century. Pearl caught a glimpse of the dark water behind the barn and shuddered. The farmers were returning from a block, heading in the newcomers' direction, an embarrassed and suspicious look on their faces. They all seemed to be under the blow of an intense amazement. A young sheriff and a plump little man in a black suit were giving contradictory orders to the workers camped among big chalky sacks filled with earth and rubble.

"So, do we take it out or what?" a man in coveralls grumbled through his moustache.

"Bring it up!" ordered the little man.

"That's not legal," replied the sheriff. "I will put it in my report."

"Make all the reports you'd like, young man! As mayor and owner of these grounds, I demand that this body be exhumed . . ."

The laborers at work in the cellar soon brought to the surface a big canvas tarp that they were holding by the four corners. Without further ceremony, they opened up to the public view a complete, though scattered human skeleton.

The excavator come up in his turn from the cellar set down a small salesman's suitcase next to the remains.

"We found it next to the body, nestled deep into the foundations of a wall. It really took a lot of work to knock it down . . ."

Everyone a little bit of a gravedigger, the farmers came closer to get a better look.

"That goes back at least to the War of Independence," said one of them.

"You're crazy!" said an old woodcutter crouched down over the skull of the remains. "The house didn't exist back then."

"One thing is certain," declared a third man, even older. "Ghosts or not, those little Fox girls had a fine nose!"

Taken with dizziness, Pearl touched the shoulder of her companion. He immediately understood and the both of them, with his hand around her waist, walked cautiously back up to the road.

When the automobile was on its way back to Rochester, William Pill sighed with relief. He started to hum a tune known by him alone:

They were both joyful spirits
Returned from a haunted castle
They believed they were alive
Death is a well-kept secret

Pearl Gascoigne, fully recovered, apologized for her illness.

"It's bizarre," she said. "It had to happen to us today, ten years after the death of the Fox sisters, as if to mark a kind of anniversary . . ."

"I see it as a sign, Pearl, my dear. A message from the beyond. Are you finally going to start believing in spirits?"

"Not any more than you do, you damned old charlatan!"

Translator's Acknowledgments

The translator owes a tremendous amount of thanks to Megan Wilson, who helped undertake the substantial research that enabled this translation to exist.

Thanks also to Katherine Mannheimer, who helped come up with "Irondequoit" for the dog's name, and who kindly listened to numerous elations and doubts during the translation process.

Hubert Haddad was born in Tunisia and is the author of dozens of works, including the novels *Palestine* (winner of the Prix des Cinq Continents de la Francophonie), *Tango chinois*, and *La Condition magique* (winner of the Grand Prix du Roman de la Société des Gens de Lettres).

Jennifer Grotz is a poet and translator from the French and Polish, as well as the editor of Open Letter's poetry series. She is a professor of English, creative writing, and translation at the University of Rochester, and is also director of the Bread Loaf Translators' Conference.

Open Letter—the University of Rochester's nonprofit, literary translation press—is one of only a handful of publishing houses dedicated to increasing access to world literature for English readers. Publishing ten titles in translation each year, Open Letter searches for works that are extraordinary and influential, works that we hope will become the classics of tomorrow.

Making world literature available in English is crucial to opening our cultural borders, and its availability plays a vital role in maintaining a healthy and vibrant book culture. Open Letter strives to cultivate an audience for these works by helping readers discover imaginative, stunning works of fiction and poetry, and by creating a constellation of international writing that is engaging, stimulating, and enduring.

Current and forthcoming titles from Open Letter include works from Argentina, Bulgaria, Catalonia, China, Iceland, Israel, Latvia, Poland, South Africa, and many other countries.

www.openletterbooks.org